T0245976

This Is Not a
Dead Girl Story

This Is Not a Dead Girl Story

KATE SWEENEY

Viking

VIKING
An imprint of Penguin Random House LLC
1745 Broadway, New York, New York 10019

First published in the United States of America by Viking,
an imprint of Penguin Random House LLC, 2024

Visit us online at PenguinRandomHouse.com.

Library of Congress Cataloging-in-Publication Data is available.

ISBN 9780593623831

10   9   8   7   6   5   4   3   2   1

Printed in the United States of America

BVG

Edited by Kelsey Murphy
Design by Kate Renner
Text set in Garth Graphic Pro

For Billy, and all the boys of Cambridge, New York.

And for anyone who has experienced girlhood,
whether by choice or not.
May this book help you find
a little joy and violence in your heart.

PROLOGUE
JUNE

On the last Wednesday of the year, school is canceled. The diner on the corner of Third and Sycamore does not open and the parking lot of the IGA grocery store stays empty. No one is out walking their dogs or cutting the thick, fresh green grass. As Mom and I make our way down Main Street, it feels as though the whole town of Black Falls, New York—and everything in it—has been raptured.

My mother looks tired today. She always looks a little tired, but usually I can find some mischief in her face, a spark. Now her cheeks are pale and her eyes are glassy. Like she's been raptured too.

She's been up crying at night. She tries to be quiet, but I can hear the muffled sobs from her room as I curl up in my bed. I don't cry, but I pile every blanket on top of myself, until I feel sure that there's enough weight to me that I'm not going to disappear too.

When we finally pull into the parking lot of the Elks

Lodge, I see them: the mayor, the principal, the moms and dads and kids and dogs and students and teachers and gas station attendants all milling around.

Someone has set up a table with giant coffee dispensers and powdered donuts. A big, orange handwritten poster perches crookedly on a metal stand next to the doors to the lodge: SEARCH PARTY HERE.

Officer Kelly, the police chief, stands nearby, Styrofoam cup in hand, holding court with a group of younger officers. I see Zack White, Callie's brother, who has been on the force for only six months, looking handsome and clean-cut in his brand-new uniform. I see Remy's crew huddled at the edge of the parking lot. I watch them for a few moments, trying to tell them apart. They stand in a triangle, in color-coordinated, pastel jogging pants, oversize fleeces, and sports bras, like Easter-themed Bella Hadids. I study their faces: the sad downturn of Callie's lips, Liliana's delicate tears, and Kendall's blank, distant stare. I wonder. Which Remy did they know?

Two days ago at lunch, Kendall said that Remy had better do it soon, in a voice that sounded sharp as a needle. Now, as I watch her drape an arm over Lili's shoulders, I think, *Do what?*

Mom nudges me forward, breaking me out of my thoughts.

"Breathe, Jules," she reminds me. We walk over to where the crowd is beginning to come together, and she holds my hand, like she used to when I was a kid.

Officer Kelly gives the instructions and then we split into teams. Each team is sent to a different area of Turnpike and the surrounding roads to walk through the woods in long lines. *Remy would love this*, I think. Her favorite hobby is consuming anything suspenseful and gory—horror movies, thrillers, true-crime podcasts.

"Look at all these stupid, stupid dead girls," she would always say. "Taking the stairs when they should have gone for the front door."

Then she would add, "Only a man would write it like this."

Maybe this is all a joke. A show. Remy loves a twist, a spectacle, an elaborate plan. Maybe tomorrow she'll show up at school with fake blood trickling out of her ears and laugh at us all.

Mom and I are partnered with the Whites. We are a picture of contrast, Mom and me with our messy ponytails and practical jackets, Callie's family with their white teeth and clean shoes. The Whites look at us with pity and a little bit of fear. Because we have lost something precious to us. They don't want to think about what that feels like.

The six of us have been assigned to search the area of woods next to Turnpike Road between Dogwood and Maple. The morning is cool and cloudy, casting the forest in an eerie darkness, as if the sun will not come out without her. As we walk into the forest, the air smells like wet earth, last year's rotten leaves, this year's flowers. Life. Death.

This is perfect, I hear Remy saying in my ear. *Almost poetic.*

She's right. The chill in the air worms its way into my bones. Everything is quiet except the rustling of leaves under our feet.

Callie walks about ten yards away from me on one side,

my mother on the other, and we advance forward in a line, like the officers told us to, scanning the ground at our feet, trying to stay together.

"I can't stop thinking about her," Callie says. Her long blond hair is woven into two fishtail braids and she has zipped her fluffy light pink fleece up to her neck. She looks to her left, where her little sister, Marta, only thirteen, is marching somberly forward, AirPods tucked into her ears. "I can't believe she could be—"

"She's not," I say, clenching my jaw.

I don't say what Remy isn't.

"How could she have just disappeared?"

I look to the other side of me, where Mom is talking quietly to Callie's mother, and lower my voice. "If Remy disappeared, it's because she wanted to," I say.

Callie nods, straightening her shoulders, like she needed to hear this. I say it again and again inside my head because I need to hear it too. But then a worse thought appears: *If Remy wanted to disappear, then she's never coming back.*

I hear a loud cracking sound. A stick, broken underfoot, but it makes me think of bones snapping.

"You have to look carefully," Officer Kelly said as he stood in front of the people gathered in the parking lot. The top of his lip looked sweaty. "Sometimes it's the smallest detail that can lead us to a body."

I trip over something, grabbing on to a branch to catch myself, but it breaks and I fall onto my hands and knees. The ground is wet and muddy. A wave of sorrow, heavy and sickening, washes over me. *Remy is not*, I think. *She isn't.* My hands begin to shake.

"Are you okay?" Callie asks. She leaves her place in the line to crouch next to me. My mom, up ahead now, hasn't noticed us.

"I'm fine," I say, looking down to where the water has seeped through at my knees. Without warning, Callie starts to cry.

"I just have a bad feeling," she says quietly. The wind blows a strand of hair across her cheek.

Isn't this fun? Remy whispers.

Suddenly, the air is loud with the barking of dogs.

It is exactly like the scene in the movie when they find the corpse. Everyone around us abandons their place on the line and starts jogging toward the road, where a cluster of people is starting to form. Callie turns and starts to run after them. I get to my feet but can't make myself follow. I am not able to face this moment.

I watch from across the street as Zack White pushes his way through the crowd. "Don't touch anything," he says, his voice loud and authoritative. He's got blue rubber gloves on.

It's not a body, I say to myself. *It's not a body.*

I hold my breath.

It's not.

A body.

It's a cell phone.

Remy's phone with its black cat case, the glass on the front shattered.

PART 1

May

ONE

My cousin, Remy Green, exists in many forms. There is the Remy she creates for the world at large, a vision of perfect proportions and alluring angles, with golden hair and laughter like bells. She makes everyone at the sleepover watch *Pet Sematary* and play Light as a Feather, Stiff as a Board, and they all pretend to enjoy it, even if it makes them cry or wet their pants. She is brilliant. Magnetic. Fun. Knife-sharp.

She sets aside this Remy when she is with River and me, and like a nesting doll, there is another Remy underneath. This person is softer. She is silly, playful, easygoing, breaking rules, making jokes, crashing through the trees. She is clumsy and graceful, she cheats at board games, and she has the worst morning breath I have ever smelled. She is irresistible, to both of us.

The next layer of Remy is one I have known as long as myself. This Remy is more of a feeling: closeness, admiration, jealousy, anger, hitting, pinching, biting, hugging, falling down laughing out of breath, hiding under tables, drawing on skin with markers, making me promise to never tell. This Remy is rare, and she is my favorite.

Deep down, underneath all the layers of Remy, someone else lurks, a secret person nobody knows. Everyone has someone like this at the heart of them, I guess. But there is something different about Remy's. Something that scares me.

On Saturday Remy and I spend the day on the couch watching Saw movies. It is the last week in May and spring is melting into summer, warm and full of possibility. The weather is perfect, sunny and dry, but Remy likes to go against the grain, so she takes special joy in spending a beautiful day indoors. She pops popcorn, dumping a disgusting amount of nutritional yeast on top, then cranks the AC and drags every blanket she can find to the living room.

I don't like horror, but Remy is always insisting I watch it to toughen myself up. In exchange, she gives me her full attention, turning off her phone for six whole hours.

I can't stomach the worst of the torture scenes, so when they come, I let my eyes drift to the corner and allow my mind to wander off to places it shouldn't. I think about River.

My life is a triangle. I'm in one corner and Remy is directly across from me, my opposite in every way. Up at the top, right in the middle, is River O'Dell, like a star in the sky. The North Star. The most important one.

The three of us have been best friends since third grade, when River's family moved to town. But River has always loved Remy the best. And I've always loved River the best. Just like any good love triangle. River and Remy have been together for three years now. And still, my love for River is so intense sometimes I feel like I'm being strangled by it.

In our world—the one that the three of us inhabit as well as the greater world of Black Falls—Remy is the queen. Sometimes I feel like my entire life is a foil to hers, a big, long race I am always losing. I am built like a loser: frizzy hair and strange face, fingernails that are jagged from chewing. No part of me is golden. The only thing Remy and I have in common is River, and the heart-shaped birthmarks just under our collarbones.

"You're not paying attention," Remy scolds.

"I am!" I lie. In my mind, River is threading his fingers through my hair.

"You are not, you little chicken," she says. Then she launches herself on top of me and finds the tickle spot under the left side of my ribs.

Remy is relentless with tickling. She shows no mercy until I surrender, and then she stays on top of me, turning my head toward the screen with her hands. I close my eyes. She tries to pry them open. I resist.

"You're hopeless," she says. She goes back to her nest on the other end of the couch.

When the credits roll at the end of *Saw IV*, Remy turns off the TV. It's early evening and the sun is starting to bend over the tops of the trees. The light in the living room is warm. My mom will be home soon from the hospital in Albany, where she has been delivering babies for the past eighteen hours.

"You know it's fake, right?" Remy says.

I shrug. "Sure. But it feels real."

"It's not," she insists, getting up from the couch and stretching like a cat. "It's just a sick fantasy."

"Why do you like it so much, then?" I ask.

Remy grins. "Because I'm a sicko, of course."

Later, the two of us sit together in a bubble bath scented by my mother's homemade lavender oil. Mom isn't home a lot—she often works long shifts at the hospital in Albany—but her herbal remedies are everywhere. After all, she's a midwife. She has a cure for everything.

Remy's blond hair is piled high atop her head. *Lemonade* plays from across the room, out of the speaker of her phone. She is uncharacteristically quiet tonight. Usually she talks a mile a minute, and I love this because it means I don't have to. We fit together in this way. She is loud and I am quiet. She is fun and I am careful. She leads and I follow.

Tonight I have a secret. I wait for her to force it out of me, because Remy always knows when I'm keeping something from her. But now she doesn't even seem to notice.

"I think I'm going to have sex with Bailey Jensen to-night," I say, studying my fingernails. Remy painted them red during *Saw II*, but they're already chipped.

Bailey Jensen is tall and handsome, with short, neat blond hair and piercing blue eyes. He plays lacrosse with

River. He is the kind of guy who would normally never even talk to me, except in the context of my two best friends.

Remy looks surprised, and I feel a bolt of warm, victorious pleasure right in the center of my stomach. I grin; I'm not usually able to catch her off guard. I sink my knees under the bubbles, remembering the moment on Friday in chemistry when I handed Bailey a pencil and he used it to tap the back of each of my knuckles, asking, "Are you coming out this weekend?"

Bailey has been flirting with me lately. It's subtle enough that I haven't been able to uncover the motivation behind it, but the truth is that I don't really care. I need a warm body. I need to get unstuck. I am turning eighteen in seven months and have never even been kissed.

The real reason I haven't kissed anyone, though, can be found in the bottom drawer of my desk, full of lacrosse photos cut out of the *Black Falls Times*, notebook pages where I've written River's name on every line, a hundred different secret pieces of him. Maybe tomorrow I will take it all out and burn it. Maybe tonight I can finally move on.

At the other end of the tub, Remy's face turns sour.

"What?" I ask, frowning.

"Nothing," she says. "It's just . . ." She swirls a finger absently in the water. "Why Bailey? Why now?"

Remy knows me well enough to guess that I don't really care about Bailey. Even on a purely physical level, he isn't my type. I am drawn to strange details, always choosing celebrity crushes with interesting scars or a chipped tooth.

Bailey doesn't have many charming imperfections.

Except for a jagged spot on his right thumbnail from where he sometimes chews it, he is seemingly physically perfect. Almost boring.

On the surface, Bailey and River aren't that different. They both could play the prom king in a horror movie. But River is full of quirks, from the white line below his bottom lip where his teeth once broke through the skin to the ineffable restless quality that vibrates, nonstop, through his slightly gangly limbs. Bailey is like a pixelated version, with all the best parts filtered out.

I close my eyes and I am transported. Yesterday, walking out of chem class, my blood fizzing like bubbly water at the thought of finally moving on.

In my mind, River walks up beside me. He slings an arm over my shoulder and the scent of him, warm grass, is so strong it makes my eyelids flutter.

"My mind is blown," he says.

He is always saying things like this. River is amazed by everything.

"Why?" I ask, playing along. I always play along.

"Weren't you watching the movie?" he asks.

I wasn't watching the movie because I was busy looking at Bailey and deciding that he was the one.

River sighs, disappointed. "Cosmic dust!" he says. "Fucking amazing." I don't say anything, because I love to listen to the sound of River's voice when he gets going like this. "Cosmic dust," he says again, stopping right there in the middle of the hallway. He makes an exploding brain gesture.

River goes on about complicated science stuff, how we

are the dust and the dust is us, everything is everything, etc., etc. And I am only half listening because I am so distracted by the perfect sound of his voice.

I look up at him and his river-blue eyes make my stomach drop.

This. This is why.

I open my eyes again, narrow them. "Because I want to." I don't know if that's true, but it doesn't matter. I *need* to. I have to get rid of this part of me.

Remy rolls her eyes and sinks lower, causing the water level to rise. She seems irritated and I can't tell why. "Don't you want your first time to be with someone who's not so . . ."

I lean my head back onto the rim of the tub, starting to feel annoyed. Remy is six months younger than me, but she always acts like she knows more, knows better. Like it's her job to teach me, to keep me safe. "Not everyone gets the fairy tale, Rem. Some people just need to get things done."

"That is too depressing. Even for you," she says. She dunks under the water and when she comes up, eyelashes lined with sparkling drops, she says, "Sure, fairy tales aren't real. But that doesn't mean you can't have something good. You should have sex with someone trustworthy. Someone who will make you feel . . ." She stops and her eyes drop to the water. Something suddenly feels off about her. For a moment she looks too soft. Too vulnerable. Then I watch as she slowly regains control, the features of her face falling in line, one by one. "Turn around," she says. "I want to braid your hair."

Later, in my car on the way to the party, Remy apologizes.

"I'm excited for you," she says. Then she hands me a condom. It's Trojan, light blue, with spermicidal lubricant. "You have to pee afterward or you'll get a urinary tract infection."

I nod, slightly annoyed at her bossy tone.

"Make sure he touches you for a while first, and that you're into it, or it might hurt." Remy turns away from the road to look into my eyes. "I want it to be good for you."

"Thank you," I say. Her condescension is a little much. "But my mom has already given me the talk, many times."

Remy shrugs, hand on the wheel. "She's the one I learned it from."

I feel such a mixture of emotion when I hear this.

Sometimes Remy has this way of taking my mother over. I'll see them together and notice my mom giving Remy a look that she never gives me. Their relationship is uncomplicated. Easy. My mother loves me, of course. But Remy would have been the *perfect* daughter. Imagining them alone together, talking about sex, talking about River, makes me want to scratch Remy's eyes out.

Remy picks up her phone from the center console. I grab it out of her hand. "Don't text while driving."

"Fine." She grabs it back and puts it in the pocket on the driver's side door. "I'm just wondering why we haven't heard from River. I hope they didn't lose the tournament."

"We're going to see him in five minutes anyway," I say. We're going to see Bailey in five minutes too. A shiver goes through me. I can't tell if I'm nervous or excited, but

I feel a little strange. My knee begins to bounce up and down.

"Don't drink too much," Remy says. Her voice is tight.

"I won't," I say. But I do. I drink a lot. Enough to make me forget that everything about this is a little bit wrong.

TWO

I wake up to a tangled cloud of Remy's thick blond hair, right in my face. My mouth tastes sour and stale, like too much beer and not enough sleep, bitter, like regret. I close my eyes against the sun, against Remy and the truth that is slowly dawning with the morning light: River is dead.

River is dead.

River is dead.

River is dead.

Once I think it, I can't stop. *River is dead.* I think it over and over, waiting for the words to lose their meaning. *River is dead.*

The world is not the world anymore. The world can't be the world without River in it.

But somehow, sunlight is still coming through the curtains. Air moves in and out of my lungs. Downstairs, in the kitchen, my mother is opening cupboards, turning on the sink.

I press the palms of my hands into my eyes, hard. My

mind scrabbles back against the hazy memory of last night. The darkness of the woods. The sound of laughter. Bailey tugging my hand, leading me away from the fire. The clumsy weight of his body on top of mine, the smell of the latex condom. Then the sound of someone crashing through the trees. Remy, wild-eyed, too drunk. The flashing red and blue of cop cars pulling into the drive.

The only solid memory I have is of Callie White's older brother, Zack, in his police uniform, putting a hand on Remy's shoulder, looking down into her eyes. "River is dead," he said, and then I threw up on my shoes.

I reach out and gently touch Remy's back, to make sure she isn't dead too. Her breathing is steady, her ribs rise and fall. Her body is loose, open, untroubled, like maybe she doesn't remember.

I close my eyes and let the warmth of her seep into me, like I used to when we were young and I'd had a bad dream.

"I'll be your good luck charm," Remy would say. "I'll never let anything get you." Then she would wrap her arms around me and squeeze all of my breath out.

I want to leave Remy these last few moments of peace, so I creep out of bed and make my way toward the door.

"You're up," Mom says when I step into the kitchen. Her eyes are red and tired and I suddenly remember falling into her arms in the driveway of the deer camp. I can feel the three of us standing there, Mom, Remy, and me, surrounded by cars and cops and parents and dense, primeval trees, the world spinning.

Mom makes me a cup of tea, something strong and herbal.

"This will help with your hangover," she says. She sets it on the counter next to me and then presses her hands to the sides of my face, smooths my hair down the back of my head, leans her forehead into mine. Breathes me in. Like she is not quite sure that I'm really here. Maybe I'm not. Maybe none of us are. Maybe we are all dead.

But outside the water-spotted kitchen window, birds are singing. Actually singing. The too-long grass is thick and lush. The sky is blue. Everything is alive. Everything but River.

This is the first time Mom has ever said the word *hangover* to me. Last night was the first time she's ever seen me drunk. On any other morning if I walked into the kitchen with alcohol still on my breath, she would send me back to my room and never let me out again. But River is dead, so the scene can't unfold like it's meant to. Instead, she looks at me like I am fragile, like I could disappear at any moment.

Then Remy zombie-walks her way into the kitchen, dead-eyed, mascara and eyeliner smudged everywhere. She looks like she might not be breathing, like maybe she drowned too. I want her to grab me, to squeeze me, to pinch me, hard. But she just stands there.

"Oh, honey," Mom says, gathering Remy into her arms. Remy remains stiff, unyielding, like the human part of her is broken and only the inner robot is still intact.

Mom makes Remy a cup of tea; Remy doesn't drink it. She makes us breakfast, but nobody eats a thing. What's the point? River is gone. Someone tell the grass and the birds and the soft spring breeze. The world is ending any minute now. There's no reason to try.

River is not the first seventeen-year-old boy to die in Black Falls, although he is the first to die of drowning in at least ten years. Others have died of cancer, in farming accidents and drug overdoses, driving their cars around the hairpin turns on Route 31. Three years ago, Remy's brother died from an overdose, cocaine laced with fentanyl. One of many. A tragedy every year or two, since before I can remember. Being a boy in Black Falls is risky.

Still, River should have beaten the odds. He was undeniably alive. Always, always moving. I could have written poems about his eyelashes, entire love songs about the way he said the word *yes*.

I close my eyes and it's the first day of spring. River picks us up in his dad's truck and we drive fast on the back roads, windows all the way down. We sit three across on the bench seat, Remy in the middle. It is early in the morning, and it still feels like winter. Remy complains that she is cold.

River laughs and tugs her winter hat from her head.

Remy shrieks. "River!" She reaches for the hat, which River is holding outside the window with the hand that's not on the wheel. "My ears are going to fall off!"

"It's good for you," River insists.

Outside the window, green grass is pushing up through the muddy ground. The trees are bare. It's that awkward, ugly moment between the seasons.

River leaves the window down, and I know it's because he wants us to feel everything about this moment. He wants us to know how good it is. I hate March, but River can make me love any month. River is contagious like that.

Before long, Remy is laughing. And so am I. We are all shivering and laughing and it is spring and looking back on this moment now I think I understand what River was saying about cosmic dust. River is not dead. And he is dead. He is all things. He is nothing.

In the afternoon, Mom brings us to the O'Dells' to pay our respects. River's house is less than a mile from mine, but we take the car anyway, windows up and air conditioner blasting, sealing ourselves off from the world as much as we can. She drives slowly, as though she never wants to get there, but eventually we do. We sit in the car in the driveway for a long time.

The O'Dells' house is nestled back in the woods, cozy and small. It has a long drive, part pavement, part gravel, that we used to race down as kids. Now, nearly June, the lawn is green and soft-looking, and hundreds of pink hollyhocks grow on either side of the front door. I remember River falling into this grass, limbs loose, laughing, eyes the color of the ocean.

The way you said the word yes
Felt like
Petals falling from your mouth.
You said yes to everything
And the world was full of flowers.

I close my eyes. How is grass still growing? How are hollyhocks blooming? How has the sun risen and moved halfway across the sky? How can any of this happen without him?

Mom takes a deep breath, reaching over to put a hand on my knee. "Come on, girls. This will make us feel better."

What a lie, I think. *Nothing is ever going to make us feel better.*

Mom opens her door and I follow after her, but Remy stays in the back seat, head down. "Give her a minute," Mom says. She hefts a giant casserole container out of the trunk and walks up to the front door.

Mom knocks once, and no one answers, and I can see her inner struggle about whether or not to knock again. Finally, the door opens and there stands River's mother, in an outfit I've seen a million times, jeans and a gray sweatshirt, blond hair in a ponytail, herself and not herself. She looks lost, almost like she doesn't recognize us. *She is not a mother anymore*, I think.

Mom hands me the casserole dish. "Rebecca," she says. And then Rebecca steps forward and crumples into her arms.

Mom brews tea she brought in her purse and makes Rebecca drink it, just like she did with me. We sit at the banquette in the kitchen and I look out the window to where Remy has not moved, her head still pressed into the back of the passenger seat.

"Jake's down at the police station," Rebecca says. "I couldn't . . ." She runs her finger around the rim of her mug. "They're trying to figure out if it was an accident or if he—" She stops and Mom leans over and puts her hand on Rebecca's. Rebecca clears her throat a few times, as if she needs to get it out but can't. "If it was intentional," she finally says. She looks away.

"No," I say. I've had enough. This is the last straw. What happened to River was not suicide.

River is not dead.

River the Brave. Devourer of life. Human light source. It simply cannot be.

I dig my nails into the wood of the table. I've got to get away from here, from this not-mother and this not-house. I start to get up.

"I need to . . ." I say. And then I freeze, caught halfway between sitting and standing. I feel like I might throw up.

"Why don't you go check on Remy in the car," Mom says. She looks at me with tired warmth in her eyes. "I'll talk with Rebecca for a while, and then maybe we can all go for a walk to get some air."

I nod, and then leave the house as quickly as I can.

When I get to the car, I open the back door and slide across the seat, nestling close to Remy. She releases her hold on the seat in front of her and falls across my lap. She feels soft, like a sleepy child.

There's something startling about Remy's formlessness in this moment. She always has such a definite shape to her. Sharp edges. Powerful tension in every limb. Now all of that is gone. Remy closes her eyes and I run my fingers through her hair, working out last night's tangles. A heavy quiet settles over us. A gentle breeze whispers through the open door.

I feel like I should say something. I want to find a way to communicate this aching feeling in my chest. But I don't have any words for it. Remy nods, like she hears me anyway. This is how we've always been. I don't have to say anything, but still, she knows.

That night, I wake up in a cold sweat, in the middle of a memory dream. I am back at the Campbell deer camp. At the party. The fire is crackling, the darkness surrounding us palpable. I have been drinking. We have all been drinking and all of the edges are blurred with it. I am sitting on the hood of a parked car with Bailey Jensen and he is leaning in to kiss me. I can smell the wet earth of the woods, the gasoline of the engine, Bailey's hot breath. This is my first kiss. It is the first time someone has opened their mouth to mine, slid their tongue inside. Or rather, shoved their tongue inside. This kiss is sloppy.

It doesn't feel good, except in the way that checking something off a list feels good, that feeling less pathetic than you did an hour ago, watching your best friend and the love of your life leaning into one another with the casual ease of deep love, feels good, in that it feels better than the alternative.

As Bailey's sweaty hands reach up to grip the skin of my waist underneath the hem of my sweatshirt, I try to think about whether or not I could like him, could like this. A feeling at the bottom of my stomach says *no*, but I keep weathering the onslaught of Bailey's tongue, keep telling myself *maybe*.

We get into the car, which is very dark and smells like marijuana and pine-scented air freshener. Bailey lies down on top of me, still kissing me messily, and it feels a little hard to breathe. Then he parts my thighs with a clumsy palm. I hand him the blue condom package and he opens it, turning away as he puts it on.

Sex doesn't hurt, but it doesn't feel good either. It feels like it happens outside me, like I am someone else, watching Bailey heave his body over mine, still in his canvas jacket. It is over quickly, and then Bailey climbs off me and zips up his jeans, breathing heavily. *There*, I think. *It is finally done.* I don't feel reborn. I don't feel anything.

Behind us, beyond the trees, the sound of the Black River is a quiet rushing, calm and gentle. A constant sound, in our ears, our bones from the time we were born. We don't know that a few miles downstream, *our* River is under the water, dying.

THREE

At the beginning of this year, Remy started wearing a red ribbon in her hair. She looked like the girl from *Heathers*, her favorite and most-hated movie. She's always loved the croquet and the fashion and the fact that Christian Slater gets blown up at the end but hated the fact that all the girls are cruel and simplistic in the way only a twenty-six-year-old man could write them to be.

Normally, when Remy starts wearing something, everyone else will follow within a matter of days. This time, however, people seemed to know that the ribbon was just for Remy. It set her apart, a symbol of her position at the top: prettiest, smartest, most beloved.

Remy has not worn her ribbon since the night River died. It's been three days, and she has yet to say a single word, except for *yes* and *no* and other small phrases necessary for survival. She has not brushed her teeth or washed her face or combed her hair or eaten anything. She has not gone home.

Traitorously, I have consumed every meal, washed my body, conversed with my mother. I have gotten hungry, gone to sleep. Remy has not. Even in this, even in grieving, she is in first place.

The two of us lie side by side on the faded quilt that covers my bed, watching as the light slowly leaks from the room. We have lain like this thousands of nights, on our backs, talking, reading, listening to music in the dark. But the world is different now. There is nothing worth doing, and both of us know it.

Details of River's death have begun to collect, swirling through the information channels of our town, gently filtered through my mother. An accident was reported at the covered bridge at 2:30 on Sunday morning. Police found River's truck smashed into the guardrail, the driver's side door open. He had a head injury; his blood alcohol content was through the roof. The police found his body quickly, in the shallows, only a hundred feet downstream. He either fell or jumped onto the rocks. Jury's still out.

Beside me, Remy's perfect stillness is punctuated only by periodic checks of her cell phone. Texts and calls have been coming nonstop, but she doesn't seem to answer a single one. Still, every time her phone makes a sound, she tenses with expectation. As if she is waiting for a message that never comes.

River is dead, I want to say. *He's not going to call you.*

For some reason I feel impatient with her. Abandoned. *You cannot leave me out of this*, I think. *River belongs to both of us.*

In the days since River died, she's been wrestling with

something. Underneath the unmoving features of her face is a secret. It's pulling her away from me.

I watch Remy turn the phone over in her hands, tracing the edges of the scratched black cat cover.

"Why do you keep checking your phone?"

"No reason," she says. "Stop asking."

And so it goes, one more day without River. One more day of nothing.

At 7:30, the bedroom door bursts open and Kendall, Liliana, and Callie walk in.

"Okay, Remy," Kendall says. "Time to come out."

Remy never invites her friends here, and now these three girls seem out of place in my house. I stare at Kendall, with her sharp, blunt-cut chestnut hair, in a colorful crocheted minidress and green eyeshadow; Callie with a long, blond braid over one shoulder, in cutoffs and a delicate white tank top; and Liliana, in a short skirt and baggy Nirvana sweatshirt, her long, black hair loose and wavy. It's like seeing celebrities at the grocery store; something doesn't quite fit. They are too perfect, standing in the doorway, appraising the scene. When I see my floral wallpaper and childish pink curtains through their eyes, I want to shrivel up and die. Luckily, they don't seem to notice me at all; they train all of their attention on Remy, who has yet to acknowledge their presence.

The girls move toward the bed in unison and I get up to make room for them, following some kind of unspoken command. "Oh, babe," Liliana says, sitting down on my bed and stroking her hair like she's a doll.

I watch them all together, fascinated as always by the subtle power dynamics. There should be a shift; Remy is the victim now, she has been laid low by tragedy. But through her stiffness, her silence, she maintains control. They comfort her because she allows it, and only to the extent that she is willing to let them.

I don't like seeing these girls in my bedroom, with Remy. This has always been *our* place.

"Remy," Kendall says, looking worried. "You need to go outside or something."

"I don't want to go outside," Remy says. Her voice is lifeless.

"We could drive to Peterson's for ice cream," Callie offers.

Remy doesn't answer.

Kendall makes a frustrated sound. "I'm not leaving until you get out of this bed. At least come watch a movie with us. We don't have to go anywhere."

"We just miss you," Liliana chimes in.

Remy rises onto one elbow, sighing deeply. Then she lifts the covers and stands up, seeming to have realized that it will be easier to just go along. Remy's plaid pajama pants are wrinkled and her shirt is stained, but no one comments on this. They all file out into the hallway, seeming to have forgotten me.

But as Remy passes by my chair, she reaches out for my hand and tugs me after her. Her hand is warm and her grasp is tight, and it feels good to know that she needs me in this way.

Mom is working tonight. She took Sunday and Monday off and has been paying for it all week.

She used to work at the hospital in town, and when I was little she was around a lot, doing mostly clinical visits and a few births each month. Then, a couple of years ago, the hospital closed down and she took a job in Albany. Now she works two or three overnight shifts each week, on top of clinicals, and she is always tired to the bone.

I can tell she feels awful about leaving us at home the past couple of days. She has left homemade meals with carefully written instructions and refreshed the flowers on the table, forget-me-nots and edelweiss from her garden. She calls a few times a day, just to check in.

In the kitchen, Kendall rummages around the fridge until she finds the strawberry crumble my mother made last Saturday morning. Before. She digs a spoon into the middle of it and then heaps a giant bite into her mouth.

"Wow," she says to me. "Your mom is a magician."

Kendall and I sit at the same lunch table every day, but she rarely addresses me so directly. To these girls, I'm a weird appendage on Remy's side. Callie and I used to be friends in elementary school, but like most people, she was eventually pulled into Remy's orbit and we drifted apart.

If it weren't for Remy and River, I might not have any friends at all. I am painfully awkward. Shy in an almost physical way, like my voice won't work when people are around. Most of the time when I'm in large groups, I sort of leave my body and drift off somewhere else. Or I just stare at one person, looking at the pores in their skin and the beds of their nails, marveling at each tiny detail until they notice me and move away. Afterward, my head and limbs buzz and my mind tells me terrible things about how strange I am, how nobody will ever like me.

"You should have some," Kendall says to Remy, holding out a spoon. Remy shakes her head and pulls at her stringy hair.

Callie and Lili grab forks and dig in, and then Remy and I watch as they polish off the entire thing. For a moment, it feels like we are connected the way we used to be, like we are thinking the same thought, at the same time: *I wish these people would leave our house. I wish they would stop being so fucking alive.*

The experience of watching a movie with Remy and her friends is overwhelming. As usual, I can't stop looking at Callie's shiny hair, Liliana's arched eyebrows, the way Kendall's top teeth bite into her lower lip when she says "Fuuuuuck," which she says a lot.

Another thing that's hard to keep track of with other people is the talking. There's too much to think about— what I'm saying, what everyone else is saying, the subtle rhythm of listening and replying that seems like it should be easy but isn't. I can never tell if I'm sweating or have bad breath; I don't know how to move my body without feeling like a monster; I don't know how to wear normal clothes without feeling like a part of me is naked.

For my own safety, I have always kept Remy's crowd at a distance, slightly blurred in the background. Now that they are on my couch I feel overstimulated and lost.

I must fall asleep eventually, because my eyes close and when I open them the movie is over and the house is dark except for the light from everyone's cell phones pointed at their faces. I lie still for a moment, head in the crook between the armrest and the cushion, trying to orient myself.

"Talk to us, Remy," Liliana says, a look of concern on her face. "What happened?"

Remy ignores her and picks up a kernel of popcorn from the floor. "I'm tired," she says, voice flat. And then she stands and walks up the stairs to my bedroom. I close my eyes again, hoping that the girls will go home.

"I'm worried," Kendall says. I think it's Kendall. It's hard for me to tell them apart by just their voices.

"Me too," says Callie.

Everyone's quiet then. My leg begins to itch, but I don't let myself reach for it. I lie perfectly still, willing them to leave.

Kendall says, "She was the last one to see River before he died. Something must have happened."

Callie shifts next to my feet and says, "She'll tell us when she's ready."

An uneasy feeling begins to creep into my stomach. It's clear that the girls think I'm still asleep, or else maybe I'm just that invisible.

"Or she won't," Liliana whispers. "It's Remy we're talking about."

"Well, either way," Kendall says. "She needs to figure this out. People need to get paid."

Before I can think about what she means, someone else says, "Jesus, Kendall, can you not?"

I open my eyelids halfway to see a blurry Kendall drop her face into her hands. "Sorry. You're right. I'm just worried."

Liliana puts an arm around her shoulders. "I know. This is a lot more than what we signed up for."

Kendall swipes at her eyes and the sparkles on her fingernails glow in the darkness. "Everything is just so fucked up."

"I know," Liliana says again.

Then Kendall straightens and takes a deep breath. "Come on. Let's get out of here."

I listen as the girls get up, gather their things, knock on the door of my room to say goodbye to Remy. I don't move until they are gone.

Over the next few days, Remy somehow retreats even further into herself. She goes home a few times, to get clothes, to check on her mother, and every time she leaves, I worry that she's not going to come back. It starts to feel a little like both of them are gone.

On Friday, while Mom is at work, I lie alone in the backyard, listening to the birds. Overhead, a giant oak tree spreads its arms skyward. Its leaves are fresh and green and new. I close my eyes, trying to imagine that River and Remy are there beside me.

We used to come out here a lot when we were kids, to lie in the grass under this tree. River called it the Birding Hour. He had an old nature guide from his grandfather that he'd bring to my house, and we'd use it to try to identify all of the birds in my yard.

"Shhh. Listen," he would always say when Remy and I started talking. River was always listening. Watching. He was special in that way.

When we got older, Remy would sometimes steal a bottle of Canadian Club Whisky from her mother and we would do Birding Hour: Night Edition. Once River got so drunk he threw up all over my mother's azaleas.

I think about these two Rivers, the one who noticed every beautiful thing and the one who sometimes drank until he couldn't remember who he was. I've always thought that all the parts of River fit together in a way that I could know and understand. But now I can see that I was missing something vital.

How could River, who loved all life more than any of us, have killed himself? My throat burns with how wrong it feels.

I close my eyes, my body heavy in the scratchy grass. My eyelids squeeze against the sting of tears. I reach for River's warmth beside me.

I hear footsteps, and then the soft rustle of Remy sitting down nearby.

"Birding Hour?" she asks.

I nod.

"Can I join you?"

"Sure."

Remy leans back and kicks off her shoes. "I can't believe he's missing spring," she says.

It's the first time she's mentioned River out loud since he died.

"It's the worst thing I've ever heard," I reply.

Remy watches as a small brown chickadee hops through the grass. But I watch Remy, holding my breath. Because it has become so rare to truly see her anymore. My mind fills with questions. *How are you?* I want to ask. *Where are you? Did something happen? Don't you know that you can tell me anything?*

My hand stretches toward hers. I feel like, even right next to me, she is somehow not close enough. But then her phone begins to ring. "I should get this," she says. And she gets up and walks toward the house.

Six days after River dies, the O'Dells hold a wake at Clancy's Funeral Home. Clancy's is the place where all the boys of Black Falls go when they die. It's at the very end of Main Street, where the town gets reclaimed by the forest, and the only thing that sets it apart is a giant muddy parking lot big enough to hold most of the cars of Black Falls. From the outside, it looks like a regular house. But inside, Clancy's has the customary dim lighting and ancient cherrywood furniture you'd expect from a funeral home. The heavy gold and green drapes keep out the early June light, which is much too bright for the dead.

The only time I've ever been inside Clancy's was when my cousin Scott, Remy's brother, died. He was much older than us, by seven years. He wasn't a very big part of my life, but I remember sometimes he'd come by the house to pick up Remy and he'd tuck her under his arm and ruffle her hair and I'd feel awed by his beauty and sharply jealous that Remy had a man in her family who loved her like that.

Remy and I both have deadbeat dads. Remy's parents weren't married and mine were never even together. Both of our fathers were out of the picture while we were still babies.

Scott's death changed Remy. She seemed to grow up overnight. That's when she began to wall herself off into sections. Each person would only be allowed to see a little piece. Maybe that was the only way she could keep things from hurting too much.

Remy's mother, my aunt Stephanie, became completely submerged in grief. Her skin tightened. Her bitterness deepened. She quit her job managing the IGA. She closed the curtains and turned on the television and let grief grow up around her, holding her in place. Like vines.

When Mom and I get to Clancy's, Remy's already there at the front, standing with River's family like a grieving widow. She wears a black sundress I've never seen before, and her knees look stark white where the hem cuts across them. She feels so distant I begin to wonder if we were ever friends, the three of us. Maybe I made the whole thing up.

A long line of people stretches all the way to the doors and I'm resentful that Mom and I have to stand in it with everyone else, while Remy is there at the front, next to River's mother, holding her hand. I look at River's parents, who aren't really parents anymore. Mr. O'Dell stands on the other side of Rebecca and there's a space between them, like they can't bear to touch. Both of them look pale and robotic, shaking hand after hand, like they are waiting for this, for life, to be over.

We cross the threshold into the giant parlor just as Rufus

Wainwright's version of "Hallelujah" begins to play, and then the line seems to speed up, moving us forward like a conveyor belt. I don't think I'm ready for this. The whole thing feels absurd and surreal, standing in line behind my history teacher to view my dead best friend's body. The air in the funeral home is artificially cold and the last thing I think before I see him is *I wish I'd brought a sweater*.

And then we are in front of a large wooden casket lined with cream satin, and there, lying inside, is a wax statue of my best friend River. He's wearing the suit he wore to the spring formal two weeks ago and his hair is neatly combed and the color of his skin is not right—too much makeup and not enough blood. He looks perfect, and monstrous, and for a moment I am frozen and can't look away.

This is a sick joke, I think, and then, inexplicably, I start to feel laughter bubbling up inside me. I begin to panic, and then Mr. O'Dell is there, pulling me toward him, into an awkward embrace. His head sort of falls down onto my shoulder and then he begins to cry. He feels somehow small and young. Gangly, like River. He smells like mint Trident and aftershave. We are both shaking, me with laughter, him with tears. I think that neither of us can believe this is happening.

The moment stretches, and I begin to feel strangely trapped. I don't know how to get out from under this man's grief.

When Mr. O'Dell finally lets me go, I look up to see Remy, staring at me. Her eyes are narrowed and her mouth is twisted in a grimace and it feels like she's telling me in our lifelong telepathic language to leave.

I feel baffled. Angry. River was *our* friend. I am a part of him, whether she wants me to be or not.

But the truth is, I don't want to be here with deadRiver and notRemy. So when my mom tells me she's going to stand up with the O'Dells for a while, I tell her I'll come back to pick her up later.

I walk back toward the door and then I turn around to look at them one more time. Remy's mask is back in place. She greets person after person with an expression that perfectly mimics both warmth and controlled, quiet grief. Something about her sends a shiver down my spine.

I'm halfway to the car when I see Bailey Jensen with his mother, getting out of a red pickup truck. He is wearing a crisp white button-down and dark jeans and his hair is wet, like he just got out of the shower. I haven't seen him since the night River died, and now he feels like a part of a different reality that has accidentally crossed over into this one. How is it possible that seven days ago I had *sex* with this person? I stare and stare at him, but he doesn't meet my eyes.

As I watch him walk away, I remember the feeling of his damp palms on me with sickening clarity. *Stupid*, I think. *You are so, so stupid.*

Sitting alone at the edge of the parking lot, I watch the dark woods across the road, trying to get the blurred image of Bailey out of my head. But when I do, all I can see is River's corpse, lying still in the coffin. I shake my head, hard. No. *River's not dead*, I tell myself. *None of this is real.*

I will myself to think of him alive: his easy laugh, his mismatched socks, the way he would say *C'mon, Jules* and I would always give in.

Behind me, a mourning dove calls out, long and slow.

And then suddenly, a miracle. I'm looking at a patch of deep green trees, my eyes hazy and unfocused, and he comes walking right out of it. It's like a hologram, the way he emerges, bit by bit through the shivering leaves, long arms pushing tree limbs out of the way. But I can tell he is real by the way the forest moves around him. He's dressed differently, all in black, and his hair is longer, more unruly, like he's crossed to the underworld and come back different somehow. My heart, which has been stopped for six days, kicks back to life with a somersault and then it finds its old favorite rhythm: *River, River, River, River.*

He steps up to the edge of the road and a gasp catches in my throat. And then a truck passes in front of him and when it is gone, when I've caught my breath and rubbed my eyes, I can see that it's not River at all, just a look-alike, frowning slightly and squinting into the sun.

"You look like you've seen a ghost," this person says once they've finally made it across the strip of gravel and into Clancy's parking lot.

I open and close my mouth a few times, but no noise comes out. My brain is stuck on repeat, my heart still beating: *River, River.* I am overcome, filled with longing and sadness, clasping my fingers tightly so as not to reach out and touch the face of this strange person, pull him into me, bury my face in his hair.

He rolls his eyes, which are not blue like River's but a

deep, bottomless black-brown. "I know," he says, frowning. "River, right?"

River.

I nod. *River.* If he notices how lost I am, he pretends not to. He grabs a joint out of his shirt pocket and tucks it between his lips.

"He was my cousin," he says, fumbling around for a lighter.

"Oh," I finally manage. Nothing more, nothing less, just *Oh.* Another truck rattles by out on the road.

"You're Jules, right?"

I nod. "How did you know?"

"We met a long time ago." He seems to give up on searching for the lighter but keeps the joint at the edge of his mouth. "I'm Sam," he says, holding out a hand.

I hesitate, afraid to touch this person who is so like River and so not. I must wait too long, because Sam drops his hand and I feel suddenly like the weirdest person in the world.

"Are you going to the wake?" I ask, awkwardly.

He looks toward the door of Clancy's, where the line has begun to stretch outside. "No," he says.

"Then why are you here?"

"My parents are in there and I don't drive."

He sits down beside me, picks up a tiny piece of gravel, and throws it into the center of the parking lot. "We were twelve. You wore the same Universal Studios T-shirt every day."

I nod, remembering the shirt, black with neon blue writing on the front. River had gotten Remy and me matching ones when he went to California with his family, and I'd liked it so much I'd stolen hers.

"I had two of them," I say, trying to remember him.

Another car pulls in, and we watch as Callie and her family climb out. Callie, her mother, and her little sister, Marta, are like a set of matching dolls in different sizes. They wear dresses that fall to the middle of their shins, each with a different floral pattern, and crisp white sneakers.

Sam and I are tucked between two cars, but somehow Callie's dad spots us anyway. He must see the joint between Sam's lips because he gives him an angry look. Sam takes the joint out of his mouth and tucks it behind his ear. He seems like he's nervous but he's trying not to be.

"Can you drive?" he asks.

"Yeah," I answer, watching as he picks up another piece of gravel.

"Can I have a ride?" He starts to stand up. "I need to get out of here."

Normally, I would never get into a car with a person I don't know. Especially not a person with drugs. But when I think of Remy and River and Bailey Jensen, all inside that airless funeral home, something possesses me and I pull my mother's keys out of my bag, spinning them around my finger.

We get in the car and I turn the engine. Sam hooks up his phone to the stereo and scrolls through his music, finally settling on something instrumental and futuristic, turning up the volume so loud I can't hear my own thoughts.

As I drive us away from Clancy's, I feel a strange pull in my stomach. It doesn't feel right to be leaving. When I watched Remy next to the casket, I was filled with a confusing anger, but now I see that she was doing the right thing. She was holding herself together. For all of them.

Why can't I be strong like her? Why can't I ever do or say what's needed? River is my best friend and he is dead. I should be there next to his coffin too.

Sam reaches over and taps the center of my forehead with one finger. I flinch. He turns the radio down.

"Your eyebrows are all pinched together," he says. "Are you okay?"

"I'm fine." I suddenly don't want to be here with this stranger. "Where do you need to go?" I ask.

"Not sure," he says. He looks out at the horizon like the world is full of possibility.

"Well, I should probably head back soon," I say. "So . . ." I tap my fingers anxiously on the steering wheel.

"Just turn left up here."

We turn, and follow Route 22 as it heads north, out of town. Sam reaches for the joint and I say, "Don't smoke that in here."

As the road begins to widen, I steal a few looks to study Sam's profile, which is actually quite different from River's, sharper. And then I see him, a boy with knobby knees and a buzz cut, visiting from New York City the summer after sixth grade.

"I remember you," I blurt.

He doesn't say anything.

I keep driving, a tense ball of anxiety in my belly. It's a warm day and the windows are down; the music flows into the breeze and everything feels like it belongs together, the movement of the long grass and trees, the insects, the music, the wind, the light. It makes me think of River.

"See," says Sam after a while. "Isn't this better?"

It isn't, I think. I don't say anything.

Still, as we drive, the thread pulling me back to Clancy's begins to weaken. The guilt and regret fade, leaving behind a pure, heavy sadness.

"Here," Sam says after about ten minutes, gesturing to a pullout at the side of an endless green field. We are almost at the New York–Vermont border, well out of Black Falls. "Stop here."

I pull over on the small patch of gravel, confused. "Here?"

"Yep," he says, absolutely certain. He reaches for the joint again. His eyes look tired and wary, ringed with dark circles. "I'm going to smoke this out here. You can go back if you want."

I watch as he unplugs his phone, unbuckles his seat belt, and steps out of the car, stretching his hands high above his head. I can't tell if he wants me to stay or go. I feel deeply uncomfortable.

"How will you get back?" I ask, leaning across the car.

He bends down so that the window frames his face, and I notice a small freckle just above his lip. A beauty mark. "I'll figure it out."

Suddenly my sadness feels like it's gotten much too big. This moment is a version of the past, disjointed and strange. How many times have I sat by the side of a road like this, even this road, with River in my car? We have been here in summer and fall and winter and now it is spring and the field is full of wildflowers. How?

"I can't believe it, Jules," said River. So. Many. Times. He was bowled over by everything, every plant, every season. He told me about the way wildflowers drop their seeds at the end of the summer and then they just wait there, all winter long, in the dark. He made it sound like the most romantic sacrifice anyone has ever made. I was sure my love was like that seed, waiting for him, under the soil.

Now it's hard to breathe in the tiny space of the car. I unbuckle my seat belt and get out.

I remind myself: this is not the past, it's the present. There's Sam, rummaging through his backpack, tossing a sweatshirt and black sketchbook out onto the pavement. "Aha!" he says a moment later, producing a small green lighter. He bends over the joint, turning his back to the breeze. "You want any of this?" he asks through a cloud of smoke.

"No," I reply.

"Okay."

He picks up his backpack and starts walking off into the field, notebook in hand, like he's Henry David Thoreau. Like he's River. I stand with my back against the car for a while, trying to catch my breath.

He calls back to me after a second. "Do you have a blanket?"

I walk around to the back of the car, opening the trunk to find the quilt I keep there. Beside it, in a crumpled ball, is River's rust-colored barn jacket. I imagine picking it up, lifting it to my face, breathing him in. It's what I would do if he were still alive. It feels pathetic now. I slam the trunk shut again, clutching the quilt to my chest.

As I spread it on the grass, the scent of spilled beer and campfire wafts up in a cloud. I remember the party—Bailey and kissing and then Remy crashing drunkenly through the trees. "River is gone," she'd said. And it felt disorienting, like maybe she was saying that by having sex with Bailey I'd managed to rid myself of this painful crush that felt like a curse, and at the same time it felt like maybe she was saying that River was dead, even though at the time all she was really saying was that River had left the party, drunk and alone in his truck.

I lie back on the blanket and close my eyes against the sun, and the feeling of missing him is so overwhelming that I start to feel dizzy. I don't know how to do this. I don't know how to exist anymore.

Sam comes back after a while and sits down on the blanket, opening his sketchbook.

"You look sad again," he says.

I ignore this, pressing my palms into my eyelids, trying to block everything out. But in the darkness I see Remy's angry face at the wake and I feel even more alone.

"Aren't *you* sad?" I ask.

Sam doesn't respond.

For a while he's quiet, except for the scratching of his pen on the paper. I think I start to fall asleep, the warmth of the sun giving me a hazy feeling. Minutes pass, or maybe hours, of lying on this blanket with this stranger. A flock of crows flies by overhead.

Then suddenly he says, "The thing I don't get is why everyone is talking about him like he's this hero. He was seventeen years old and just as messed up as the rest of us."

I am stunned by the incorrectness of this statement. I sit up, feeling all the blood rush to the surface of my skin. "No," I say, sun-printed shapes dancing in front of my eyes. "River was . . ." I don't even know how to finish this. River was *everything*.

Sam's cheeks redden with frustration. "Yeah," he says. "I know." I think I hear sarcasm in his voice.

I look at Sam, burning with anger, and I try to think of a way to defend my friend. My perfect, heroic, *dead* friend. But I'm so angry that all words fly away like dust.

Sam laughs, bitterly.

"What is wrong with you?" I ask.

"Lots of things," he says, leaning back on his hands.

I roll my eyes.

"No, really," he insists. "I'm totally fucked up."

Sam turns away from me, looking out at the million white flowers dotting the tops of the grass. "I used to love it up here," he says. "It's so beautiful and quiet." He picks a blade of grass and splits it with his thumbnail. "But now it just seems . . . I don't know." Sam looks back at me, his brown eyes cavernous and dark. "There's something wrong about this place," he says.

I stiffen. Black Falls is my home. Mine and River's and Remy's. This place made us. I reach for my anger, but I can't find it again. I'm too tired to argue. Instead, I stand. It's time to go.

We fold up the blanket without talking, and then Sam follows me to the car. He's quiet as we make our way back into town. As we drive past the police station, the grocery store, toward Clancy's, the knot of tension in my stomach remakes itself again. I park a block away from the funeral home, still not sure whether or not I want to go back inside. Sam takes his time climbing out of the car and I sit in the driver's seat, watching him.

"Jules—" he says as he stands next to the open door. "I—"

He stops, something solemn in his eyes. I am angry at him still, but I can't help wanting to hear whatever it is he's going to say. But then he takes a step back, closes the door, and walks away.

FOUR

The next afternoon is River's funeral, at the Episcopal church in the center of town. The building is a jewel on an otherwise drab street, with a gleaming white spire that rises up into the heavens. It's one of my favorite buildings, even though I've never been inside. When I was younger and my mother stopped at the gas station across the street, I used to look at the church and fantasize a wedding, walking down the aisle toward River, who would be wearing a suit the color of his eyes.

We get there early, but the parking lot is already full. My mother parks down the street and the three of us make our way down the cracked sidewalk—Remy's mother has decided to stay home. Remy wears a simple but elegant sleeveless black dress that flutters just above her knees, and natural makeup—flushed cheeks and a few swipes of mascara. Her hair is back in a French braid, no ribbon. She looks like a mix between Audrey Hepburn and Princess Guinevere. Timeless and classically beautiful. I'm not sure how to feel about her today. I think I can see her purpose now, in all of this. Survival. And duty. Still, her distance confuses me and makes me angry.

I am wearing black pants and a short-sleeve black blouse my mother picked out and I feel awkward, uncertain of whether I've left the right number of buttons open at the throat, self-conscious about the red bumps on the back of my upper arms. Unlike Remy, I feel like my grief is spilling out everywhere.

Rebecca invites us to sit in the family pew, right behind the O'Dells. Next to Rebecca and Jake are a good-looking middle-aged couple, who must be Sam's parents. His mother has blond hair pulled into an elegant low bun, and her back is perfectly straight. Sam's father is tall and thin, with short salt-and-pepper hair and square glasses. When he turns, I see that he has sparkling blue eyes. River eyes. I crane my neck, looking for Sam, but I don't see him anywhere.

The music in the church is more formal today than it was at the wake, and the organ plays a wandering melody as everyone comes in and finds their seats under the beautiful tall, wooden ceilings. Spring air wafts in through the open doors at the back, adding a freshness to the clean scent of the polish on the shining pews. I think about Scott's funeral, at the falling-down Catholic church on the other side of town, the way Remy's mother smoked cigarettes, one after the other, in the family lounge until the service began.

I lean close to Remy, wanting to rest my head on her shoulder. I know that she is hurting. She's the only other person in existence who can understand this yawning emptiness I feel inside. But she stiffens against my arm until I move back.

Then the music changes, to the melody of "Amazing Grace," and the pastor motions to suggest we should all sing along, using the lyrics printed in our programs, as the pallbearers—seven members of the boys' lacrosse team and Sam—begin to bring River's body down the aisle. Remy and I stand there, silent, as everyone around us starts awkwardly singing.

Remy looks angrily at the boys and whispers, "We should be the ones carrying his casket."

This momentary glimpse of her makes my heart skip a beat. But then they come closer and I remember that River's *body* is inside that box.

I am on the aisle and when Sam passes me, he turns toward me and winks. He's close enough that I can smell liquor radiating from his body, and he weaves a bit under the weight of the casket as he climbs the steps to the altar.

"What was that?" Remy whispers.

"Nothing," I say.

Normal Remy would reach down and pinch my arm and say, "Don't lie." But normal Remy has disappeared again, so she turns away and watches as the pastor takes his place at the head of the congregation.

Pastor Hall leads a prayer, and then various people from town get up to speak. The principal, Mr. Meyer, the lacrosse coach, Mr. Valdez. Rebecca asked my mother if I'd like to speak, but the thought of getting up in front of the entire town and trying to verbalize the experience of losing River felt like torture.

In front of me, Sam sinks down into the pew, and I wonder if he is actually sleeping. He lets out a small snort and his mother elbows him. He jolts upright. I can see her jaw clenched tightly with anger.

Then it's Remy's turn. She stands up, back straight, and walks slowly up the altar steps. She stands at the front of the church in her black dress, and in the diffuse light coming through the windows she looks like an angel. Like yesterday, her features are neatly arranged into an expression of perfectly calibrated sadness, like you'd see in a movie, no tears, nothing too over the top.

Where are you? I think.

The organ plays the first chords of a slow, somber version of the Beatles' "Let it Be."

As Remy starts to sing, I hear Sam whisper under his breath, "Jesus Christ."

His mother angrily whispers back, "Would you stop?"

Sam laughs darkly. "I refuse to believe that anyone likes this song. Not even River."

He's right; River hated this song and Remy knows it and this whole thing is ridiculous. But the way Sam says it—*not even River*—feels unkind.

I watch Remy until the song is over, waiting for a glimpse of the real person underneath. Her voice is beautiful, and even though several people around me are moved to tears, something about her performance feels fake, almost calculated to me. Finally, she returns to sit beside me and Jake O'Dell gets up to give the eulogy.

If Remy is artfully held together, Mr. O'Dell is completely blown apart. His hair is rumpled, his tie is crooked, he's cut himself shaving, just under his chin. Suddenly, for the first time in days, I am drawn out of myself and my heart actually aches for someone other than River.

He takes a paper out of his pocket and unfolds it carefully, setting it on the lectern. The whole congregation feels like it's collectively holding its breath.

"River was many things," he begins. "He was a student, an athlete, a friend, an unruly teenager." He laughs unsteadily at this. "He was messy. And very funny. And—" He pauses. "He was my son." Mr. O'Dell's voice breaks on the last word.

"I remember the night that River was born. We drove down to Albany twice over the course of two days before they would admit us." Another small laugh. He seems to be getting his footing now, regaining a bit of that famous O'Dell charisma. The side of his mouth tips upward in a familiar gesture. Like father, like son. "We were nervous parents from the start. But from that very first moment I held him in my arms, I knew that River was going to be something special."

Suddenly, Sam stands up, right in the middle of the eulogy. I see his mom pulling at the back of his jacket, but he resists her, swaying drunkenly on his feet. "This is bullshit," he says, just loud enough for the people sitting around him to hear it.

Mr. O'Dell looks genuinely confused. "I'm sorry, what?" he says. His voice is polite, uncertain.

"You're a hypocrite," Sam says, his voice louder now. He turns himself in a drunken circle, arms outstretched. "You all are."

For a moment, everyone is stunned silent. No one moves. I watch Sam's face as it changes from defiance to the slow realization of the enormity of what he's just done. Momentary regret. Then defiance again. "Fuck it," he says, more to himself than anyone else.

He makes his way out of the pew and then walks quickly toward the back of the church. Everyone watches. Then, just as he crosses the threshold to the outside, he leans over and pukes his guts out.

That night, after we pile a thousand casseroles onto plates in the church receiving room and watch River's body get lowered into the earth, Remy and I find ourselves back in my room. We lie across my bed, the same way we have done every day since River died; we are still and lifeless, barely breathing. A text comes in and Remy jumps. Like she's seen a ghost. Then, when she sees that it isn't whomever she's been waiting for (that it isn't River), she throws her phone back onto the mattress.

It never used to be like this with us. Remy was always an open book, at least on the surface, every dazzling detail of her life laid bare for me to see and covet. She would talk for hours. I would listen. But now she hasn't said a word in a week and I feel so lonely I could die.

Without River, without Remy, I have started to feel like I actually don't exist. I wonder if Remy even sees me in her peripheral vision as she stares distractedly at the ceiling, out the window.

Finally, when the room is completely dark except for

a long stripe of moonlight across the bed, Remy seems to get the text she has been waiting for. But it isn't elation that crosses her delicate features as she reads it, angling her phone away from me, it's something darker, sadness or maybe even fear.

I wonder who this notRiver person is. I remember the girls on my couch in the darkness. *People need to get paid.* Since when does Remy have so many secrets?

"Can you give me a ride to town?" she asks once she's carefully returned the mask of indifference to her face.

"Why?" I ask. The loneliness inside me begins to boil. I feel angry, really angry. I'm sick of being on the outside. I want in.

But Remy doesn't answer. Instead she gets up and heads toward the doorway and the warm triangle of hallway light falling into the room.

"Why?" I say again, more insistently this time.

"Because," she says, her voice betraying the smallest hint of anger.

I can feel the balance of power in the room. As always, it flows toward Remy, even though I'm the one with the car and she's the one who needs a ride. Remy has the information, the secrets, she has always had the life I want and she knows it; I'm always left feeling like a child who can't get a turn, who's about to start screaming and biting and pulling hair.

I dig my toes into the rug. "Tell me what's going on."

"Don't be dramatic," Remy says, leaning down to tie her sneakers. Her hands are so delicate.

"Don't be dramatic?" I feel myself losing control even

as it happens, my nails filing themselves down into sharp claws as I slip into Remy's trap. This is the moment when I say something mean. This is the moment I'm going to regret. "I watched you perform today," I say. "I watched your perfect, fake, sad face, the way you said 'This is for River' before you started singing. He didn't even like that song."

I feel the truth of Sam's words as I repeat them.

Remy rolls her eyes and says nothing. She is a wall of apathy, honed by a lifetime of my petty barbs.

"Is it real?" I ask. "Do you even miss him at all?" I heave myself up from the bed and start stalking toward her. "Really, Remy. Is there any part of you that actually feels anything?"

For once, my words hit home. It's rare that I'm able to wound Remy, but I have. Her shoulders fall.

"Forget it," she says. The mask drops and I see actual, honest-to-god regret on her face. "Good night, Jules," she says. Then she turns and walks out the door.

FIVE

The next morning, Monday, is the first day back at school for Remy and me since River died.

"You need to get out of this house," Mom says as she sets a steaming bowl of oatmeal in front of me on the kitchen table. She looks toward the stairs. "Where's Remy? She's going to be late."

I shrug, feeling guilty. "She went home last night. I think she's sick of me."

Mom frowns. "Everyone deals with grief differently," she says, like I should cut Remy slack for the way she's been shutting me out.

What about me? I think. *What about how* I'm *grieving?* And then I think, *How* am *I grieving?* And then I feel like I can't breathe.

"Eat," Mom says. "I added a little bit of yarrow. For courage." Mom is always sticking extra ingredients into things to fortify us against the world. Sometimes I think it's silly, but other times I feel a darkness in Black Falls, in the thick, dense forests, the burned-out buildings on Avenue B, the oppressive wave of bodies in the halls of the high school, all following the same intangible thing.

I think Mom can feel it too. She never talks about growing up in Black Falls. Or about my father, who I know grew up here too. All I know about him is that they weren't friends, and that he died of a heroin overdose when I was seven. But sometimes we'll be driving by the high school or the police station and she'll get really quiet, and I know she's thinking about the past.

Mom is one of those people who actually got out of Black Falls, once. She went to college in North Carolina on a scholarship. She stayed away for an entire year. Then she came home on winter break of her sophomore year and got pregnant with me. She might have been able to keep going, but then her mother got cancer and Stephanie got pregnant too. My mom couldn't leave them.

After I was born, Mom got her associate's degree at a community college and then finished her bachelor's and completed nursing school by commuting to Albany. When I was four, she took me to Connecticut for nine months while she got her midwifery degree. And then we came back again.

I don't know how Mom really feels about coming back home. But I can tell by the small ways she tries to protect Remy and me, with yarrow or chamomile, long walks and stern warnings, that she has never fully settled into this place.

On the way to school, I drive past Remy's house without picking her up. I almost circle back, but then I change my mind. I remember how angry and hurt I feel and I keep going.

I drive slowly, reflecting on the silence in my car, which is now so empty and quiet that I can hear a faint squealing in my brakes when I slow at the stop sign on Spring Road. Three weeks ago, I drove this route with Remy and River lounging back in their seats, complaining about a quiz in chemistry, me trying not to look at the way they held hands across the space between front and back seat. Now it's hard to believe that anything like that ever happened.

All night I thought about Remy, restless in the tangle of my bedsheets. I can tell that something is wrong with her. Something bigger, even, than this unspeakable loss. I want to reach her. I need to reach her. But she feels farther away than she's ever been.

I get to school and look for Remy in the stream of students coming in from the parking lot. When we fight, she takes the bus and always arrives first. I look for her in the hallway, at her locker, in homeroom, but she isn't there. One class passes and then another.

In the hallway, the memorial posters of River's face are already a little bit battered. People walk by them without even looking. Every time I see one, I stop and stare at it until someone nearly runs into me.

I stand at my locker after second period, thinking about how two weeks ago, River and I stood here together. Last period of the day.

"I need to get out of here," he said. "Let's cut PE."

We snuck out the doors next to the gym, going the long way around to the parking lot. River's dad teaches English and coaches cross country at Black Falls and could have easily spotted us from his classroom windows if we went out the front. We drove to Peterson's to get soft serve, even though it was cold and cloudy. River got chocolate swirl and I got plain vanilla. We sat on top of one of the beat-up picnic tables, me in my puffer and River in a short-sleeve T-shirt.

"Aren't you cold?" I asked, shivering a little.

He shrugged. "I like to feel the air."

"You're so weird," I said, and then he pulled me into him, right under his arm, and rested his chin on the top of my head.

Looking back, I think there may have been something strange about him on this day and the ones that followed. A residue of sadness that dimmed his usual glow. But I didn't notice because I was so overcome when he touched me.

I wriggled out from under his arm when I didn't think I could take any more. "We should head back," I said. "You're going to be late for practice."

Moments like these—just River and me—were rare and special, but they made me a little uneasy. I always felt like I was taking River away from the rest of his life. And maybe some part of me *could* sense that there was something wrong this time. But River pulled me back again, like maybe he needed this more than I realized.

"Nah," River said. "Let's take our time. I don't think I'm going to go today."

An hour later, at lunchtime, I sit at my usual spot at the very edge of Remy's friends' table, next to where River used to sit. Nobody has filled his space yet, so there is some distance between me and the rest of the group.

"Where the fuck is Remy?" Kendall asks. Today she is wearing a long-sleeve blue crop top and low-slung jeans, a gemstone winking from the piercing in her belly button.

"I don't know," Callie says, tapping her clawlike fingernails on the table. "I've been texting her all morning. Not that she ever replies anymore." She takes a bite of a waxy-looking apple and then frowns and puts it back on the table. I listen to them, and I wonder where Remy might be.

"Well, I want my money back," Bailey says. "This is bullshit."

I look over to where he is sitting at the other end of the table, golden arms and rumpled T-shirt and perfectly combed hair. He still hasn't looked at me since we had sex. I knew better than to expect anything from him, but the lack of eye contact and basic greeting feels egregious. *Am I actually invisible?* I wonder. *Do I not exist without Remy and River here?* What would happen if I picked up Callie's apple and chucked it at his face? If I stood up on the bench and said, *YOU WERE INSIDE ME, YOU DICKHEAD.* I hold my own hand up in front of my face, just to make sure I'm real, then I grip it over my mouth to make sure I don't really throw anything.

Around me, without me, the conversation continues.

"Calm down," Liliana says, rolling her eyes. She is wearing her Nirvana sweatshirt again. "She'll fix it."

"She'd better do it soon," Kendall says, attempting a disaffected-looking yawn. "Bailey's not the only one."

Callie clears her throat, loudly, gesturing with her head

to where I am sitting in the corner, trying to disappear into my half-eaten sandwich. Over the years I've become an unobtrusive feature of the table, like a clump of moss. But sometimes Callie still sees me. "Let's talk about this later," she says.

Bailey scowls. "Fine." He still doesn't look at me.

As I walk from lunch to my next class, an uneasy feeling starts to stir in my chest. I am unnerved by the conversation. And I miss Remy.

I open my phone and check her social media sites, the Instagram and TikTok pages with the same profile pictures of the bottom half of Remy's heart-shaped face, bubblegum-pink lipstick and blond hair. She hasn't posted anything since the night River died.

I open the message window and type a text: I'm sorry I didn't pick you up.

I wait for Remy's reply. I've seen her ignore thousands of texts in the last week, but I want her to make an exception for me. I need her.

I slip into my seat in Spanish as the bell rings. All through class I furtively check my phone. The text box stays empty. Regret starts to seep in, and worry.

I text again in English class: Are you okay?

Nothing. I sit staring at the screen until the last bell rings, a rock in my stomach.

After school I drive to Remy's house. Rain clouds gather at the edge of the sky, thick and violet gray. My hair is pulled back into a tight ponytail, the way I always wear it, but I can feel unruly curls beginning to spring out at my hairline, reacting to the humidity. I look into the rearview mirror, catching my own eyes there. *It's okay*, I tell myself. *Everything is okay.*

Nobody answers Remy's door, so I let myself in. The house is empty and quiet, the smell of cigarettes settling in an invisible film over everything. The coat rack by the door is covered in old purses and jackets. Empty Diet Coke cans line the edge of the coffee table. Dishes lean in a haphazard stack at the edge of the sink.

I try to remember a time when the house wasn't like this. Before Scott died things were different. Remy's house wasn't cozy like mine, but at least it was clean.

When she lost him, Aunt Stephanie stayed in her bedroom for a year, her hair turning brittle and her mouth sagging into a deep, sad line. At first, Remy was afraid to leave her side. But eventually it became clear that Stephanie wasn't going anywhere. Remy wasn't going to let herself get stuck like that.

I knock at the door to Remy's room, but she doesn't answer. When I crack the door open, it's like I'm entering a sealed chamber. The air in here is cleaner, the space sparse and neat: soft bed, clear desk, fluffy white rug. I'm almost never in Remy's room and it feels like I'm doing something secret right now, something forbidden. I want to open her notebooks, to rifle through the papers in her drawer, but something holds me back. I stand in the doorway. Outside, rain begins to drum on the windows.

I look at the neat stack of textbooks on the desk, at the backpack hung carefully on the back of the chair, at the closet, door ajar, dresses hanging perfectly on their hangers like doll's clothes.

"Remy?" a raspy voice says behind me. I startle, banging my foot into the doorjamb. I turn in the dim light of the hallway to see Stephanie, in baggy sweatpants and a pink Victoria's Secret tank top. She looks exhausted, the skin under her eyes bluish and heavy.

She puts a hand to her chest. "Oh. Jules. It's you. What are you doing in here?"

I feel like I've been caught doing something wrong. The guilty feeling in the pit of my stomach spreads to my limbs.

I walk past Aunt Stephanie and head toward the living room, toward daylight. "I'm looking for Remy," I say.

Stephanie follows, rubbing the edges of her forehead and then reaching into her pocket for her cigarettes. "She's not here."

I swallow. "Have you seen her?" I ask.

"Not in a few days," Stephanie says. For a brief moment, I wonder if she even knows that River is dead. If she cares.

"I need to go," I say. "Tell her to call me if she comes home, okay? It's important."

Stephanie nods absently, then sinks into the couch and turns on the television.

Outside, I sit in my car and try to breathe. Rain streams down the windshield and the air is thick and hot and it feels like I am choking it down, like I might be drowning.

PART 2

June

Remy Valentine Green
Prettiest girl you've ever seen
Hair of gold, eyes of blue
Where, oh where, oh where are you?

SIX

The next twenty-four hours pass in a blur. Remy is gone, vanished, disappeared like a cloud drifting out of the sky, vaporized by the sun.

On Tuesday morning the police come to take our statements. Outside, rain falls; the sky is heavy and gray. Officer Kelly and Zack White knock on the front door, in pressed police uniforms and shiny shoes.

Ever since Scott died, even before that, Mom has been suspicious of the police in Black Falls. But she settles them down at the kitchen table anyway. She brings everyone big mugs of dandelion nettle tea, then she slides her chair up right next to mine.

The officers tell us that, at this point, it looks like I'm the last person to have seen Remy before she went missing. They relay this information without a hint of accusation, and I watch them from a million miles away, at the edge of a yawning canyon in my mind. Remy is gone. It's all my fault. I can't seem to grasp on to anything else.

Officer Kelly brings his mug to his lips, then seems to change his mind, setting it back down at the table. Zack crosses his ankle over his knee and sits there quietly, taking up space. "Can you tell us what happened, Jules?" Officer Kelly says. His face is round and red cheeked, his hair thinning at the back. His eyes are small, watery, light blue.

I open my mouth but can't make any words come out. I close it again, afraid I'm going to scream.

Zack looks at me with friendly, clear blue eyes. "It's okay, Jules," he says. "Take your time."

My mother reaches over and grabs my hand. I begin to tell them. "We'd been up in my room, basically all afternoon. Not really talking or doing anything." I clear my throat. "It's been like that since River . . ." I can't say it. "She got a text message and she wouldn't tell me who it was from. We fought about it. She asked for a ride to town." I swallow. "I kept asking her to tell me why. She wouldn't. I got mad. And then she left."

A wave of nausea washes over me. Mom squeezes my hand.

"Was anything off about her?" Officer Kelly asks.

Everything, I think. I look away.

"The girls just experienced a huge loss," Mom says, voice impatient. "Of course Remy wasn't acting like herself."

Zack gives us a look that is almost conspiratorial, like he knows how much of a clown his boss is. Like he understands. Callie is his little sister. He grew up with Remy and River too. "Right," he says. "Of course." His voice is deep and comforting. He gives Mom a small smile and takes a sip of his tea, trying his best not to grimace at the bitter herbs.

"Do you remember if she said anything else? Anything that could have been a clue about where she was going or who she was meeting up with?"

The memory of two nights ago starts playing again in my mind. Remy asking me for help. Remy leaving. I feel vomit begin to rise from my stomach and I run for the bathroom.

That night, when I am walking to the kitchen to get a glass of water, I hear my mother sobbing behind her bedroom door.

I lie awake in my own bed for hours, one hand on the spot in my comforter that is still Remy-shaped. The pit of grief that opened for River widens, yawns, sucks me inside. An icy numbness starts in my toes and spreads up through my body.

I curl my knees into my chest, feeling the smallness of myself. I have never felt particularly small, but without my two best friends I feel like I have begun to shrink. They are gone now. Both of them. More than anything, I want to follow, but I don't know how.

I bury my face into Remy's pillow. Already the scent of her is fading. "*Please*," I whisper. Over and over again. But I don't know what I'm asking for.

All night, I torment myself with visions of what might have happened as Remy walked five long miles in the darkness toward town. Because of me.

In my mind, a car pulls over, Remy gets inside.

"No," I say. "No. No. No." I keep saying it until I am screaming, sobbing, and my mother bursts through the door.

The next day the whole town searches the woods for Remy's body. I feel like I'm in a nightmare as Callie and I walk through the woods side by side. After Officer White finds Remy's phone, everyone stays clustered by the road for a while, talking in small, quiet groups about what it might mean.

I don't want to hear what anyone has to say. I slip out of my mother's arms, which are holding me too tightly. "I need a minute," I tell her, and then I walk down the foggy road, away from the crowd.

"Remy is not dead." I say it out loud to myself, to cover the sound of all the voices that seem to be speculating otherwise.

I walk until I round a bend in the road and can't see them anymore. Then I sit down in the wet grass and drop my head into my hands.

I think the thought that's been throbbing against my eardrums for two days: *This is all my fault.* The moment replays in my mind again and again: Remy walking out my bedroom door. Me letting her go.

I breathe. Long, shaky breaths of damp earth and new grass. I think of all the things that have died to form the soil underneath me.

"Everything dies," River said once.

"Not Remy," I say now.

"Not Remy what?" a new voice says. I open my eyes. River's cousin Sam stands on the edge of the asphalt, hands in his pockets. He looks tired, and his hair is sticking up on the side.

"Nothing," I say.

Sam takes a step toward me. "Are you okay?"

I don't answer. He comes closer and sits down. He smells like stale alcohol again.

"That was a stupid question," he says. "I'm sorry."

"Are you drunk?" I ask.

Sam shakes his head. "Last night I was. Now I'm just hungover."

"Shouldn't you be in New York City right now? In school?"

Sam laughs and I feel anger begin to flare in my chest. But I'm grateful. Because Sam is real. Alive. And this pulls me back from the panic I'm feeling.

"I got expelled," Sam says. He watches my face as if expecting a particular reaction. But I just shrug. I have nothing to say to this.

"Can I sit here for a few minutes?" Sam asks, leaning back on his hands.

I want to say no, but I know if I do that I'll be alone again, with this loss that is too deep to survive. "Okay," I say.

Sam stretches his legs out in front of him, crossing his feet at the ankles. Above our heads, a bird calls out.

"Red-winged blackbird," Sam says. He seems to catch himself, like he might be embarrassed for blurting that out. "My grandfather taught me."

"Your grandfather taught me too," I say. I smile, thinking about Birding Hour. But then I remember that I will never sit with River again, listening to birdcalls. "River had this book from him. A guidebook."

Sam looks up into the trees. "I had one too."

Sam pulls a sketchbook out of his backpack and begins

to draw. I watch over his shoulder as a bird appears on the page. It's small and delicate with dark, shining eyes.

"You like to draw," I say. It isn't a question, just an odd statement. I cringe inwardly at my awkwardness. But Sam smiles.

"I do."

"You're really good at it."

"Thanks."

I look down, flustered. "Sorry. I'm so awkward."

"No you're not," he says. He looks at me. "You just like thinking more than you like talking."

I nod, surprised. "Yeah."

He starts filling in the feathers on the blackbird's wing. "Nothing wrong with that." He says this like there actually might be something *right* about it. I suddenly feel even weirder. I don't know what to do with my hands.

We hear talking, and then a small group of people comes walking around the bend. One of them calls out to us—my history teacher, Mr. DiMarco—"They're starting up again!"

The surrealism of the moment almost makes me laugh out loud. And then the awfulness of it begins to sink in again.

"I don't think I can keep going," I say to Sam. I don't know if I'm talking about the search or if I'm talking about something bigger.

"That's all right," he says. "Let's just stay here until it's over."

We sit by the side of the road for a long time. I watch Sam as he finishes the drawing, filling in the scales on the feet, erasing and smudging until everything is just right. The bird looks real. Alive.

When he's done, he tears the paper out of his sketchbook and places it in my hands.

That night, everyone descends on Remy's small house on Lakeview Road. It's been years since my family was anywhere together and it feels strange. Stephanie is Mom's only sister, but they have three half brothers between them and Remy and I have lots of cousins, mostly older boys.

People bring food, a box of wine, a few cases of beer. The gathering swells into a strange sort of party. Nobody seems to know how to process what's happening. Remy is missing. Gone. All that anyone found today was a cell phone. There has been no conclusion.

I keep hearing small snatches of conversations. People say things like *She shouldn't have been walking alone at night* and *You know how these kinds of stories play out.* I can tell that they are thinking the worst, but nobody will say it outright.

Today, after the search party disbanded and Mom and I drove back to our house on Turnpike Road, when I was finally all alone in my room, I made a decision, reached a conclusion. This is not a dead girl story. This is not a horror movie or true-crime podcast. This is my life, Remy's life. She is alive and I'm going to find her.

Eventually almost everyone is drunk enough to get loud, to start making jokes, to demolish the buffet and turn on the

Red Sox game. They aren't here for Remy anymore. Not really.

Mom and Aunt Stephanie and I eat alone in the living room. People avoid us, like we are stained with a depth of misfortune they do not want to touch. I sit on the floor next to the couch and try to ignore the smell of cigarettes coming from the overflowing ashtray in the center of the coffee table. My mother and Aunt Stephanie eat quietly as the raucous sound of men in the next room grows louder and louder.

Then my cousin Bobby walks in the front door with Derek Stevenson. Bobby is small and clean cut and Derek is tall and rangy, his long hair pulled back into a low ponytail. Derek's brother, Tate, is the one who sold the bad drugs to Scott. My mother and I both freeze, waiting for Stephanie's reaction. But she just nods at them and turns back to the television.

Bobby says, "Is my dad here?"

"Fuck if I know," Stephanie says.

Bobby and Derek head into the kitchen and the three of us are left alone again. Mom and I stare at Aunt Stephanie.

"What?" she says, reaching for a cigarette. "Derek's a good kid. It's not his fault what Tate did."

This is the most she's talked about what happened to Scott in years. Stephanie lights her cigarette and a curl of smoke wafts up around her face. Her skin looks blue in the light of the television.

The smell of smoke and menthol quickly becomes overpowering, but Mom and I don't say anything. We wait, as if knowing there's more.

"What I can't forgive," Aunt Stephanie says, tapping her

cigarette against the ashtray, "is Remy getting up and walking out of here." She looks up and says, "She's ruined my life."

Mom closes her eyes, as if she is praying for restraint. "I know you're upset, but come on."

Stephanie picks up her fork and points it toward the door. "I'll never get over how ungrateful she's been. To just leave me here in this house."

I see this comment register on Mom's face, her composure beginning to slip. "Aren't you worried?" Mom says. "She could be anywhere."

Stephanie shrugs and waves her cigarette in front of her face. "She'll be fine," she says.

"She's sixteen," Mom says, gritting her teeth.

As Aunt Stephanie and Mom's voices become louder, I feel my chest begin to tighten. I'm not ready to witness the fight that's about to unfold. I quietly excuse myself and tiptoe down the hall to Remy's room.

This time, I go all the way inside, closing the door behind me. I walk up to the closet; I run my hands over her clothes. River's lacrosse sweatshirt hangs at the end of the rack, a little apart from everything. I hold it up to my face, inhaling deeply. Grief wells inside me, for both of them, thick and confusing. "Remy," I whisper. "Please."

Are you sure you want to find me? Remy's voice whispers inside my head.

Always, I whisper back.

Then look, Remy says.

I nod. Then I begin to search. I look around for anything out of place, but Remy's room is maddeningly perfect. I grab her planner and notebooks, shoving them into my backpack. I rifle through the closet and pull River's sweatshirt off its hanger, and then I take Remy's sleek, black makeup box down from the shelf.

I wonder if the cops have been here yet, if Zack White's gloved hands have thumbed through Remy's delicate dresses.

I turn to the jewelry on top of the dresser. A tiny cross from Remy's first communion, River's State Championship ring, a pair of fake diamond earrings her dad gave her before he left. I have spent my life coveting all of Remy's things, knowing they were precious to her, and now she's left every single one of them behind.

I search the bookshelf and nightstand. I slide my hand under the mattress. I find nothing.

Finally, I crawl over to the loose floorboard behind Remy's desk. This is where Remy keeps her contraband—gum and candy when we were little, vape pens and condoms now that we are grown. Like she's pretending she has the kind of mother who would care about any of these things.

I use my fingernails to pry the board up, unsure of what I'll find inside. My heart begins to pound. The board comes loose, and in the space below I see a journal and a neat roll of cash, bound up in a rubber band. I lift out the money and hold it in my hand for a moment, feeling its weight. *People need to get paid*, I remember Kendall saying.

What is Remy involved in? It couldn't be drugs. Not after what happened to Scott. But what else is there?

I put the journal and money in my backpack. I try not to listen to the voice that tells me Remy would have brought her cash if she'd run away.

The door opens, suddenly, and I jump, trying to shove the board back in place. Then Derek Stevenson slips inside and I freeze. For a moment I think I can hide behind the desk, but he spots me immediately.

"What are you doing?" Derek says. His hair is down now and falling partially across his eyes, making him look almost menacing. He eyes my backpack, Remy's makeup kit, me.

"What are *you* doing?" I reply. I cross my arms, as if to protect myself.

"Just escaping the crowd for a minute," Derek says, pushing his hair out of his face. His voice is low and a little scratchy. His eyes are beautiful.

I tighten my jaw. "This is Remy's room. You shouldn't be in here."

Derek smiles. "Oh, I know this is Remy's room." He takes another step inside. "What's under that floorboard?"

My pulse flutters in my throat. "Nothing."

Derek raises an eyebrow.

With shaking hands, I lift up the board to show him. "Whatever it was, she took it with her."

He tilts his head to the side.

"What?" I ask.

"I'm trying to figure out if you're lying."

There's something threatening in the tone of his voice. I force myself to hold my voice steady. "You should leave."

Derek holds up his hands. "Easy," he says. He walks slowly across the room and sits down on Remy's white bedspread. "Remy and I were friends." I don't like the look on his face when he says this. A small smile, like he's remembering something secret. And then it disappears, and he says, "I was Scott's friend too."

Derek gets up and starts walking slowly around the room, looking at Remy's things. He lifts up one of the fake diamond earrings. Then he opens each of her dresser drawers. I watch him, even though I'm scared, because I desperately want to know what he's looking for. If it's this roll of money, I want to know what that means.

"You can tell a lot about a person from what they've left behind," Derek says. He stops and looks at me. "Don't you think?"

I clench my backpack to my chest. Derek takes a step closer.

"DEREK!" My cousin Bobby's voice echoes down the hall. "LET'S GO."

Derek holds my eyes for one second longer, then turns and begins to leave the room. He looks back as he reaches the door. "Come find me," he says. "If you change your mind." I'm not exactly sure what he means. But when he closes the door behind him, I realize that he was talking about Remy and Scott the same way, as though both of them are dead.

It takes a few minutes for my body to stop shaking. I get up, placing my backpack carefully next to the door. And then I walk over to Remy's bed, turning on the TV, suddenly exhausted. I lie down, pretending she is next to me. I flip around the channels until I find a scary movie. One Remy would love.

Forty-five minutes later, my mom comes to find me. She

lies down in the blue light of the television and smooths the hair back from my forehead. "I love you, honey," she says. Her voice is tired, fragile.

I scoot my head into the crook of her neck, smelling her lily of the valley perfume. "I love you too," I say.

"It's going to be okay," she says to me. I can hear in her voice that she doesn't believe her own words. But I do. Remy is alive. I am going to find her.

At home, back in my room, I take out Remy's things, one by one. I put her journal inside my nightstand, not ready to open it yet.

I turn to her planner instead. It is full of notes, symbols, hearts, flowers, groupings of words like *what if I* and *how can we*—thoughts with no endings or explanations. And then, after River died, a brief trickle to nothing. I go through the pages again, looking for patterns. Thursday night shifts at the diner. Cross-country practice every afternoon. River, everywhere plans with River. To-do lists: *Talk to M, Buy a green sweater, Sephora sale, paper for AP Lit.*

The book lists nearly every detail of Remy's life, but there is nothing to hint at the vast, deep expanse of mystery underneath. I close the planner, holding it to my chest. I will some essence of Remy to come seeping out of the binding. I miss her. I miss her so badly. I feel lost; I don't know where to begin.

Just look, Remy says. *Look and find me.*

SEVEN

When a child goes missing, the first seventy-two hours are critical. This is what Officer Kelly said, the day of the search. For the first few days after Remy disappears, everyone in town seems to buzz with urgency. An Instagram post goes viral, the local news comes to Black Falls High, and members of the police force work double shifts, cop cars circling everywhere like sharks. A few people call in to report sightings of a blond sixteen-year-old, in an old car, at a gas station. Seventy-two hours pass, then ninety-six.

Another thing Officer Kelly said, quietly to another cop at the water table, is that most girls are killed within two days of being kidnapped.

Mom calls the station every night for updates, and soon it becomes clear that they are investigating Remy's disappearance like it's a murder. All of the leads have gone cold. Remy's phone is being tested for DNA. In the grocery store, at school, people talk about her like she's one of those dead girls on *Dateline*.

On Saturday morning, the first weekend in June and six days since I last saw Remy, I pull my car into the gravel parking lot of the Mather Farmstand, just as the sun is rising. Out front stands Rebecca Mather, River's mother, whom I have not seen since the funeral. She has aged hundreds of years in just two weeks, gray hairs sprouting among her long blond waves, deep rings settled in below round blue eyes. She wears a faded blue T-shirt dress and dusty work boots.

The Mather Farmstand has been in River's family for four generations. The small wooden building perches on the side of County Route 33, the long road that leads into the center of Black Falls. Behind it, fields of crops stretch in long, neat, green rows. On the other side of the street is forest, deep and unending. A path through the trees leads to River's house.

The stand itself is closed on three sides with an open front that faces the road and the woods beyond it. A long, narrow wooden counter takes up most of the back, a very old cash register on top and all different sizes of baskets below. The rest of the room is a maze of tables for fruits and vegetables, jars of honey and balms from another farm down the road.

Since we were thirteen years old, River, Remy, and I have spent our summers working at the stand, among the vegetables, playing vicious rounds of speed with an old, bent deck of cards. Remy and I were deadly competitors, but sometimes I'd lose to River just to feel the sharp sting of his hand slapping mine.

Rebecca pulls me into her wiry arms for a hug as soon as I am within reach, and her body shudders once, then catches itself, going rigid against me. I hold my breath until she lets go.

"Any word?" she asks.

I shake my head.

Rebecca closes her eyes, makes almost the same bereft expression as my mother. "I can't believe . . ." she says, and I nod, a giant glob of guilt beginning to rise in my chest. Then she clears her throat and the moment passes; there is work to do.

Today is the first day of the season, and Rebecca takes me through the familiar routine of opening up, not talking much or even looking at my face. It must be hard for her to see me, here in the stand, alive, alone.

"I'll be back at four to help close up," she says. Then finally, she meets my eyes. "Thank you."

"Of course."

"I'm trying to find more help, but it's . . ."

"I know," I say. "It's okay."

I listen to her car pulling out of the lot and then it's just me. I stand there, in front of the counter, overwhelmed by how alone I feel.

"Everyone is alone," River said once, just a few days before he died. "We only pretend we aren't to make ourselves feel better." We were sitting on my porch steps in the morning sun, waiting for Remy to get ready. I remember looking over at him. He was looking away from me, but I could sense a strangeness about him. It made me uneasy; I wanted to make him laugh again.

"That's so depressing," I said dryly, poking him under the ribs.

River laughed, and when he turned back to me he was smiling. "Actually, it's kind of comforting when you think about it," he said.

At the time I thought that this was one of River's usual philosophical moments. Now I wonder if he was trying to tell me something important about himself.

I force myself to swallow back the unending grief and spend the first few minutes of the day walking along the tables of produce, straightening pint boxes and crates, touching the tiny, perfect seeds on shiny red strawberries. In June the stand is full of early summer vegetables: beets, tender greens, broccoli, garlic blossoms, green onions, peas. It's all so beautiful I almost can't look at it. I don't feel like I deserve beauty today. Not after letting Remy go like I did.

When I am done setting up, I sit down on the wooden stool behind the counter and wait. Cars pass, one after the next after the next. My mind wanders and I find myself thinking of Sam. I haven't seen him since the search party, and I don't know if he's still in Black Falls or if he's gone back to the city. I've taped his drawing to the wall above my desk and now the blackbird's dark eyes follow me wherever I go.

Nine o'clock comes without a single customer, and then ten. June isn't usually the busiest month at the stand, but after an hour I start to wonder if people are avoiding this place because of River.

I stare out across the road, at the edge of the forest. It's dark, thick, loud with birds and insects. I've grown up playing in these trees, but from this angle it feels like the kind of woods that would suck you inside and spit you out a hundred years later, a completely different person. I let my eyes focus and unfocus on the layers of green, feel the pull of it, the way my mind clears and I start to disappear.

The feeling of missing Remy and River is starting to take over everything, to make me feel like I might not even be real. When you define yourself by your love for someone else, and that person ceases to exist, do you stop existing too? I've been sleeping with River's sweatshirt on, clinging to one of Remy's old T-shirts, to smell their scents and remind myself that they were here, that they were a part of me, that I was a part of me. The quiet in my room, my house, my head is unending.

Remy is not dead. Every time I hear someone whisper otherwise, I become more certain of this. The fact that no one can find her just seems like a failure of imagination. In my bed, at night, I willfully imagine Remy climbing onto a bus, arriving in another city. When River came back from his California trip, Remy made him describe every ride at Disneyland again and again, in excruciating detail. Now I imagine her riding Space Mountain, her face glowing in the darkness.

It isn't hard, imagining Remy leaving all of this behind. Black Falls has always depressed her. She always longed to be somewhere else. I just need to figure out where she's gone to.

A car pulls into the parking lot, startling me out of my thoughts. I watch as a young father pulls two small children out of his SUV, carrying one in his arms, holding the other by their small, dirty hand. It's a moment before I recognize

Mr. Bellamy, who teaches biology at Black Falls K–12. He was our teacher last year, in tenth grade. He gets to the stand and lets the children loose to paw through the produce.

Mr. Bellamy is handsome, if a little bit disheveled. He has stylish glasses that suit his face and sweat stains in the armpits of his gray T-shirt that have spread outward into visible territory.

"Jules," he says with a strained, overly enthusiastic smile. "How are you?"

I'm not sure what to say to this, so I stand there staring awkwardly at his left shoulder.

For a moment I imagine what it would be like if Remy were here instead of me. She would tell a story, make a joke; she would be captivating. Mr. Bellamy's eyes might stray momentarily to her chest, then back up to her face. Lost in the moment, I look down at my own chest, where my breasts have been stuffed into a sports bra like sausage into a casing, under a plain blue T-shirt. When I look back up, Mr. Bellamy is still there, his smile barely hanging on, waiting for my reply.

Stop being weird, imaginary Remy says.

I clear my throat. "I'm all right," I say, looking at the numbers on the register as if there is some task there that must be completed. I reach around my mind for something else to say.

Mr. Bellamy clears his throat and says, "The strawberries look perfect this week."

He puts two pints in his basket. His older child reaches grubby fingers inside and takes two strawberries, shoving them into his mouth, leaves and all. Mr. Bellamy picks up two bunches of chard and a fist of garlic, clearly rushing to get this over with, and then puts the basket on the counter.

"Any plans for the summer?" I ask, trying to make things less deadly awkward as I run his card through the Square chip reader on my phone.

"You're looking at it," he says, then half sighs, half laughs.

"Well, I guess I'll be seeing you around then." I try to smile, but it feels unnatural on my face.

He nods and smiles too, though it doesn't really feel like he'll be coming back.

Three days later, I am sitting in English class, watching the movie version of *My Antonia*. It is Tuesday, the last day of school, nine days since Remy disappeared, and for reasons I don't understand my mother has made me come here and sit in this room of people and pretend I am still a functioning human being. Outside, summer is coming; I can feel it. The smell of life, thick and green, drifts in through the open classroom windows, mocking us all.

I lay my head down on my desk, pressing my forehead into the backs of my hands, my nose into the cool laminate of the faux wooden top. I force myself to take long, slow, even breaths. Everything is so alive. Alive, alive, alive. Sometimes it's hard to remember that River is not alive like me. Sometimes it's hard to remember that I am not dead like River.

And what am I? Remy asks.

I trace my finger on the tabletop. *NOT DEAD*, I write.

Just before lunch, all of the non-male students are called into the gym. We sit on the sticky bleachers and wait while Mr. Meyer, the principal, talks with Officer Kelly near the podium. Both men are mostly bald, and their heads are shiny on top. Mr. Meyer wears a baby-blue polo shirt and belted khakis and Officer Kelly wears his uniform. It is hot in the gym, and before long the sound of everyone talking around me, echoing all over the walls, begins to become overwhelming. I want to put my hands over my ears, but I know that wouldn't be normal.

I'm about to get up and find a way to sneak out of here when Callie slides in next to me. I haven't talked to her since we were paired up in the woods. I've been eating lunch in the parking lot this week because I can't sit in the cafeteria without River and Remy anymore.

Kendall and Liliana are a few rows down, heads together, whispering. I am distracted by how shiny their hair looks in the low light of the gymnasium, Kendall's brown and Liliana's black.

"Hey," Callie says, her voice low. "How are you doing?"

I shrug, unable to answer with words.

"Me too," she says. She looks over to the men at the front. "This feels like a bad dream." She leans down to cradle her head in her hands and I find myself wanting to touch her— like Remy or my mother would, to offer comfort. Callie and I used to be friends. I tighten my grip on the edge of the bleacher.

Mr. Meyer steps up to the podium then, tapping the mic with his hand.

"Good morning," he says into the microphone. He says a few other awkward lines of greeting that I don't listen to, because I am distracted by all of the other noises in the room. My attention returns just as he says, "Due to recent events, we've decided to go over some safety tips before we let you go for the summer. Please welcome Officer Kelly of the Black Falls Police Department."

Officer Kelly steps up to the podium. "Hello, ladies." He grins, oblivious to the fact that this greeting is gross and that he is misgendering several of the people in this room, and the tired, sweaty mass of girls and nonbinary students on the bleachers does not offer any greeting in return. For the next ten minutes, Officer Kelly drones on about all the things that we, as "young girls," should not do.

Don't go out alone, especially at night.

Don't drink anything anyone else gives you.

Don't get into cars with strangers.

Don't. Don't. Don't.

Where are the boys? I wonder. It seems so insulting to have grouped us like this. I pinch the bridge of my nose, feeling a confusing, tight, angry sensation begin to build behind my eyes.

Finally, Mr. Meyer says, "That's all, ladies. Have a great summer and stay safe."

Callie frowns down at the podium. "That was unnecessary."

I nod. "Very."

"Every time he used the word *ladies* I cringed a little." Callie is trying to sound strong, detached, but I can tell she is just as shaken as I am.

The two of us make our way down the bleachers together, following the line of students heading out of the gym. As I near the open double doors, I spot Ms. Canary and Mrs. Mills standing on either side, handing each girl a rape whistle with a bright red ribbon.

When we get out into the hallway, we become caught in the crowd again. I lose Callie and end up behind a group of seniors who are talking about Remy. I try to tune them out—enough is enough—but then one of them says, "Did you hear that her phone was missing its SIM card?"

For a moment I stop breathing. I feel weightless, as if carried forward only by the momentum of the crowd.

Remy's SIM card. It feels like a sign of life. If Remy ran away, she would have taken her secrets with her.

"Maybe that's why she was murdered," someone else says. The casual tone in their voice is like a slap across my face.

"Remy isn't dead," I say out loud, without really realizing what I'm doing. All of them stop and turn and I realize how weird I must seem, walking behind them, acting like I'm part of their conversation. "Sorry," I say quietly, and then I back away and start to run for the parking lot.

I don't even bother to stop at my locker and pack up my things. They'll be thrown away over the summer, but I don't care.

As I open my car door, I hear Remy in my head. *Let's get the fuck out of here*, she says.

I drive around town for a while, not ready to face my empty house. I never used to mind Mom's overnight shifts, but now I miss her so much when she's gone that I can't sleep.

Remy isn't dead, but I can't make the pieces she's left behind fit into any kind of meaningful shape. She took her SIM card but left her cash. She was involved with Derek Stevenson and had over two thousand dollars rolled up under her floorboard. She owes people money. She was the last person to see River before he died. Each detail seems to point in a different direction.

I weave up and down the small maze of streets that emanate from the single stoplight at Main Street and Route 22. I am adrift, a seed in the wind, a leaf in a river. River. I wonder if this sticky dead feeling will ever go away.

When I find myself on Derek and Tate Stevenson's street, I slow down. There are two cars in the driveway. Without letting myself think too hard, I park across the street.

As I walk up the front porch steps, I think about Derek's face in Remy's room. *Come find me.* For what? I don't know what I'm looking for.

That's not true. I'm looking for Remy.

Maybe this is where it all begins. I don't know. I really don't. I feel like all of the parts of me are disconnected. My body is just moving in space, without understanding why.

The door opens in a cloud of smoke so thick I almost start laughing. It's all a bit obvious and I'm feeling kind of hysterical. Derek is there, tall and dangerous, dark hair loose around his shoulders. His eyes seem to glow in the afternoon sun. "Jules Green," he says, raising his thick eyebrows. "To what do I owe the honor?"

I smooth my hands down the front of my shorts and Derek watches, standing in the space between the door and the frame, leaning on his elbow, body bent casually. I momentarily forget all thought. Derek waits.

"I want to know what you were doing in Remy's room," I say, finally. My voice is surprisingly sure, even though my hands are trembling.

He laughs. His laughter is full of darkness. "That's funny, because I wanted to know the same thing about you."

I swallow.

"Maybe you should come inside," he says.

In this moment, I leave my body and I see myself, teetering on the edge of something. Remy is down at the bottom of the rabbit hole and she is beckoning me to follow. *Walk back to your car*, says my mother's voice inside my head. *Live a little*, laughs Remy. I let Derek lead me inside.

Everything in the living room is old, left over from the time when the Stevensons' grandparents owned this house. The deep green sofa has some kind of satiny rose pattern on it; the drapes are pink velvet. In the center of an old wooden coffee table carved with roses sits an ashtray with a smoldering joint.

Derek sits down, picks up the joint, and holds it out to me. I shake my head.

He takes a deep hit and then lets his mouth fall wide open, smoke drifting out. His lips look soft. His eyes look clever. Dark stubble dots his jawline. "You first," he says.

Derek is sitting in the center of the couch so I sit down on the end, as close to the arm as I can. "I was waiting for my mom," I say, looking at my bare knees.

Derek leans a little closer. The sticky-sweet smell of marijuana surrounds us like a cloud. "That's why you were crouching over a secret compartment in the floor?"

I twist my fingers together. "I don't know why I was doing that."

The frustration of Remy's secrecy comes back to me all at once. A strange jealousy sizzles in the pit of my stomach. Why does Remy have so many secrets when I don't have any?

"It doesn't seem fair." I don't mean to say this out loud and I immediately feel childish. My cheeks burn.

I can feel Derek looking at me, even though my eyes are fixed on a small porcelain angel in the middle of the dusty windowsill. He taps his fingers on his thigh, letting the silence stretch.

I realize in this moment that now, because I'm here, I do have a secret. Is this what it's like to be her?

"Did you take it?" he finally asks; there is an edge to his voice now. I think of the wad of cash stuffed into my nightstand drawer.

"Take what?" I ask. I feel my underarms growing sticky with perspiration.

"The SIM card," he says.

I look at him, stunned. "No."

He rolls his lips and nods his head. "Again. I'm not sure if I believe you," he says. He's drifted closer to me during our exchange, making the couch feel smaller. I shift against the corner. He leans closer still. I can hear honeybees buzzing around the rosebush outside the window.

I wonder again if this is what it's like to be Remy. There is danger in this moment, but there's something sweet about it too. People don't usually want me. And I think Derek wants me. This knowledge makes me feel powerful.

When I feel his breath on my cheek, I start to close my eyes. Then his fingers grab on to my thigh and I remember Bailey's hand on me in back of the car. The sweet feeling in my belly turns over, too sweet now, making me sick.

Then I hear the sound of feet clattering down the stairs. I startle upright, not wanting anyone to see me like this, but Derek just leans back slowly, leaving his arm on the back of the couch behind me, as if all of this is normal for him.

"Hey, man—" a low voice says. Then, "What the fuck?"

I look up to see Tate and Sam O'Dell standing in the middle of the living room. It takes a minute for the images to line up, for Sam to make sense here in the Stevensons' house. He looks at me, angry.

"What are you doing here?" he asks.

I am baffled by the disdain in his voice and embarrassed by how obvious it is that I do not belong in a place like this.

"Dude," Tate says, eyeing me warily. "Isn't she a little young?"

"This is Remy's cousin," Derek says. There is some kind of hidden meaning in his voice, which suddenly breaks the spell. I remember that I am here for a reason. I remember Remy.

Sam looks at me meaningfully and says, "I need a ride."

The implied order in his voice makes me angry, but the anger orients me, and for a moment I am back in my own skin, all the parts of me together. He slaps Tate on the shoulder, slipping something from his hand into his pocket. "Thanks, man," he says. He nods at me. "Come on, Jules."

I smile, but my teeth are clenched. "I'll be out in a minute," I say. "Wait for me on the porch."

Tate walks into the kitchen and Derek and I are alone again. This time I stand up, smoothing my hair down and stepping away from the couch.

"It's your turn," I say. The anger is still there, between my teeth, giving me purpose. "Why do you want Remy's SIM card?"

Derek takes another hit of the joint and laughs. "The same reason everyone else does, Jules. If you think about it, I'm sure you'll figure it out."

"Let's go, Jules!" Sam calls from the porch. The anger fizzles into humiliation.

"Come back anytime," Derek says, smiling knowingly.

When I step back through the front door, my body starts shaking again.

We drive in silence. My brain is reeling, trying to understand why Derek wants Remy's SIM card so badly. Was she dealing drugs? That feels impossible to believe. Remy has always hated Tate for what he did to her brother. We always swore that neither of us would ever touch any of it.

Sam directs me down Turnpike to a trailhead in the woods not far from where we sat by the road the day of the search for Remy's body. I felt a strange connection to Sam then. A pull. But now I am angry at him again, embarrassed by the way he spoke to me in front of Derek and Tate.

"Walk with me," he says as he opens his door.

I turn to him, nostrils flaring. I am tired of being ordered around.

"Tell me what you put in your pocket," I say.

He pulls out a plastic baggie with four pre-rolled joints neatly tucked side by side. "Nothing serious," he says, waggling his eyebrows. "Don't worry."

I clench my jaw. "Pretty cool that you've been here two weeks and already know where to get drugs."

"It's a gift." He smiles. "I started young." It sounds like he's joking, but I'm not sure.

I think about Scott, who started young too. There's a reason I don't do drugs. I've seen where the impulse to numb your boredom can lead.

We get out of the car and make our way through the trees, walking until we are fully submerged in the forest. I watch the back of Sam's head, the way his long, darker-than-River's hair falls to the tops of his shoulders. His all-black wardrobe and non-athletic shoes are out of place in this town. His clothes fit differently than everyone else's too, closer to his body, making a more graceful shape of his limbs. But underneath, there's no denying that he is made in the spitting image of River. It's a little hard to look at him. He looks back at me like he knows, is disappointed by this.

We walk on, and I watch the way his scuffed Doc Martens

eat up the ground. And in watching Sam, I don't think of Remy. The woods feel safe again. Not exactly familiar, but better than before.

The feeling that's tugging some part of me toward Sam begins to come back as I follow him through the forest. I remember the way he sat with me for more than two hours while the search party finished and walked me down the long stretch of road back to where my mother was waiting at her car. Every morning, I look into the eyes of the blackbird drawing, wondering what it's trying to tell me.

Eventually we stop, when we are in deep enough to almost feel lost, and Sam leans against a tree, lighting up a joint.

"Why are you still here?" I ask.

He takes a deep hit, breathes it out. "My aunt and uncle needed help," he says. "And my parents didn't want to miss their summer in Europe just because their nephew is dead and their son is a fuckup. So they decided to send me upstate."

I look away, not sure how to reply.

"Yeah," he says. "They suck." He takes one more hit. I wait for him to offer me some. He doesn't. Instead, he stubs it out against the tree trunk and then places it in an Altoids box he pulls from his pocket.

"You're staying with Rebecca and Jake?"

"Yep."

I think back to the empty feeling of River's house the day we visited his mother. "That must be . . ."

He flips the box around his finger. The movement is graceful, almost magic, but when he does it again he misses and it falls to the ground. "Suffocating? Creepy? Depressing? Definitely." He shoves off the tree and starts walking around the clearing, placing one foot exactly in front of the other, like he's on a tightrope. For a moment he looks like maybe he's going to reveal something. I hold my breath. But then he seems to lose the thread of his thoughts.

His face shifts. "I can't believe that Remy died right after River," he says.

I take a step back, the words hitting like a punch.

Sam's voice is looser now, as if the joint has slowed down everything about him. "It's some real Romeo and Juliet shit," he says. "Except you all have the wrong names."

He stops for a second. "Get it?" he says. "Because your name is Juliette." He starts to laugh. And then a part of him seems to realize that he's said something awful. He pauses, running a hand down his face. "I'm sorry. I am really high."

This steadies me, blunts the disorienting, awful feeling of Remy and River and death in the same sentence, and I find myself again. "Remy isn't dead," I say.

"Sure." He laughs again, but this time it's more cynical. "And River didn't kill himself."

Another blow, straight to the gut. I almost double over. "What is your problem?" I ask.

"I don't have a problem," he says, backing away now, into the trees. "I just think it's ridiculous how everyone is romanticizing their story when it's obvious that something so fucked up is going on."

I look away from him, because it feels wrong to see such bitterness on a River-shaped face.

"I need to get home," I say. I suddenly feel like I'm going to cry.

"I'm gonna stay," he says. He sounds almost bored. "I'll walk the rest of the way."

"Fine." I start back along the path we've broken through the woods, trying to keep it together until I get to the car. I'm almost there when I hear Sam behind me.

"Jules," he says.

I turn around to see him standing at the edge of the forest. He looks worried and lost.

"I really just want to be alone," I say.

"I know," Sam says. "I just—I'm sorry. That was fucked up."

"It was," I agree. I close my eyes, feeling so tired. "I gotta go."

"I know," Sam says again. He shoves his hands into his pockets. And then I leave him there, standing by the side of the road.

On the drive home, the sadness begins to recede, a wave of anger rising in my chest, growing and growing until it feels like it might burst through my skin. I'm angry with Remy for keeping so many secrets from me. I'm angry with Derek for thinking he can manipulate me into giving him what he wants. I'm angry with Sam because I wish he would just leave me alone.

By the time I get home, I am shaking with how angry I feel. Fuck it. I take Remy's journal from my nightstand. I want to throw it out the window. I grip the pink notebook in my hands, my knuckles turning white. Fuck Sam. Fuck him for being right. Fuck Remy for hiding everything. Fuck River for dying. Fuck them both for leaving me.

I sit down on my bed. Fuck Remy. I can handle whatever it is she's said in here. I can handle it. I need to know.

I crack open the book, slowly. But instead of Remy's looping, perfect cursive, I see page after page of numbers and letters, like a coded, handwritten Excel sheet.

My mind swims. As I stare at the writing, my anger begins to drain and cold fear seeps in to take its place.

I suddenly realize that Remy could be anywhere. She could be in danger. She could have spun a web of lies so complicated and messy that she'll never get out. She could be dead.

I slam the book closed.

No.

This is not a dead girl story.

"Remy is alive," I say to my empty room.

I lie awake at least half of the night, counting the hours until Mom comes home. The house seems to grow around me. The air is hot and still, and everything is quiet. When I close my eyes, it's easy to pretend the world has disappeared. I imagine that I am floating in the middle of space, that I am a tiny speck of dust in a vast expanse of nothing. It feels good for a while, but then the emptiness turns and begins to close in on me like a coffin, squeezing until I can't breathe. I open my eyes and sit upright, touch my face, my bed, to make sure I'm still here. Then I go down to the door and slip on my shoes.

As I make my way through the wet grass of the front yard in the darkness, I think of Mr. Meyer in the gym this morning.

"Don't go out alone at night," he said.

I turn left, following Remy, and I begin to walk.

EIGHT

The next morning I arrive at the farmstand in a strange mood, eyes puffy from a lack of sleep. Something about the feeling of emptiness I experienced last night has stuck with me. I walked in the darkness until my legs throbbed, but I couldn't get rid of it.

Rebecca gives me space as we open the stand. I want to ask her about this feeling. Does she have it too? But it's as if she can sense my need, as if it repels her, because she barely talks to me at all. Right before she leaves, she says, "Sam will be helping out today. He should be here in a few minutes."

I nod, feeling uneasy as I remember the awful things he said to me yesterday. Sam gives me this horrible feeling I used to get sometimes when I was a kid, when someone was unkind or unsafe and I wanted to tell but knew I wasn't supposed to. It has always made the world feel so out of control, to know that people can just allow themselves to do things like that.

When Rebecca is gone, I sweep the stand, break down boxes, dust the register. I complete each task with love, care, trying to regain a sense of control. This place is sacred to me. To my friends. I can't let Sam to come here and ruin it.

When Sam finally arrives, it is after 10:30 and the sun is already past the line of the awning out front. I watch him cross the road in his black T-shirt and pants, his Doc Martens. Like on the first day I saw him, he looks like an apparition.

He walks into the stand, taking his time, looking around at the produce on the wooden table. He frowns like he is studying the plumpness of each tomato, the color of the eggplant. He looks at things like an artist. Like every detail is equally important. When he gets to the counter, he stops and crosses his arms, looking at me in the same way. Since last night I've been wondering if I'm invisible, but now it feels like he is seeing every broken, ugly part of me. I begin to shrink back from his gaze, but then I stop myself. What does this person want from me?

"Look," he says, running a hand back through his hair. He looks pale this morning, like a vampire. His eyes are full of regret, and when he pauses, mouth open, I wonder if he's going to apologize again. But then he takes a deep breath. "I'm supposed to be working today, but I have some things I need to do." He looks down at the counter. "If you could just tell Rebecca I was here, that would be awesome."

My mouth falls open at the audacity of his request. I feel immediately angry and also secretly a little disappointed.

But then he smiles mischievously and for an instant I'm looking at my best friend. *River*. My knees go weak.

He turns and walks out of the farmstand, turning right, making his way up to the crossroads, then over the hill. I watch him until he disappears, captivated by his loping stride, long like River's but slower, like he doesn't care if he's late. When he's gone, I sit for a long time, just staring at the spot where he disappeared.

At 4:30, Rebecca comes back to the stand.

"Where's Sam?" she asks.

Even though I want to rat him out, I don't. Instead I say, "He needed to leave a little early."

Rebecca eyes me skeptically and then takes a deep, sad breath. "I'm sorry, Jules. I knew I should have come with him. He can be a bit . . ." She doesn't finish. "My mom had an appointment today and it ended up taking longer than I thought."

"It's okay," I say, straightening a pile of receipts on the counter. I look at Rebecca, the way her clothes hang on her frame, her eyes dark under the brim of her faded baseball hat. "You know, I really don't mind working alone."

Rebecca frowns. "Yeah, but you shouldn't have to. I'll talk to him."

"Please, don't," I say.

She sighs. "Okay. Let's see how it goes tomorrow."

Together, Rebecca and I close down the stand in silence, wiping surfaces, breaking down boxes, then locking the doors and standing together in the parking lot.

"Thanks again for doing this," she says.

"Of course," I reply.

And then, quietly, we go our separate ways.

That night, I go out on the road again. Mom is home, so I have to be quiet as I slip out the front door. It feels like an invisible force is propelling me from the house, out into the darkness. I don't know why I'm doing this.

I've always been afraid of the dark, of getting kidnapped or murdered or snatched out of my bed by some awful, unknowable thing. I have nightmares of terrible images from Remy's movies: a pair of hands squeezing around my neck, a knife biting into a patch of soft skin, visions of my own corpse, bruised and rotten and left in the woods. When this happens, I pull the covers up over my head until I almost can't breathe. Then I toss and turn until Remy, crabby and warm, wakes up and I curl into her side, knowing that she is angry enough to protect us both from anything.

Remy isn't here now. I'm the only one left. I can't just wait until whatever it is I'm afraid of comes for me. I need to do something now to remind myself that I'm still alive. So I jump into the cold water of my fears. I step off the grass of my front yard, onto the gravel of the road.

I walk until I get to Turnpike, then make my way along the cracked shoulder, noticing how everything is made silvery by the moonlight, shivering a little even though it isn't cold out.

It's good for you to face fear, Remy says. *Otherwise your life will get really small.*

I walk slowly, with purpose. I watch the way the tree-tops bend gently in the wind. I remember that this world is a soft place.

My life is not a true-crime podcast.

Remy is not a dead girl.

I don't have to make my life small.

I repeat these truths to myself like a mantra. I try to call Remy to me as I walk down the road.

I see it now, the way they try to make us scared. Mr. Meyer in the gym on the last day of school.

Don't go out alone.

Don't stay out too late.

Tell someone where you are at all times.

Make your life as small as possible.

I've been following these rules my whole life, hiding my head under the covers, being cautious of strangers, never going out alone. But now that Remy is gone, I don't want to do it anymore.

Tonight the air is hot and humid, and the crickets are loud. The world feels full and alive. Not safe, but not small either.

I've been out for a long time, long enough to lose track of how far I've gone, when I hear the hum of an engine in the distance. I freeze, turning my head toward the sound, body still, like a bird.

So far, I haven't seen any cars on my walk. Not last night either. Black Falls is a sleepy place. People don't go out at night. I shrink at the sound of the car, and then I rebel against the shrinking. I have a choice to make. I don't want to make myself small again.

In the end, though, instinct wins. At the last moment, maybe even too late, just as the headlights come over the crest of the hill, I crouch down behind a low shrub and hold my breath until the car passes.

Who could be out at this lonely, middle-of-the-night hour? I close my eyes and try to calm my heartbeat, the short, quick gasps of my breath. I try not to think about whether or not they saw me.

When the air is quiet again, I get up and keep walking. This is not a horror movie. I am not a dead girl. This road is mine. I can walk it if I want to.

But then I hear an engine sound again, driving from the other direction. Is it the same car? Why would they be coming back? They wouldn't. Unless, maybe, they saw me. A girl. Alone on the road at night.

As the headlights come around the curve, I jump like a jackrabbit, diving into the low ditch by the side of the road. I press my belly into the gravel; I make myself as small as I can. I try not to panic as it becomes clear that I've been spotted. The car slows and stops, spraying a few sharp pieces of gravel into the skin at the backs of my legs.

And now, maybe I *am* a dead girl. Maybe my life is the size and shape of the person inside this car.

I hear the door open and close. Gingerly. Gently.

"Remy?" the voice says. It's low, familiar, cracked with grief. "Remy? Fuck. Oh fuck."

I hear footsteps walking toward me. I am still trying to decipher the voice when the person, the man, stops at the edge of the road, just above my prone body. Every instinct tells me to be still. To not even breathe.

But then the person sinks to his knees. "Oh my god." He gasps. "Oh my god." And he begins to sob.

I lift my head slowly, turning to see the man, forehead on the ground, hands splayed on the pavement, body shaking.

"Mr. O'Dell?" I say quietly. He looks up, in shock. His face is white as a sheet.

"You're alive," he whispers, clutching at his chest. He closes his eyes and then opens them again, as if trying to clear his vision. Then I see sadness descend over his features again. "Jules," he says. "It's you."

It's not Remy. That's what he's really saying.

I make my way awkwardly to my feet and he watches me. My heart is pounding and my mouth is dry.

Slowly, my brain begins to make sense of things. Mr. O'Dell thought I was Remy. Dead Remy, and then alive Remy.

Mr. O'Dell slowly gets up too. I watch as he puts himself back together, brushing the dirt from his knees, clearing his throat, smoothing his hair, sliding his hands into his pockets.

"I'm so sorry," he says. "I thought you were . . ." He stops, mouth opening and closing. "I thought I'd found—"

"I know," I say. I swallow, hard. "I'm so sorry for scaring you."

We look at each other for a moment in the moonlight. Our losses, his child, my best friends, seem to hang in the air between us.

"I just . . ." Mr. O'Dell pauses, running a hand through his too-long hair. There is a part of him that looks so much like River. "You kids grew up together. I can't stand the thought of losing another one of you."

Then Mr. O'Dell opens the passenger door to his car and the moment ends. I have no choice but to get inside. To leave this big world and return to the safety of my bedroom. To shrink back down.

When he gets into the car, he sits for a few minutes with his hands on the steering wheel, staring into the middle distance. "I don't think I can take much more of this," he says. He closes his eyes. "I haven't been able to sleep for days. I thought that maybe if I got out of the house for a while it would feel better."

I nod. *Me too*, I think.

"Jules," he says. My name sounds strange the way he says it. Because to Mr. O'Dell I have never been just myself, only ever RiverRemyJules. One of three. "What were you doing out here walking by yourself?"

I try to think of the right answer. I could say that I was walking to meet a friend. To buy drugs. To find a party. Something normal. But the truth is I was walking to convince myself that my cousin is still alive. That I'm still alive.

In the end, I just give a half-hearted shrug and he starts the engine of the car.

"It's not safe," he says. I have heard these words so many times, but now, after the taste of freedom, they sit heavy on me. I want to tell him everything I've been thinking. This is my body. My life. Why can't I be the one to decide if I'm safe or not?

Instead, I say, "I know."

He makes me promise I won't do this again. I say the words.

The drive home takes less than three minutes. He pulls

over by the edge of the road in front of my house, turning off his headlights. Then he waits as I cross my yard and slip in through the front door. I look out the window when I get to my bedroom and he's still there.

The next morning Rebecca arrives at the stand with a tired-looking Sam behind her. I brace myself for a lecture, wondering if Mr. O'Dell told her about finding me last night. But she is quiet again, like yesterday, busy with her morning tasks until it's time to go. As soon as she leaves, Sam props himself up on a stool in the corner and falls asleep.

I spend the better part of an hour just looking at his face. Even though I am angry at the way he's behaved, I can't help but feel drawn to him. Maybe it's River.

It's hard to compare a living person to a dead one, but the task feels somehow necessary. Sam's nose is crooked in the middle, as though it's been broken, where River's was straight as an arrow, but they have the same long face and sharp cheekbones and black, feathery eyelashes. If I squint my eyes so that my vision blurs a little, I can't really tell the difference between them. But when I focus them again, the contrast is clear. The animating force behind Sam's features is unfamiliar in every way.

"This is getting creepy," Sam says in a voice that is flat and sleepy. I jump and fall backward over my stool, clattering down behind the counter and banging my elbow on the floor. I stay down there for as long as I can, lying on my back and staring up at the ceiling, which is covered in cobwebs. I will myself to disappear. But then a customer comes in and I am forced to get up, dusting off my jeans and smoothing back my hair.

"You all right?" Sam asks.

I don't answer. I can feel his eyes on me as I try to make small talk with the elderly woman and her wife, who are on a road trip to Canada. I watch them admire the greens and touch the jars of honey, refusing to look toward his corner.

When they leave, sending up a cloud of dust in the parking lot, Sam takes out his sketchbook and begins to draw without saying anything.

An hour passes; a few more customers come. I busy myself with small tasks, like turning all the jam jars label out, while Sam draws in the corner. Then, at twelve o'clock, he looks up and says, "This is boring. We should get out of here."

I turn to him slowly, gritting my teeth. "Why are you being such an ass?"

He snorts, looking back at his drawing.

I take a step closer. "Really, though. I thought you were here to help."

Sam's face shows no reaction to this. "So that's a no, then, I'm guessing," he says. He puts his sketchbook away and pulls out his phone.

I go back to organizing the pantry shelves, feeling my stomach fill up with a bubbly kind of rage. Then I hear Sam get off his stool and walk toward me, across the room.

"I'm sorry," he says.

I watch as he takes down a jar of last summer's strawberry rhubarb that River and I made in my mother's kitchen. He begins turning it in his hands. "I told myself I wasn't going to say anything dickish today."

I watch the jar rolling back and forth, from palm to palm. "You failed," I say.

Sam sighs. He holds the jar as if he's feeling the weight of it, like he can see River dropping the wooden spoon onto the floor, the jam splatter making our bare feet sticky. I look away, toward the woods across the street. "Sometimes you just look so sad," he says. "I mean, of course you do. Everyone does. Everyone is sad. But you . . ." He pauses. "When I look at you, I remember how sad *I* am. And I don't want to feel how sad I am. So I panic."

A long silence follows this admission. I slowly turn my head to look at him. His dark eyes are asking me if I understand. I do. He hands me the jar. I shake my head.

"You can keep it," I say.

At 3:30, a brand-new Jeep Cherokee pulls into the parking lot and Liliana, Callie, and Kendall climb out of it. They are wearing cutoffs and bikini tops and bright, interestingly shaped sunglasses. They look sun-kissed and full of life.

I haven't seen the girls since school let out, and I wonder if a few days of summer are all it has taken for them to forget about their missing best friend and her dead boyfriend. But when Liliana walks up to the counter, I see that her nails are bitten to the quick.

"You okay?" she says to me, her voice tired and scratchy. Her long, dark hair is hanging loose and some of it has fallen into her eyes. Then she surprises me by reaching over and covering my hand with hers.

"We came to see how you're doing," Kendall says as she walks over. She leans gracefully against the counter. "We haven't seen you since that creepy assembly on Tuesday. Can you believe that shit?"

I'm momentarily surprised that she even noticed that I was there.

"I wonder if they took all the boys aside and told them not to sexually assault anyone this summer," Liliana says, cheeks flaring with anger.

"Probably not," I say, not realizing at first that she's being sarcastic. "These things are usually our fault, right?"

Callie, who has been hanging back a little, laughs at this.

"You're funny when you talk," Kendall says.

Sam has been organizing boxes out behind the stand and now he walks into the front, earbuds in.

"Hey!" Kendall says. "It's you."

Sam takes out an earbud. "What?"

"It's you," Kendall repeats. "The kid from the funeral."

Sam closes his eyes, regret flashing on his face. "Yep," he says. "It's me."

"This is River's cousin," I say. "Sam."

Kendall looks Sam over appreciatively. Liliana's expression is somewhat more suspicious.

"Sam's working at the stand with me this summer," I say. It feels unnerving to say all this. *Sam. With me. This summer.*

Liliana turns back to me. "You doing okay?" she asks again.

I look down at the counter. "I guess."

"This is all just so . . ." Her voice drifts off.

"Yeah," I say. "I know."

We stand there awkwardly for a few seconds, neither of us knowing what to say next.

"We're having a get-together at Top of the World tonight," Kendall says, breaking in. She looks at me. "In honor of Rem and River. You should come."

This feels like a slap. People mourning Remy like she's dead.

"A little ironic, isn't it?" Sam says. "A bunch of drunk kids getting together to celebrate their friend who died at a party?" Kendall looks a little crestfallen and Sam's face softens. "Just kidding," he says, and he looks up at me. "We'll be there."

If I were someone else, someone more like Remy, with her kind of backbone, I might say, "Speak for yourself," or "Not me," but I just sit there watching it all unfold.

Kendall smiles and then pushes his shoulder. "I like this one."

He laughs darkly, still looking right at me. "I'm glad somebody does," he says.

At 5:30, Rebecca calls and tells me she won't be able to make it by to lock up the stand. I tell her I'll do it and then walk over to Sam. He seems lost in his drawing, lost enough for me to peek over the edge of the notebook to where a dark scrawl of forest looks like it's about to come off the page. I want to look closer, longer, but I step back. *Don't be a creep*, Remy says in my head.

"HEY," I say, loud enough for him to hear through whatever awful music is blaring from his earbuds.

"WHAT?" he says back, equally loud, as if unable to gauge the level of his own voice.

"I NEED YOU TO HELP WITH THE GRATE." I motion exaggeratedly with my arms.

He rolls his dark eyes and sighs, slowly getting off the stool and putting his phone away.

"Have you ever actually worked before?" I ask him.

"Come on, Jules," Sam says. His voice is quiet.

It takes both of us to pull down the creaking metal grate, Sam on one side and me on the other.

"You don't know anything about me," he says when we're done. I don't know what to say to this, so I turn to walk to my car. Sam follows me.

We both stand outside the driver's side door, the sun at Sam's back, making a glow around his whole body. Again, I think of River, returning from the dead. As if he can read my mind, a line forms between Sam's eyebrows and he says, "Don't do that."

"Do what?" I ask, even though I know.

"I'm not River," he says.

"You aren't River," I repeat.

He clears his throat. "Pick me up at eight," he says. Then he turns and walks back toward the O'Dells'.

NINE

I lie in my room until 7:30, curled up like a wood grub. I scroll through Remy's TikTok, endless snippets of dancing and laughing and putting on makeup. She has a lot of makeup videos, mimicking some of the influencers she follows. I watch these the most, studying her face. I look into her eyes for some kind of warning, a hint or clue. *Why did you leave me?* I ask.

Her voice comes swiftly. *Why would I stay?*

I switch over to Instagram, study Remy's grid of selfies. I stop on a close-up of her in a flowery white bikini top. Remy's rib cage is pushed forward, chin tilted; a line of soft pink lipstick covers over the indent of her Cupid's bow, making her top lip look puffy. I tap on the next square, a reel captioned Five-Minute Face!

As Remy begins to talk, I push myself upright and walk over to the mirror that hangs on the back of my door. I remove my shirt, angle my body into a more pleasing shape. I study myself. I have an ugly brown mole on my shoulder.

My skin is pale, with red marks where my jean shorts dig into the soft flesh at my waistline. My breasts feel pendulous and disgusting under my sports bra.

I remember when they first arrived, my breasts, the summer after seventh grade. It was the one time Remy was jealous of me; she was a late bloomer, willowy and smooth. She already had River by then. She already had everything.

I was revolted by the way my body changed. Everything felt wrong: the blood on my underwear, the dark hairs sprouting between my legs, the grease on my skin, the smell of my sweat, my breath.

On the first day of eighth grade, I wore a bra my mother had left in my bedroom, a delicate, feminine sea green underwire with a pink rosebud between the cups. The straps just peeked out from under my tank top and when I got to school, Rylen McAdams's dad slowed as he passed me in the parking lot, eyes scanning up and down my body. The way he looked at me was so different from the reverent way the boys at school watched Remy. There was something wrong with that look, something that left my mouth dry. When I got to class I put on my sweatshirt—even though the room was not air-conditioned—and hunched my shoulders, wanting to crawl out of my skin. I never wore that bra again.

From my phone, which is sitting on my desk, Instagram Remy says, *Always, always blend with a brush.* I put my shirt back on and turn to her makeup kit, which is open on my desk. I pull out a tube of Chanel lipstick. *Remy's going to kill me*, I think. And then, *No she's not. Remy's gone.*

Still, as I swipe the color across my lips, I swear I can hear Remy's voice say, *Don't.*

An hour later, I knock on the door to River's house, feeling like a different person. My eyelashes are curled and my cheeks are contoured and I am wearing Remy's favorite blue sundress. It feels like the inverse of a moment I've lived before, with Remy standing on the porch and River inside and me waiting in the car.

Jake O'Dell looks confused when he opens the door. He is wearing khaki shorts and a crewneck sweatshirt for the New York City Marathon. His face is covered in stubble and he looks tired. The two of us stand there, awkwardly, as if an invisible movie of last night is playing in the air between us, me lying belly down on the gravel, Mr. O'Dell crying on his knees.

"Jules!" he finally says. He's smiling, but his eyes are empty.

"Hi, Mr. O'Dell!" I say, my voice sounding shrill. I pull at the hem of my dress.

I feel as if I need to cheer him up somehow. His sadness visibly consumes him, like he is a child, leeching into every feature of his boyish face. There is something so charming about him, something so *River* about him, that his sorrow reaches in and tugs at my own.

"Call me Jake in the summertime, kiddo," he says, leaning over to ruffle my hair.

When school is out for the summer, Mr. O'Dell leaves his teacher persona behind, working on his novel and helping Rebecca run things on the farm. He wears casual clothing and insists that we call him Jake. He's been a part of my life since I was eight years old, but somehow I still have a hard time with it.

"Got it," I say. He nods.

I can see on his face that he is trying to make out why I am here; his son is dead. And then it registers: there is a River look-alike living in his house. He clears his throat, still standing in the doorway. "You here to get Sam?"

I nod. "He needed a ride." I twist my fingers into one another.

"Ah," Mr. O'Dell—Jake—says, turning his body and gesturing to invite me in. "Thanks for hanging out with him," he says. He leads me into the kitchen, which is lit only by a small bulb hanging over the sink. The counter is covered in crumbs and dishes.

I peer into the living room, looking for Rebecca. The curtains are closed and the lights are off, and I wonder what it's like for the two of them, being in this dark house all day and night with a nephew who looks just like their son.

"Want something to drink?" Jake asks. He leans against the counter and a shadow falls across his face.

"No thanks," I say.

I close my eyes and then, suddenly, I am sitting at the table by the window with River, three days before he died. Sunlight floods the room and we are laughing about something. I can't remember what it is.

I stop to look at him, because I love looking at him, and then I notice something heavy behind his eyes.

"What?" River says. In this moment, everything stops: the birds, the clouds, the humming of the refrigerator. I see now that I have a choice. I could say, "What is it?" I could be like

Remy and pick at the scab until it bleeds. But I look down instead, embarrassed to be caught looking. I say, "Nothing."

Sam comes into the kitchen now, freshly showered, wet hair clinging to his forehead. I actually feel grateful to see him, present and alive in all of these shadows.

"Want something to eat before you go, Samalama?" Mr. O'Dell says. His voice is sweet. A dad's voice.

Sam frowns and says, "No thanks." He barely looks at Mr. O'Dell, instead cocking his head toward the door to signal me it's time to go. If he notices my makeup, Remy's clothes, he doesn't show it.

I follow him out, turning back to wave. "See you later, Mr. O'Dell."

"It's Jake," he says, smiling. He stands on the doorstep and watches us walk out to the car. "Be careful out there," he calls as I open my door. Then he turns and goes back inside.

"What's this?" Sam asks as I close my car door. He's got Remy's journal and is thumbing through the pages.

"Did you take that out of my bag?"

He shrugs. "It fell out when I was moving your stuff."

I sigh, annoyed, and turn the engine.

"It's Remy's," I say. "I have no idea what it's for."

Sam runs a finger down a line of numbers. "I don't remember Remy that much," he says. I wonder if he's lying. Everyone remembers Remy. He turns to look at me. "It seems like she's really important to you." He pauses, looking down at the notebook again. "Do you think all this has anything to do with her disappearance? Missing SIM card. Mysterious codes."

"I don't know," I say. I pull out onto the road and begin to drive. It's almost dark, and the forest that lines the road looks blue in the changing light. "I also found a giant wad of cash under her floorboard," I blurt without meaning to.

Sam's quiet. Something has suddenly changed between us. I've told him a secret. I wait to see what he will say. For some reason I want to trust him.

I feel the weight of Sam's stare on the side of my face. I'm not used to people looking at me like this and I bring a hand up to touch my hair.

"So are you going to try to figure out what happened to her?" he asks.

I look out at the dark road in front of us. "I am."

"Maybe I can help," he says.

Top of the World is a giant hill at the intersection of Turnpike and County Route 135. It's an old pasture, and in June everything smells like the fertilizer wafting over from the Johnsons' farm. Thick forest covers the backside of the hill, hiding it from the main roads. It's the first place I ever got drunk, in the back of River's truck, from a six-pack of White Claw Remy stole from Cumberland Farms.

I turn onto the narrow gravel road, driving up the switchbacks until I see the line of cars against the dark trees. I park at the end, on the side of the muddy drive.

"It smells like shit out here," Sam says as he climbs out

of the car. Something about the way he stands on the slope of the hill makes me remember how long-limbed and loose-boned he is. "This is where you guys party?"

I shrug. "Sometimes."

"Is this where you were when River—"

"No," I say, cutting him off.

I've been to a lot of parties at Top of the World. I've lurked and watched and passed the time here on many nights, downing warm beer until everything felt like a blur. I'm not sure if I liked it or not. I'm realizing now that I feel this way about a lot of my life before.

Ever since Remy disappeared I've been playing back snippets of memory, trying to place myself. But all I can see is River and Remy. River and Remy at a party. River and Remy at a football game. River and Remy in the farmstand. My life is, was, has always been River and Remy. I'm not a part of it.

I suddenly feel like I can't be here. Like I can't be anywhere. I hesitate, wondering if I should just turn back.

This is too pathetic, Remy says in my ear. *Even for you.*

Come back, I say to her, in my mind.

Not a chance, she replies.

Sam watches me as I start trudging up the road again, like he can see this conversation happening.

Then we crest the hilltop, enter the clearing, and suddenly kids are everywhere, in clusters in the dark grass, in a ring around the firepit, swarming the keg.

I look at the students of Black Falls High, trying to see them through Sam's eyes. But I can't; something about the shape of the crowd is not right. This whole party is in River and Remy's honor, but their absence permeates everything. How can it be that these people, this place, the entire world, is still here without them?

I feel for Remy's journal in my bag. It reminds me that at the heart of all of this chaos, all of these people, there is a secret. And I need to find out what it is.

"Give me a lay of the land," Sam says, shoving his hands into his pockets.

"Well, you've got your stoners, your jocks," I say, looking at the mass of kids. "Most athletes play more than one sport, because there aren't that many of them . . ." I look down at my shoes, the only thing I'm wearing that's mine. I suddenly feel foolish for dressing like this. Did I think it would make any of this feel better? "I don't know. Everything sort of runs together."

Sam runs a hand through his darker-than-River's hair. "What about you and Remy?"

"Well, Remy is friends with everyone." I look away, scanning the crowd again. "And I'm . . . not, really. I mean—" I pause awkwardly. "Remy and River and I were . . ." *Jesus*, I think, adjusting the strap of Remy's dress, which feels too tight. *You are such a fucking loser.*

My sentence dissolves into a long silence and Sam watches me, looking puzzled, as if he's not quite sure where I've gone to.

Luckily, we are interrupted by Callie, waving at us from the keg line. "You made it," she calls out. She runs over and folds me into a hug. I feel stiff and awkward. I haven't been hugged by Callie White since we were little kids. She must be drunk.

"Here, let me get you guys a beer," Callie says, leading us back to where Lili and Kendall are waiting, looking like gazelles in their short sundresses.

People have begun to notice Sam by now and they are all gawking. All thinking the same thing: *River*. Sam's face remains blasé, as if he is used to it. But by now I am beginning to realize that there's always more below the surface.

Callie finishes pouring the last beer just as Bailey Jensen walks up to our circle, looking at me for the first time since Remy pulled me out of his car the night River died.

"Can we talk?" he asks.

I swallow, frozen.

Callie gives me a meaningful look. "I'll show Sam around," she says. I follow Bailey away from the group, heart thumping, and then he turns to me and we are alone in our own tiny circle of two.

Bailey looks handsome enough that I can't even believe I've touched him before. His shoulders are big and strong and his jaw is square and his thick blond hair is just long enough to brush the tops of his perfect ears.

"Hey," he says, his blue eyes serious, leaning his head down. I feel confused about why he's being so nice to me and why I suddenly like it. "How are you?"

I don't know how to answer that question, so I just shrug and say, "How are you?"

He sighs, looking back over his shoulder, toward the bonfire. "It's been a weird few weeks."

Without meaning to, a loud laugh bursts its way out of me. Bailey looks at me like he's not sure how to respond.

"Sorry," I say, looking down at my feet. "I'm just . . ."

I don't know how to finish the sentence. God. I am the worst.

He takes a step closer and I can smell his sharp deodorant. He looks down at my lips in a way that makes me remember the red lipstick I applied in my room.

Careful, Remy whispers into my ear.

Bailey glances at the dark line of trees behind us. "I've been meaning to talk to you," he says, and suddenly a million possibilities burst into my mind. I think of the first moment he kissed me. How, for a second, everything else got quiet. *I could do this,* I think. *I could like Bailey Jensen. I could move on.*

He runs a hand through his perfect hair and says, "I want you to know that I had fun with you. And I'm really sorry I didn't text you or anything afterward. Everything seemed really . . . complicated."

I stand there, nodding, trying to forget all of the times he didn't even look at me. I just want to hear what he'll say next. *Maybe,* I think. *Maybe this is the good part.*

But then he rubs the back of his neck and says, "I just. I wanted to tell you that I'm not, uh, I mean. I'm just not really looking for a relationship or anything right now. You know?" And I remember that these kinds of conversations never have a good part. Never.

I told you so, Remy says.

I take a sip of my beer, not knowing how to reply, and some of it goes down my windpipe. I burst into a fit of violent coughs, flinging tiny droplets of spit onto Bailey's shirt. He waits patiently as the coughs subside, quietly witnessing my humiliation.

Finally I manage to say, "I'm all right. And yeah, that makes sense."

We both stand there for a few more seconds, not sure how to get out of this conversation. Then he sort of nods and backs away.

For a moment I am all alone in a sea of people. Everyone seems to have gotten drunker in the past five minutes and the volume has begun to rise. *What am I doing here?* I think.

"So which part of this do you think is meant to memorialize them?" A low voice sounds in my ear. "The keg, or the flip cup table they set up between those two cars over there?"

I laugh in spite of myself, and I can almost feel Sam smiling behind me.

"You were right about the irony," I admit, turning around to face him. I have to tilt my face up, just a little, to look into his eyes. "Why did you want to come here?" I ask.

Sam shrugs. "I'm bored out of my skull."

"It's probably the drugs," I say wryly.

"What do you have against drugs?" He laughs.

"Everyone I know who takes them eventually ends up dying."

Sam's smile fades and he gets that look that I now know means he's about to say something he shouldn't. *You look so sad*, he's telling me with his eyes.

"Don't you know that half of this town is on drugs?" he asks.

"Exactly," I reply. "That's why it's so dangerous here." I start walking away from the keg, toward the edge of the tree line. I feel uneasy in this conversation. When I think about drugs, I think about death.

Sam follows close behind me. "Did you know that they found heroin in River's blood?" he asks.

I stop walking. Shock makes the world tilt and I feel unsteady on my feet. No. It's not possible. Not River. But it's too late. Sam's words have already begun to leak into all of my memories, turning them the wrong color.

Sam puts a hand on my shoulder. It feels heavy and warm. I take a step away from him.

"Sorry," he says. "I don't know why I told you that."

I lift my cup to my mouth and drink down the rest of my beer. It's bitter on my lips.

"I want another one of these," I say. Sam nods and gives me his. He watches me as I drink it. It's darker over here and I can't quite make out his expression, but I feel the intensity of it.

"I don't know how to even think about him," Sam finally says. "It's too much."

"Me too," I agree, squeezing my eyes closed.

"I just feel really angry that everyone is lying about him all the time."

"But what if they're not?" I ask. "River was . . ." I try to think of the right word. "Good. He was good."

"I know," Sam says. We stand there looking at the fuzzy, dark forms of each other, a giant sadness taking shape between us.

Then there's a crashing in the trees nearby and three people come running out of the woods, drunk and doubling over with laughter.

Sam looks back toward the party. "Look, I think I'm going to get out of here. That's what I came over to tell you before."

"We just got here," I say, confused. I look down at my blue Remy dress.

"I know," he says. "But I ran into Derek and . . ." His voice trails off.

I think of Scott. River. And I wonder if Sam is going to slip through the same cracks. I don't know how to stop it.

"I guess I'll see you tomorrow, then," I say. Sam seems hesitant to walk away, but I wait him out, not moving until he's gone. Then I lie down in the dark grass.

I think back to the Saturday morning of the bonfire. River and I had eaten breakfast at the diner at 6 a.m., before he'd left for his tournament. Remy was home sleeping in my bed, because the only person who would wake up that early for River was me. He had looked tired, more tired than usual. I'm sure of it now; there'd been some kind of secret sadness in his eyes. For a couple of weeks maybe.

We'd ordered the usual, two short stacks of chocolate chip pancakes and two sides of bacon. Half coffee, half hot chocolate, whipped cream on top. River had been so quiet. A few times, it had seemed like he was going to tell me something. I'd waited, holding my breath. But just like that day in River's kitchen, I didn't say anything. And then he'd changed the subject, made a joke or asked me a question.

When we left the diner that morning, he'd hugged me so hard it hurt a little. And when he'd driven out of the parking lot, he'd turned right, away from the school and the bus that was waiting to take the players to Schenectady.

Was he really doing *heroin*? I shake my head, hard, trying to forcefully remove this possibility. But it's there now. There's nothing I can do.

I hear a quiet rustling in the grass behind me and then Kendall sits down, followed by Callie and Liliana. They don't say a word; they just lie back next to me, all of us looking up toward where the edge of the tree line meets the sky.

Kendall reaches over and grabs my hand. Hers is smooth and warm, except for the cold press of her rings and the points of her fingernails. I'm not used to people like Kendall touching me, and I feel like my skin is crawling.

"God, it's so weird," Kendall says. "One minute they were here and then the next . . ."

"I know," Liliana says. She takes my other hand. I wonder if my palms are sweating.

I don't know why they've come over here. Why they invited me to this party in the first place. In my mind, Remy's friends are an amorphous blob. Not quite threatening, but almost.

I guess now the four of us have something in common. For all of us, the center is gone. I don't think anyone knows how to move on from here.

I look at Kendall's face, waiting as her features become clearer in the darkness. For the first time, I allow her to be a person, an individual. She looks sad, and something else too, like she isn't used to feeling like this.

"She'll be back," Kendall says, turning to look at me, trying to look confident. "It's Remy, after all."

Liliana laughs softly. "She's probably just fucking with us," she says.

At the edge of our group, Callie is quiet. I wish I could study her too, to notice more fully who she's become since I used to know her. Does she still love *My Hero Academia*? Is her dad still an angry jerk? My head begins to fill with questions. There are so many things I don't know about these girls I grew up with. For the first time, I find myself regretting the way I've sequestered myself from their world. Maybe if I hadn't, I wouldn't feel so alone right now.

After a while, the heaviness between us begins to dissipate. The girls begin to talk about other things and I go in and out of the conversation. I don't understand most of what they're saying; it almost feels like they are talking in code.

"Seems like things are beginning to fade," Kendall says. "Thank God."

Liliana sighs thoughtfully. "I'm almost glad it's over," she says.

"Too stressful," Callie agrees.

"It was fun in a way, though," Kendall says. Her voice is thoughtful. "Wasn't it?"

"For once, it felt like *we* were in control."

Kendall pauses. "We still are."

"It doesn't feel like it."

Callie sits up a little. "At least I can stop being afraid of my parents finding out."

"You didn't even have your own page, Cal," Kendall says, sounding a little annoyed. "I think—" Her voice catches and she looks at me, as if only now remembering I'm here. "Hey. What did Bailey want before?" she asks.

It's the perfect diversion—I was just at the edge of understanding, but now I close my eyes, cheeks warming with regret as I remember our earlier conversation. "Nothing," I say. I try to hide how disappointed I am about what he said, but my voice betrays me.

Liliana squeezes my hand a little tighter. "He's an ass," she says.

"A creep," Kendall agrees.

"The worst," Callie chimes in.

I hold my breath until the conversation moves on.

Soon it becomes clear the girls are talking about something secret. Every time they get too close, someone remembers I'm here and the subject of the conversation shifts. I follow along, trying to figure out what they're not saying—it's something that's gone now, that they are relieved about, that was exciting at first but had grown bigger than anyone could handle. I can't tell if it's money or drugs or something else. I begin to feel a sense of urgency. Like I need to figure it out right now.

I sit up, reaching into my bag. I take out Remy's journal, and before I can say anything, Kendall reaches for it, as if to pull it out of my hands. I tug it back and bring it up to my chest, hugging it tightly.

"Where did you get that?" she says. There's something in her voice that I don't trust.

"Remy gave it to me before she left."

Kendall looks at me like she knows I'm lying. Her eyes seem to glow in the moonlight. I swallow, hard. "Can you explain it to me?"

"Let me see it," Callie says, breaking the tension. I hand her the book and she opens it, leafing through the pages.

"Weird," she says. "I have no idea what this means." Now two of us are lying.

Suddenly, a swirling flash of red and blue lights breaks through the trees.

"Cops!" someone yells.

"Oh fuck," Callie says, her face turning white.

The girls jump up, and everyone starts running in different directions. Everywhere, kids are darting into the woods.

Suddenly, Callie and I are alone. "Shit," Callie says. "Shit. Shit. Shit."

TEN

I grab Remy's journal and Callie's hand and tug her toward the woods, just as the cop cars pull up on the other side of the clearing. The party has splintered off in all directions, leaving us behind.

Callie and I run together into the heart of the forest. I wonder if she is thinking the same thing I am—these are the woods where we searched for Remy's body.

When I can't run anymore, I stop, tugging Callie's hand. Around us, everything is still and quiet; we are alone.

The leaves above us are dense and the woods around us are dark. The scene is like one of Remy's horror movies—the kind that I've been forcing myself to watch since she's been gone—two girls in short dresses, inching our way through the forest, holding hands. My blood is humming from the beer and the sips of whiskey I took from Kendall's flask, and I can't help thinking, is this how it was for them, before they died? Did River feel the heat rushing to the surface of his skin? Was Remy stumbling through the woods, unprotected and alone?

I'm not that girl, Remy says. *The one from the movie. And you aren't either. That girl doesn't exist in real life.*

"I know," I say out loud.

"Know what?" Callie whispers. She is standing very close to me.

"Nothing," I say. "I don't know anything." I start walking again.

"How do we get back to the road?" Callie whispers. Her voice is trembling.

"It's okay," I whisper back. "We just have to keep going downhill."

By the time we make it to the road, my legs are scratched and Remy's blue dress is ruined. Callie and I walk for a while in silence until we find a small, abandoned shed. We sink down behind it, facing away from the road. The moon paints the grass silver, casts the trees in a dark shadow.

We sit for a long time, unsure of what to do next. The cops are probably out on the road, looking for stragglers, so it will be a while before it's safe to head back to the car. "My curfew was ten minutes ago," Callie says, looking at her phone. She drops her head into her hands, starting to cry. "I'm in so much trouble."

"It's going to be okay," I say, putting a hand on her shoulder. I wonder if her brother is one of the cops looking for us.

"No," Callie says. "It's not. Nothing is going to be okay ever again."

We wait behind the shed for a long time. I want to talk to her, but I don't know how to anymore. She's changed so much since we were little. She is beautiful, calm, at home in her skin. Almost as good as Remy. They are the same kind of girl. And I'm a different kind of person altogether. I'm the person with lumps and pimples and old cotton under-wear and embarrassing thoughts about sex. I shouldn't have come tonight. Not without Remy.

I listen to the night sounds, the crickets and the rustling of small creatures in the grass. I try not to look into the black mass of trees in the distance. Now that we are no longer in danger, the questions from before begin to resurface again.

Finally I say, "What about the journal?"

"What about it?" Callie asks, lifting her head. Her eyes are wide with feigned innocence. She has always been a terrible liar.

"Come on, Callie," I say. I try to make my eyes sharp, like Remy would. "I know you know."

Callie relents almost immediately. She looks down at her folded hands. "Remy didn't want us to tell you."

"Remy is gone," I say, feeling a lump rise in my throat. I try to ignore how angry and sad I feel. I need to focus right now. "This could be the thing that helps us get her back."

Callie leans back against the wall of the shed, looking up at the stars. "It started about a year ago, last August. Do you remember when Brandon Parks sent out that topless photo of Stella?"

I nod.

"Remy was furious," Callie says. "I have never seen her that angry." Callie pauses, looking off into the woods. "She fumed for days. And then she got an idea."

I look at Callie when she says this, and for a moment I almost see Remy's face in the moonlight, that slightly evil smile she gets when she thinks of something good.

"Remy thought, why let the guys have all the power? So." She takes a deep breath. "We started taking pictures ourselves." Callie looks straight ahead. Her body looks pale in the moonlight, her limbs perfectly angled, like a doll's. I feel my cheeks grow hot as I try to process what she is saying. "Remy created a whole system and Kendall's cousin helped us make an app. Kids could subscribe to see the pictures in exchange for a monthly fee. We called it Fawn."

Callie turns to me, misreading my shock for judgment. "I know what you're thinking. But it made sense. If our pictures were going to be out there, at least this way we could control them. Get something in exchange.

"Remy was . . . forceful. About maintaining the safety policies. Invites only, no screenshots, no sharing. She made examples out of anyone who broke the rules. She made it feel safe. And we made a lot of money." Callie looks down. "*Remy* made a lot of money. She took a cut of everything."

As Callie talks, I feel the blood drain from my face. Everything around me takes on a surreal quality. It reminds me of the morning after River died, when the world was all wrong.

"Remy didn't want you to know," Callie says. She puts a hand on my arm, as if she feels sorry for me. I pull away. I feel sick. "You know how she is," Callie explains.

I look down. "It seems like maybe I don't."

"Jules, I am so sorry," Callie says, her voice miserable.

I'm not, Remy says in my ear.

"What about River?" I ask, ignoring them both.

Callie looks away, then nods. "He knew."

I get up and walk a few yards toward the trees, feeling like I can't breathe. The world has begun to spin, but I can't tell if it's the alcohol or just the destruction of reality. River. Heroin. Remy. Fawn. I wait for vomit to surge up my throat, to purge this feeling out of me, but it doesn't.

I stand there for a while, my brain trying to catch up. Remy *lied* to me. For months. And she was posting naked photos of girls at our school. For money. So that the girls could have more *power*? It doesn't make any sense.

I go back and sit down beside Callie.

"For what it's worth," she says, "I wanted to tell you."

I look at her face, trying to see if she's telling the truth.

What would it have been like, to be included? What would it have felt like to take a photo of myself like that, to know that someone was looking at me?

Stupid, I think. *Nobody would want a picture of you like that.*

"We should walk back," I say, standing up. "I think it's been long enough." I don't care if it has or hasn't.

We are almost back to the gravel road when a cop car pulls up behind us. "Fuck," Callie whispers. Her face looks ashen. I feel numb, not caring if I get in trouble or not.

We turn around as the door opens and Zack White steps out.

"Callie?" he says. He runs a hand down his face, through his short hair. "Jesus Christ."

He gets back in the car and Callie and I walk silently over to it, sliding into the back seat. He does not say a word to me.

He pulls out and does a U-turn, driving in the direction of the Whites' house. I'm grateful for the partition separating us from the front; Zack is radiating anger. We ride in silence for a few minutes, and I feel the car filling up with it.

"How could you be so stupid?" he finally says. His voice is too loud for the small space we are in. "A girl your age was just *murdered* out here."

This word—*murdered*—pushes the air out of my lungs.

"She wasn't a girl," Callie says quietly. "She was Remy. You knew her." I want her to say, *She wasn't murdered*, but she doesn't.

"It doesn't matter," Zack says. "We're talking about *you* right now. Anything could have happened to you out there." He rubs a hand over his face. "Why were you even at a party tonight? Your friend just died and you are out here getting drunk and running from the police. You're lucky I found you."

I recoil from the judgment and fury in his voice. It reminds me of Callie's dad, yelling at her when we were little and had made a mess of something.

"And why are you wearing that *skirt*?" Zack sneers. "Jesus Christ."

"Fuck you, Zack," Callie says, rolling her eyes. I'm proud of her. She never would have said that when we were kids.

"Dad is going to kill you," Zack says.

Callie pales again at that. "Don't tell him," she says. "Please."

"I don't have a choice, Cal."

A small, delicate tear slides down Callie's cheek. I feel like I should comfort her, should put my hand on hers or my arm around her, but I don't.

I wait in the back of the cop car for a long time while Zack brings Callie inside. I watch the house, the serene white paint glowing in the front porch light. Zack left the window cracked and I can hear shouting. I look away.

What will my mother say when she sees me in this makeup, at this hour, on the front porch with Zack White? I look at the rearview mirror, trying to see how bad it is.

Something catches my eye. A ribbon. Tied in a neat bow around the stem of the mirror. Remy red.

Just then, I hear the front door close. Zack White comes jogging back toward the car.

"You live out by the O'Dells', right?" he says, opening the car door. He doesn't look at me.

"Yes," I say, voice trembling.

"Buckle up," he says.

I can't hear anything but the thudding of my own heart as we pull back onto the road. I am afraid to look back at the ribbon; I don't want Zack's eyes to catch mine in the rearview mirror. He turns on the radio, as if he can hear my heartbeat too and wants to drown it out. "Black Dog" by Led Zeppelin comes blasting into the car.

My stomach clenches with every turn we make. I follow the route in my mind, making sure he isn't taking me somewhere else. When he pulls up in front of my house, my entire body goes limp with relief.

Then my mother opens the door and I do not feel relieved at all.

"Oh my god," she says as she drags me over the threshold into her arms.

"Do you mind if I come in for a moment, ma'am?" Zack says.

"It's late," Mom says, not letting me go. Her heart is hammering against my ear.

Zack White nods. "Listen," he says. "I found Jules and my sister walking down Turnpike, alone, after we busted up a party over at Top of the World." He clears his throat. "This concerns me, especially after the disappearance of your niece." I notice that he doesn't use the word *murder* with Mom.

Because I'm not dead, Remy whispers in my ear.

"You can rest assured that I will discuss this with my daughter," Mom says. Her face doesn't give anything away. "Is there anything else you need from me tonight?"

"No, ma'am." Zack bows his head a little. I try not to look at him, but he puts a hand on my shoulder, drawing my eyes upward. "You get some sleep now," he says.

ELEVEN

Upstairs, I scrub Remy's makeup off my face. *Stupid,* I say to myself. *Stupid stupid stupid. You will never be like her. Or them. You will never, ever understand.*

I lie in my bed for a long time, angry, confused thoughts racing through my mind. I pull up Remy's Instagram, then Lili's, Callie's, Kendall's. I study the shape of their bodies, the pout of their lips. I try to imagine what the pictures are like on the app. Are they wearing underwear? Do they show their faces? I search for Fawn but find nothing. It was encrypted, and now it's gone. I have only my imagination, which is completely failing me. I've never thought to look for naked photos on the internet; I have no idea what an app like that would even look like.

It is infuriating, humiliating, being completely blocked out of this world that everyone else is somehow a part of. Even River. I feel like a child.

And that's the thing, isn't it? I *am* a child. So is Remy. What the fuck is wrong with just being what you are?

I am so angry that I don't know what to do with myself. My blood boils. My skin burns. I kick off the sheets. *Fuck you, Remy*, I say in my head. She doesn't say anything back.

The first thing I see when my alarm wakes me at 6:30 a.m. is Remy's blue dress, crumpled on the bedspread. My eyes feel like they are full of sand; my stomach churns. Why did Zack have that ribbon on his mirror? *A girl your age was just murdered.* His words feel sticky in my mind.

Last night has opened up a deep chasm of questions, ones I don't have answers to. And worse than that, it's washed away everything I thought I knew about Remy, and about River. I feel lost and betrayed and angry. I want to yell and scream and kick and punch, but there is no one there to absorb the blows. I am alone.

I open my River drawer, looking at all the pieces of him in the soft morning light. I close my eyes and go back over every memory, searching for signs. But I can't find any. Heroin. How did I miss something like this? How is it possible that the River I saw was so different from the one who was really there?

Eventually, I drag myself down to the kitchen, to face the inevitable conversation with Mom. She has made a lemon poppyseed cake with vanilla icing. She must have been up all night.

"Jules," she says, looking up from her coffee. "What were you thinking?"

It sounds so different coming from her than it did from Zack, and I let the relief of that, of my mother, pour over me.

I sit down at the table across from her. I am so tired. "I don't know," I say. "I don't know what to think about anything anymore."

She takes a deep, slow breath. "I know that this is hard for you," she says. "Impossible. I wish I knew what to do."

I feel so guilty when she says this. I know it's hard for her too, and I hate thinking that I've made it worse.

Mom takes a knife and slices the cake. She places a small, neat piece on a plate and pushes it toward me. Mom's cakes always have secret herbs in them, for healing or good luck or whatever the moment needs. I take a bite, and the tart bitterness of the lemon peel feels like protection.

"I'm going to stop working overnights for a while," she says. I feel guilty again, but also relieved. "The hospital said I can pick up some extra clinical shifts."

Mom watches as I eat another bite of cake.

"I should have done that from the beginning. I'm sorry. I should have been here."

"No. It's okay," I say. "I know this is hard for you too."

Mom reaches toward the cake with her fork, not bothering to use a plate. "I think I just wanted to be at the births. To watch life coming *into* the world." She closes her mouth around the bite and then shuts her eyes while she chews and swallows, as if she is focusing on just that one thing. "Did you know that Remy's birth was the one that made me want to be a midwife?"

I shake my head.

"Stephanie and I never got along, but when Remy was born she *wanted* me there. For nine hours I was useful to her in a way I'd never experienced. And then, right before Remy came, everything got so quiet. The sun was coming up, and the room was filled with golden light. I'd never experienced anything like it."

Mom smiles. "Except when you were born, of course. You were a midnight baby, but you lit the room like a little star."

She puts her fork down, eyes full of tears.

"You have to be careful with yourself," she says. "You are so precious."

I look away. "No I'm not."

"You are," Mom says. Her voice is certain. "I couldn't live without you."

I pick a piece of icing off the top of my cake and put it in my mouth, feeling the sweetness dissolve against my tongue. I close my eyes to savor it, but the image of the red ribbon is still lurking behind my eyelids.

"Is Remy dead?" I ask.

Mom closes her eyes. "I don't know." Then she asks, "Why were you wearing her dress?"

I look down, thinking back to yesterday afternoon: watching Remy's TikTok, seeing this part of her that had always seemed so unknowable to me. And I wanted to know. Now I see how foolish that was. "I don't know. It was silly."

Mom taps her fingers on the table.

"You know that you are perfect the way you are, right?"

I don't say anything, because I don't know how to feel about myself right now.

"Last night," she says. She pauses, as though searching for words. "Please don't do that again."

"I won't." I get up, bringing my half-eaten cake to the sink.

As I drive to the farmstand, everything from last night begins to pile up in my mind. Fawn. Heroin. The red ribbon. I feel distracted and overwhelmed as I park my car and walk across the gravel lot.

A girl was murdered out here, Zack White said.

I wasn't murdered, Remy says in my ear, sounding annoyed.

"I know," I tell her.

"Who are you talking to?" a voice says. It's Jake O'Dell, wearing a red plaid flannel and a pair of beat-up leather gloves, leaning over to inspect the lock on the front grate.

"Just myself," I say, feeling embarrassed to have been caught.

You were talking to me, Remy says.

I ignore her.

Mr. O'Dell smiles and turns to crank the grate upward. It makes an awful screeching sound and I put my hands over my ears.

"I guess I should probably grease that a little," he says when he's done. He looks a little better this morning, like he's been enlivened by the fresh air. But the image of him sobbing by the side of the road at night still hangs in my mind.

"Where's Sam?" I ask.

"He's coming. Eventually," Mr. O'Dell says. He turns toward me, taking off his gloves. "He got in late last night." Mr. O'Dell looks at me meaningfully. I can't tell if he's scolding me or trying to tell me something else. I wonder how it must feel to watch all the other kids of Black Falls gallivanting around when his own kid is dead.

Mr. O'Dell adjusts his dusty blue ball cap, seeming to snap out of the moment. "Welp, I should head out. We need the tractor today and I have to get a part from town to get it running again."

"Okay," I say. "I'll see you later, then."

He crunches off into the parking lot and I start filling boxes of yellow wax beans. But then, a couple of minutes later, Mr. O'Dell comes back. His hands are black with grease.

"I think my alternator died," he says, frowning.

"Oh shit," I say. Then, "Sorry for swearing." I look down. "Do you want me to call Rebecca?"

"Nah," he says. "She's off with her mom this week." He scrolls on through his contacts for a few seconds, aimlessly. "Fuck," he says, running a hand down his face. And then, "Sorry, I shouldn't be swearing either."

"It's okay."

He rubs the back of his neck, seemingly unaware that he is leaving grease marks all over his skin. "Any chance you could give me a lift into town? Sam should be here any minute and can cover until the morning rush starts."

I nod, relieved to not be alone with my thoughts. "Sure."

I make a small cardboard sign that says BE BACK SOON and then Mr. O'Dell and I get into my car.

As we drive along Route 22, he seems restless. He fiddles with the radio stations until he finds a song he likes, then he taps his fingers on the dashboard, on the window, on the center console. He reminds me so much of River, sitting here in my passenger seat, constantly moving. It makes my heart ache.

"How was the party?" Mr. O'Dell asks, breaking into the silence.

I shrug. "It got busted up by the cops."

Mr. O'Dell laughs. "Seems fitting." He reaches out and turns the volume knob down a little. "You got home all right, though."

It's both a question and a statement. A worry and a reassurance. I think of Zack White, how that felt like a close call, and the warmth leaves my cheeks.

"Everything okay?" Mr. O'Dell says. He is looking at me now.

"I don't know," I say.

We slip into quiet again, but it feels more awkward this time, and I wonder if we are both thinking of our middle-of-the-night run-in, the way we were both out there at the same time, trying to escape reality. He reaches for the radio dial again.

We pass a police cruiser. I look to see if it's Zack, but the reflection of the sky obscures the driver from view.

"Did you ever have Zack White in your class?" I ask.

Mr. O'Dell smiles. "I'm pretty sure I've had every rotten kid in Black Falls come through my class."

"Was Zack White a rotten kid?" I keep my eyes focused on the road, trying not to give anything away.

"Oh yeah," he says. "I can't believe they gave that guy a firearm."

I don't think he notices the shudder that goes through me at that. I try to remember Zack White as a kid. I saw him sometimes at Callie's. He graduated with Scott. They were friends. But he's kind of a blob in my memory, never really standing out.

We pull up in the parking lot in front of the Stevensons' hardware store and I wait in the car while Mr. O'Dell goes inside to get the part he needs. The morning sun streams through the windows, but I can't seem to warm my body up.

Imagine what it's like to be dead, Remy says.

I rub my arms vigorously. *You're not dead,* I think in reply.

Something catches my attention at the edge of my vision, a squad car parked in the accessible spot, Remy-red ribbon hanging from the rearview mirror. I shudder, remembering last night and feeling as though I've somehow summoned Zack by asking Mr. O'Dell about him.

I watch the car for a moment, and then I see Zack, in regular clothes, walk out of the store and around the edge of the building.

I get out of my car and start to follow behind him. It feels like a bad idea. I don't know what Mr. O'Dell will think if he comes back to the car and I'm not there, but I'm compelled in a way I can't explain.

I pass by the Stevensons' German shepherd, sleeping in the sunlit walkway at the corner of the store. I wait until Zack is out of sight, and then count to ten before entering the narrow alleyway between Stevenson's and the post office. I try to walk quietly, but my heart is pounding loudly in my ears, making it hard to gauge sound. When I get to the back corner of the building, I hear voices. I stop, pressing myself against the cool bricks.

"What the fuck are you doing here?" It's one of the Stevenson brothers. Tate, I think.

"You weren't answering my calls," Zack says. His voice is quiet. Angry.

"Look," Tate says. "You shouldn't be calling me right now. The best thing that any of us can do is to just chill the fuck out."

"That's not what we agreed on."

There's a long, tense silence. I hold my breath.

"Look," Tate finally says. He sounds resigned. "None of this has worked out the way it was supposed to. She shouldn't have been—" He pauses. "Fuck," he says quietly. "This is all so fucked up."

There's a deep sadness in his voice that sends a shiver down my spine. Are they talking about Remy?

I dig my fingernails into the palm of my hand. Remy. Is. Not. Dead.

She. Is. Not.

"Just find it," Zack says. He sounds menacing. "Soon."

I hear footsteps coming toward me.

Run, Remy whispers.

I turn and hurry back down the alley as quietly as I can. But just as I get to the parking lot, the German shepherd comes around the corner and starts to snarl, tugging on the end of his chain.

I feel a heavy hand on my shoulder.

"Easy," Zack says, his voice calm and low. He takes a step forward, and the dog relaxes.

Did he see me coming out of the alley? My whole body tenses, recoiling from his touch.

Zack lets his hand fall away and steps backward. "I didn't think your mom would let you out so quickly."

I am still frozen, afraid to even look at him.

Then I hear a bell jingle, and Mr. O'Dell walks out the front door of the hardware store. He looks between Zack and me, frowning. "Ready to go?"

I nod.

Zack reaches over again and squeezes my shoulder. "You be good, now," he says.

On the way back, Mr. O'Dell is quiet again. His forehead is creased, and his hands are gripped into fists, as though some stressful thought has taken hold and he is trying to physically overpower it.

Finally he says, "Listen, I don't know why you were asking about Zack. But you should be careful. People aren't always what they seem."

My stomach turns, still feeling Zack's hand on me. "I know," I say.

He looks at me then, sadness radiating from his eyes, his mouth, every part of his face. "You're the only one left."

It feels excruciating to have someone else acknowledge it. That I used to be one of three little kids, riding down the dirt road behind the stand in the back of his truck. I almost can't look at him; it hurts too much.

But then Mr. O'Dell seems to remember himself, a stiff kind of composure coming over him. He steps back into the suit of good humor he always wears, the one I'd never seen broken until he cried on my shoulder at River's wake. The radio switches songs, from the Eagles to the Rolling Stones. Mick Jagger sings "Under My Thumb."

"This is a good one," Mr. O'Dell says, turning up the volume again.

Back at the stand, I wait while Mr. O'Dell gets out of the car. Through the windshield I watch as he disappears down the hill of young sunflower stems, toward the barn. I feel unsteady, watching him walk away from me. Something has come loose inside my chest and I feel somehow even emptier than before.

I'm the only one left. The only one.

I want to run after Mr. O'Dell and ask him, "How did you do that back there? How did you put yourself back together like that?"

Instead, I sit for a few minutes in the front seat, my arms wrapped around myself.

I squeeze my eyes closed. I miss Remy and River so much that I want to disintegrate. But the fucked-up thing is, I don't really know if I knew either one of them at all. For me, our friendship has been a strong, steady line, stretching from childhood into the present, each of us always ourselves, complicated and inconstant but essentially unchanged. But at some point, Remy and River got away from me. They left their old selves behind, and I was so wrapped up in our world that I didn't even realize they were gone.

I shiver, thinking about Zack and Tate's conversation. Why were they talking about Remy like that? What else was she involved in?

A knock at the passenger window startles me out of my thoughts. It's Sam.

"Can I come in?" he asks. I nod.

He slides into the passenger seat. Not River. He is not River. He smells like summer, like life, fresh air and sharp sweat. I wrap my fingers around the steering wheel.

"I heard about the party," he says. "I'm glad you're all right."

"Thanks. I guess you left at the right time."

"Yeah." He picks at a string on his shorts. His fingers are long and knobby. "I'm on probation, so I can't get caught drinking or anything."

He shares this fact like it is not a secret, like he is not ashamed. "What are you on probation for?" I ask.

He looks out the window. "A fight." The fingers of his right hand close down into a fist, and I imagine him smashing it into someone's face. "The same reason I got expelled."

"Oh," I say. Sam's hand uncurls again, and he runs it through his hair.

"I'm sorry about last night," he says. "You should know that I asked Tate about it and he said that River didn't usually do that kind of thing."

I frown, afraid to let the relief of this in. "And you believe him?"

Sam looks off into the field, where Mr. O'Dell disappeared. "The day River died, he called me three times. I'd just gotten arrested, and expelled, and my dad had taken my phone away." He closes his eyes. "It's weird because we hadn't really talked in years. Our dads had a falling-out. It's complicated.

"Anyway, when I got my phone back I saw that he left these voice messages. They were long and rambling and almost manic. It was hard to understand. He said something about his dad and my dad. About how they were the same. About how he and I were the same. About how it was all fucked up.

"And he kept talking about Remy. About how she was the one. About how he was going to get her out of here." I look down at my hands, thinking of the two of them. Gone.

He looks at me. "He talked about you too. He said you were his best friend." He reaches out one finger and taps it on my knee. Then his face falls. "I just wish that I had been there. I wish I had done something, you know?"

I think of the night of the bonfire, how I was with Bailey while River took his last breaths. "I know," I say.

Sam takes a deep breath. "There's something else I wanted to tell you," he says. He shifts in his seat. "When my parents and I came up for the funeral, River's room was locked from the outside. When I came back again last week, I broke in. The whole thing was destroyed. Just completely torn apart. He must have been angry. Really, really angry." He looks thoughtful. "Anyway, I think you're right. River was good. But I also think there was something dark in him, in his life, that nobody was willing to acknowledge. I think that's what killed him. Not heroin."

I look out the window. I feel like I am drowning in this conversation, like I need to get back up to the surface of the water. But I can't. "My dad overdosed," I say. "I didn't know him or anything. He left when my mom was pregnant. But that's how he died." For a moment I wonder if it was more complicated for him too.

Sam looks into my eyes. The morning sunlight makes the brown of his eyes look lighter today, warmer. "I'm sorry," he says.

We sit there for a while without talking, letting all of what we've said sink in. Then I open my door, and the morning air rushes in. "I want to see River's room," I say.

Sam and I don't talk much for the rest of the morning. But we watch each other. I watch Sam's long arm moving back and forth as he makes lines on the page of his sketchbook. He watches me through the dark hair falling over his face.

We know things about each other now. There's no going back.

At lunchtime, Callie comes by the stand with Liliana. They are wearing running clothes, with white headbands over sweat-slicked hair.

"What's up, bitches?" Liliana says. Her voice is scratchy and tired. She puts a big Tupperware on the counter and begins pulling out peanut butter and jelly sandwiches.

Why are they here? I ask myself. I still can't figure out why Remy's friends are suddenly so interested in me.

Sam hops off his stool and grabs a sandwich.

"This is so nice," he says around a mouthful. "Thanks."

"Hey," Callie says, looking from Sam to me. "You guys are matching." I look down to see that I'm in an old black

T-shirt and cutoff black denim shorts, just like Sam.

"You are too," Sam says, gesturing at the girls' workout gear. Callie laughs.

I smile at her, relieved that she seems okay after last night. "I can't believe you went running this morning," I say. "You drank a lot of whiskey."

She pushes back a piece of hair that's fallen out of place. "It's the only way my parents would let me out of the house." She takes a step forward, and I notice a few small, round bruises on her left arm. "Anyway, we came by to apologize."

I frown. "For what?"

Liliana glances over at Sam. "For not telling you about Fawn," she says. "Remy wanted to keep it a secret, but after she disappeared we shouldn't have kept hiding it."

I'm glad I'm on the opposite side of the counter, because the girls suddenly feel too close. "You don't owe me anything," I say.

Callie looks at me meaningfully. "But we're friends, right?"

I don't know what to say to that.

"That's not the only reason why we're here," Liliana says. "We were wondering . . ." She takes a breath. "If it's okay with you, we'd like to look at Remy's book."

"Sure," I say, relieved at the change in subject. I go to my backpack and pull out the journal, handing it over to Liliana.

"What is that, anyway?" Sam asks.

I look at Liliana and Callie, not sure what they want me to say. But Liliana doesn't miss a beat. "Remy started a DIY OnlyFans app at our school," she says.

Sam drops his sandwich.

"Yep," I say.

"Wow."

I watch him bend down to clean up the crumbs, grateful that someone else is as shocked as I am.

Then Sam's phone rings. He looks down at the caller ID, seeming annoyed, and then he walks out toward the parking lot to answer it.

Liliana opens up the book and starts flipping through the pages.

"Do you know what any of this means?" I ask.

"No." Liliana puts the journal down. "Look," she says. "I think that whatever happened to Remy had to do with Fawn. It's the only reason someone would want her SIM card."

I flinch at the insinuation in her theory, that someone has done something to Remy. Then I remember Derek, Zack, and Tate. *Find it. Soon.* Something clicks in my mind.

Liliana says, "I think Remy might still be out there. Maybe this information can help us figure out where she is."

"You're trying to find her too, right?" Callie says. "That's why you showed this to us."

I nod, feeling suddenly overwhelmed. Callie and Liliana think Remy is alive. Just like I do.

Liliana opens the book again and we all huddle around it together, studying the pages. The rows of letters and numbers swim before my eyes, but it seems like Callie and Liliana understand, at least partially.

Liliana runs her finger down a row of numbers. "Remy assigned all of the users a key based on their initials. And each of the models have a number. Subscribers are charged a monthly fee, and then additionally based on how many photos they access beyond the fifteen-photo limit. It's the same for the models. We're paid a flat fee for each photo, and then extra, depending on how many users choose to access our individual content. Remy created the algorithm, then kept track of it all on the back end and made sure everyone was getting paid."

"Wow," I say, my brain still struggling to catch up. I look down at the notebook, letting the numbers blur. "But what I don't understand is *why*."

Liliana crosses her arms. "Those douchebags used to jack off to photos of us for free. Now they have to pay. And we get to decide how much we want to share."

"But how could you . . ." I take a step back, grasping for the right words. "I mean." I look down at my legs. "I hate my body so much." I feel immediately embarrassed, having admitted this in front of them.

"We all do," Liliana says. She looks at me like she understands, even though I'm not sure I believe her. "But only because they tell us to."

"Exactly," Callie agrees. "They want us to feel disgusted by our bodies because then they can control them."

I feel confused. "Who's *they*?"

"Men, culture, society, the patriarchy, the boys of Black Falls High."

"Fawn was our way of fighting back, I guess," Callie says.

"We decided our bodies were worth something," Liliana says. She shrugs. "Turns out they were willing to pay."

My head spins with all of this. *We decided our bodies were worth something.* It sounds like something Remy would say. Remy, who is strong, fearless. Whose body can run through the woods and swim halfway across Hedges Lake and tackle me to the ground with a single screaming lunge. Is *Fawn* the thing that made her worth something? And what about me?

Sam comes back to stand beside me, pulling me out of my thoughts. I listen as Liliana explains the basics again.

"How did you stop people from just taking screenshots and sharing them?" Sam asks.

Liliana taps her fingers on the counter. "She had a way of finding out and making people regret it." She starts looking through the journal again. "I think this is where she kept track of who was accessing which photos." She flips back to the front. "This is a key of model numbers. Remy was number one, of course."

I look at the model number key. Numbers 1–12. All of them girls I know and grew up with. I wonder what could have made each of them want to do this. Was it really control? Money? Something else?

"I don't see where she lists the initial keys for the subscribers," Callie says, flipping to the next page.

Liliana shrugs. "Maybe she just knew who the initials stood for. There aren't that many people in our class."

Callie and Lili start pointing to user keys and making guesses at who each could be. There are so many of them. It starts to feel like everyone is on the site, even Tim Stewart, who barely speaks to anyone, and Devon Brown, the school valedictorian. Everyone at Black Falls was involved. Everyone but me.

"What about teachers?" Sam asks. "Could any of them have accessed the database?"

"I don't think so," Callie says. "Kendall's cousin encrypted the app pretty well. And we were clear about the boundaries when we started. Students only."

I think again about what I overheard this morning. "Are you sure?" I ask.

Liliana narrows her eyes. "Why?"

"Last week I was in Remy's room and Derek Stevenson came in looking for something." I pause, dragging my toe across the dusty floor. Should I mention Zack? I look at Callie, who is watching me, rapt, and my courage falters. "He and his brother are trying to find Remy's SIM card too."

Liliana closes her eyes. "Fuck."

I step forward, placing a hand on her shoulder. "It could be for a different reason. Remy had a lot of secrets."

Liliana nods, but she looks pale. Callie does too.

"Is the app still up?" Sam asks. "Maybe we can find a way to trace the users in real time and see whether they're involved or not."

Liliana shakes her head. "It went down the night River died." She pauses, and for a moment none of us says anything.

Liliana looks down. "Remy wouldn't say what happened." Her tone is tight with quiet frustration. "She left a giant mess. The money is gone. The server is broken. Everyone is angry."

I think of the wad of cash under Remy's floorboard and shift uncomfortably.

Sam frowns. "Do you think River was the one who took it down?"

"Maybe. But nobody can figure out when or how it happened. A lot of us were at the party and it's not like anyone else really wants to talk about what time they were jerking off at home."

Sam nods. "Do you have any idea what happened between them before he left the bonfire?"

My hands grip the counter. I feel suddenly anxious. I don't want to think about this.

"No," Callie says, looking off into the woods across the road. "I've been trying to figure it out. We were all just sitting around the fire. Everyone was wasted. Jules went off with Bailey." She looks at me. "Remy wanted to go after you guys, but River wouldn't let her. He said he had something to show her. I don't know. All night he was acting a little strange. But not bad strange. *Good* strange. Like, happy in a way I hadn't seen him in a long time." She tugs on one of her long braids, frowning. "But almost a little manic."

I try to remember River that night, but it all feels like a drunken blur. Still, this description of River doesn't make it sound like he was on *heroin*. None of these pieces make any sense at all.

"They argued a little," Callie continues. "Then the two of them went off into the woods." She looks down. "I never saw him again."

Liliana closes the book. "A little while later, Remy ran back to the campfire." She takes a shaky breath. "She was crying, saying, 'River's gone. River's gone.'"

I close my eyes, heavy with regret. Because I missed all

of this. For Bailey. Because I was too drunk to do anything to help my friend.

"Everyone was trying to calm her down," Liliana says. "She said he'd taken off in his truck, but she wouldn't say why. She wanted to go after him, but we were too drunk to drive."

"Fuck," Sam says. He looks shaken.

I walk out from behind the counter, toward the open front of the stand. I need air.

"Do you think Fawn had something to do with what happened to him?" Sam asks behind me.

"I have no idea," Lili says. "But I definitely think it has something to do with what happened to Remy."

"Okay," Sam says. "Okay." He picks up the book. "We can figure this out."

Lili flips through the pages some more. "I know that the answers are in here somewhere, but I have no idea where to start."

After they leave, Sam and I sit side by side against the wall, like we are unable to stand under the weight of everything we've just heard.

"Are you okay?" Sam asks.

"No," I reply honestly. "I'm not." Sam looks at me, and it feels so heavy. "I can't believe they didn't tell me. Both of them lied to me for months. I feel so incredibly stupid."

"You're not stupid," Sam says. I swallow hard and look away, taking deep breaths to keep myself together. My brain feels too noisy, too full of everything the girls just said. Fawn.

River. Remy. The party at the deer camp. All the threads are so tangled.

"The summer we met I was kind of in awe of you," Sam says. I can feel the warmth of his hand, right next to mine. His presence is grounding. "River kept me away from you guys. Honestly, I thought it was weird how possessive you were of each other."

"It's true." We were *so* possessive and insular. "But they grew out of it and I never did."

Sam doesn't reply to that. Instead he says, "I watched you a lot when you were around. You always stood a little apart from everyone. Like you couldn't stand how loud the world was. I felt like that too."

"I still feel like that."

I look at Sam and he looks at me.

"Me too," he says.

I stay in this moment for as long as I can, but eventually the energy building between us becomes too much, and I start to stand up from the floor.

Sam follows me back over to the counter and watches as I slide Remy's journal into my backpack. "I meant what I said. I want to help you find her," Sam says.

"Okay," I reply, avoiding his eyes. His presence feels suddenly overwhelming. I want his help. And Callie and Liliana's too. I *need* it. But these memories are personal and painful. There's still a part of me, the possessive part, that feels like Remy and River are *mine*.

TWELVE

After work, Sam and I cross the street and walk through the forest path to the O'Dells' house.

"Rebecca's staying with her mom right now and Jake is tutoring until later," Sam says. "We should have some time before anyone comes back."

We walk through the evening-dim, dusty house. It feels abandoned, almost unreal, like the set of a television show after the season has ended. I have a million questions for Sam: *How do you live here? What does it feel like?* But the hushed atmosphere of the house is overpowering.

It doesn't take long for Sam to pick the lock on River's door. He pauses for a moment then, hand on the knob. "Are you sure you want to see it?" he asks.

I don't answer.

The first thing I notice when we walk into the room is not the destruction. It's him. *River.* His posters and his dirty socks and his rumpled baby-blue sheets. His smell, faded but still *everywhere. He is everywhere.* God, I miss him so much.

"Do you want me to leave you alone?" Sam asks. I can't answer, but he seems to understand and he walks back into the hallway.

Sam was right, River has destroyed his room. A layer of torn papers, broken trophies, and clothing blankets the floor. The dresser drawers hang open. On the desk is a pile of family photographs, frames smashed. Next to the desk is a baseball bat. I try to hold my breath steady, but it's hard. Everywhere I look is River, and River's pain and anger and sadness.

Suddenly I am overwhelmed with a sense of regret and helplessness. Whether River died by suicide or overdosed or just drunkenly fell off a bridge, he was hurting so badly. He tore his entire room apart. He started doing *heroin*. How did no one see this?

We saw it, Remy says in my head. *We were just afraid to ask.*

I slowly lower myself to the floor, onto my back, careful not to touch any broken glass. I look up at the ceiling, the only place in the room that has no sign of him. I breathe in long, slow breaths, trying to get my bearings.

After a while, Sam comes back and lies next to me. He sets his hand on top of mine and the weight of it brings me back down toward earth.

My eyes stray to a smashed picture frame that's fallen from the desk to the floor. I've always envied River's family, which seemed so happy and whole. Why would he destroy all of these photographs?

"Tell me about your dad," I say to Sam. "I want to know what River meant when he said your dads were alike."

Sam blows out a breath. "My dad is a phony asshole," he says. "Obsessed with money. A chronic cheater." He laughs, moving his hand off mine, placing it on his stomach. "It's funny, because Jake is technically the black sheep in the O'Dell family, even though he's the only decent one. Everyone else went to Ivy League law schools and became corporate lawyers and Jake ended up a high school teacher and married someone with an actual family farming business."

My mind flashes back to the night Mr. O'Dell found me by the side of the road. I think that was the first time I'd ever seen him as complicated in any way. Until that moment, he'd always just been River's dad. But something about the way he looked that night, the depth of his pain, still haunts me a little.

"I don't know. Their relationship has always been troubled. Honestly, I think my dad was jealous. Not of the stand or anything." He pauses. "I think he was jealous of River. He was always telling me to be more like my cousin. He wanted me to be an athlete and honor student. To cut my hair. To say the right thing to his friends when they came over for dinner. Always to be a little less like myself. A little more like him."

I turn my head so that I am looking at the side of Sam's face. Color is spilling into the top of his cheekbone, and even though his voice is steady I can tell this is something that hurts him. I feel a pull, like I want to reach out a finger and smooth it over his skin. Like maybe this sadness is something I can draw out of him.

"I've been thinking a lot about what River meant in his

voicemail," he says. "I don't think that either of our dads really saw us for who we are. I think they both wanted us to be the same person. River was a lot more like that on the outside. But it's still a lot of pressure. A heavy weight around your neck."

I think about the responsibility on River's shoulders. About his family and his grades and his spotless image. I think about the weight I added, with the way I idealized him, my impossible crush.

"Do you think he killed himself?" I ask. I know it doesn't matter, but I can't help asking.

Sam closes his eyes. "I don't know. I think that's just a technicality. He was suffering. He died. That's what happened."

A tear slides down the side of my face. Sam's right. But I don't know if that makes it better or worse.

I start to close my eyes too, but then the room begins to spin. So I open them again, until Sam comes into focus. Without thinking, I lean over and trace my finger over the top of his cheek, where the skin is warm with emotion. He is perfectly still for a moment, and then he grabs my hand and traps it against his face. He takes a deep breath.

"This hurts so much," he says. "I hate that I don't know what to do."

I turn onto my side, resting my cheek on the carpet. "I think there's a part of me that hopes that if I find Remy, I'll find him too. But the truth is he's just gone."

Sam turns to face me. His eyes move back and forth between mine, like there's something more he wants to say. But then the moment stretches out and everything seems to slow down. Outside the window, birds are singing. Light spills in through the open windows. For a while, we are still.

Later, downstairs, Sam begins to flip on lights, puts a record on the turntable, opens up the fridge. The house doesn't look haunted anymore. *Maybe Sam is alive enough,* I think. *For all of us.*

"Tell me about your life in New York," I ask. I want to hear about something that isn't sad.

Sam pulls out a brick of cheese and places it on a cutting board on the counter. "Ugh," he says. "No."

"Come on," I say. "There must be something good about it."

Sam stays stubbornly quiet, slicing off a few pieces of cheese and then placing them on a small plate.

"Like, when everything feels shitty, what do you do to make yourself feel better?"

Sam grabs a box of crackers from the top of the fridge. He takes one out and places a slice of cheese neatly on top. "I'm guessing you don't mean smoking weed."

I smile. "No."

"Well," he says. "I keep a big map of all the museums pinned to the wall next to my bed. And sometimes I close my eyes and pick one. And then I spend the whole day there, wandering around."

"That's so wholesome," I say, laughing.

"Don't tell anyone," he says, smirking. He makes a tiny cracker and cheese sandwich and hands it to me. "What about you? What's your thing?"

"My thing . . ." I try to think. But for some reason every good memory I have includes the two of them. "I don't think I have one yet."

My phone buzzes in my pocket. It's my mom: You're late for dinner.

It's sweet, knowing my mother is waiting for me. But I feel Sam's pull again and I don't want to leave.

Another text follows quickly after the first: Don't make me eat alone.

I sigh. "I've got to go."

Sam's face falls, and it's as if the lights in the kitchen begin to flicker.

That night I sit on my bed with my computer and Remy's journal and I begin to transcribe the entries into an Excel spreadsheet. At first the work is slow and plodding. Lili and Callie have decoded a lot of the initial keys, but a few remain mysterious. After a while, though, things begin to click and flow. I feel a comforting sense of order setting in. Patterns emerge. I begin to understand.

Remy, I think. *You are brilliant.*

I know, she says.

Of all the girls, Remy is—of course—the most popular. Number 1. But most subscribers branch out, seeming to like different models at different times. A few of the subscribers, however, seem to be exclusively, excessively focused on Remy. These would be suspects, if there were a crime.

There isn't one.

Remy is fine.

I remind myself of this whenever fear begins to close in.

It's dark by the time I'm finished putting all the numbers in. I enter my formula to sort the columns by users' access of Remy's content. Two keys sit tied atop the list:

BJ and ZW.

THIRTEEN

The next morning I get a text from Callie, early, when I first wake. I was up most of the night, tossing and turning, two names rolling through my mind.

Bailey Jensen. I feel nauseous just thinking of his initials on the notebook page, knowing what we did. I wonder if he was thinking about Remy when he kissed me.

Did Remy know about him the night of the party? Is that why she tried to talk me out of it? I feel so foolish now, thinking about how she must have felt, watching me make such a terrible mistake. I squeeze my eyes shut, trying to clear the memory, and for a moment my mind is blank. I can breathe again.

But then the second name slides into the empty space: Zack White. My stomach turns.

I open my phone to read Callie's message: Want to go for a run later?

I don't know how to read this. Is it an offer of friendship? Are we friends? That's what she said when she came to the stand yesterday. Still, I can't help but notice that the thing bringing us together is Remy. She is always at the center.

Evening runs have been Remy and Callie's thing for a long time. It started freshman year, when Remy joined cross-country. I got so angry at first, because Callie was *my* friend.

"Don't worry," Remy said. "It's just running."

That's how it always was with her.

Now I look down at my phone. I hate running. But I text back: Sure. Because I don't know what else to say.

After work at the farmstand, I meet Callie on Turnpike. We park our cars in the lot for Richardson's apple orchard, which is closed this time of year. I am wearing Remy's running shorts and sneakers that I borrowed from her room. The shorts feel small and tight and the expanse of white skin on my naked legs is glaring.

I've been noticing my body in a different way since finding out about Fawn. Suddenly I can't stop thinking about how other people see my legs and breasts and skin and face.

This morning I spent twenty minutes posing in front of my mirror, trying to see myself as a pleasing object. I couldn't.

I can't shake the feeling that something about me is inherently disgusting. When I'm alone and touching myself, the fantasies I make in my mind usually feature other people, other bodies, not mine. I am not sexy. Not in any way.

What is it like for other girls, the ones on Fawn? Do they feel strong when they take the pictures? Beautiful? Is there really power in showing your body like that? Have they somehow managed to escape the shame I feel when I acknowledge that I have a body at all?

Knowing that so many people I know have taken and posted naked photos of themselves makes me feel farther than ever from the rest of the world. And from Remy and River, the two people I thought I knew best. I am beginning to think that maybe there is something fundamentally wrong with me. Something that makes me unable to understand anyone.

Callie hugs me when I get out of my car. She doesn't look at my legs. Instead, she steps off the side of the road and starts stretching, gracefully arching her long, tanned limbs into neat, angular shapes. I try to imitate the motion, my own body feeling awkward and unbalanced.

I remember someone at the party saying Callie didn't even have her own page on Fawn. I wonder what that means. Did she have any pictures? I want to ask, but I don't know how.

Callie and I begin slowly jogging toward the direction of town. My body feels uncomfortable with the motion, and I squint into the bright afternoon sun.

"We might have to walk a bit," I hedge.

"Sure," Callie says, smiling warmly. "I'm just happy you came out."

Again, I wonder what she means by this and what she wants from me.

The road, which is lined with open pastures, feels alive with birds darting out from behind trees and soaring across the road. I try to get lost in the beauty of it all, but almost immediately my lungs begin to burn and sweat slicks, sticky and wet in my armpits.

"How are you doing?" Callie asks, after we've jogged about a hundred yards.

"I'm okay," I wheeze. I'm already out of breath.

She turns to look at me. "Let's just walk," she says. "I'm pretty tired today."

"Good idea." I laugh with relief, and she laughs too. It feels familiar. I wonder if I want this run to be about more than Remy.

We walk for a while, past an old white farmhouse that sinks down into the earth. My skin is hot and sticky and the humid afternoon air feels oppressive. I feel awkward, like I want to make conversation but I don't know what to say.

"So," Callie says. "Did you find anything in the notebook?"

With this, we are back on solid ground: Remy.

My eyes snag on the bruises on Callie's arm. Her brother's name has been looping through my mind all morning like a mantra: *Zack White, Zack White, Zack White*.

"Well," I say, trying to buy time. "A couple of people stood out."

"Who?" Callie asks. I open and close my mouth. Maybe I should tell the truth. Callie and Liliana deserve to know their fears are founded; it wasn't just students who were accessing Fawn. But the words die in my throat.

"One person, actually," I say. "Bailey. He looked at her profile like thirty times a day."

"Wow," Callie says. She turns her head to study me. I wonder if she knows I'm leaving something out.

"Bailey," Callie says, shading her eyes. "That's fucked up."

Humiliation washes over me again as I remember that the first person who I ever had sex with was actually obsessed with my cousin. *It turns out that everything really is about Remy*, I think bitterly.

As soon as I think that, I feel guilty. These feelings are all so confusing. What am I supposed to do with my anger now that she's gone?

Callie wipes at sweat on her brow, even though I can't see any. "Do you think that's why she didn't want you to go off with him? The night of the bonfire?"

"Probably," I say. I feel defeated. Pathetic. Callie is watching me like I'm fragile. I see pity in her eyes. Then her face changes and I see something new.

Remember? Remy says in my ear. *Don't get mad. Get revenge.*

"You know," Callie says, as if she is thinking the same thing, "I babysit for his little sister sometimes. Maybe I can find something out."

"Okay," I say. "Just make sure you're not alone with him."

I bend down to tie my sneaker. I need a break. I take my time with the laces, trying to remember how to breathe normally.

"It was just Bailey, then?" Callie asks. She stands above me, hands on her hips.

"Just Bailey," I say. I look away. I need to change the subject. I am not a good liar. "It's kind of strange, being here with you," I blurt out. What a weird thing to say.

Callie looks at me then, like she doesn't know how to respond.

I stand up and brush off my hands, trying to recover. "I mean, because you usually run with Remy."

Callie pauses, like she might say something meaningful. Then she turns and starts walking again, seeming to change her mind. "I miss her so much," she says.

"Me too."

"Do you think she's really alive?" Callie's voice is quiet, uncertain, and the doubt in her expression makes my own sureness falter. For a moment, the awful truth hangs in the air: Remy could be dead. She could be just like one of those girls in the podcasts, brutalized, forgotten. I squeeze my eyes shut. Suddenly, the heat of the afternoon feels like it's closing in.

"Are you okay?" Callie asks.

No. No, no, no. I grit my teeth, like Remy would. I force my eyes back open. "Remy isn't dead," I say.

"Okay," Callie agrees. But I can hear the effort it takes for her to say it.

We keep walking, both of us shaken, both of us trying to pretend that this is going to turn out all right.

"I feel like Remy was changing," Callie finally says. "Before she left." She turns her head, shielding her eyes to look at something in the distance. "Usually when we ran we'd just talk about surfacey stuff. School. Fawn. But sometimes she'd go in and out of the conversation. Like, sometimes, she was somewhere else. More and more lately, you know?"

I think about the months before River died. I've always taken Remy for granted, always known that she was *right there*. But I think it's possible that I missed the signs, that she was becoming more distant, like River, and I just didn't see it.

"Jules?" River had said once, toward the end of April. It was just the two of us; we were lying in the grass at the Little League field, looking at the clouds.

"Yeah, Riv?"

His soft blue eyes scanned my face, then fell for a moment to the heart-shaped birthmark Remy and I shared.

"Do you think she'll ever let us know her?" he asked.

The question had nicked a soft place right under my ribs. "What do you mean?" I replied. I felt confused. I remember thinking, *Remy is mine. Ours.*

"Never mind," he'd said, turning his face to look back at the clouds.

Now I feel a strange, lonely ache in my chest. Remembering River and Remy, being here with Callie. Everything feels so tender inside.

I look at Callie, with her kind eyes. I realize that I've missed having a friend of my own. That I've missed Callie. But the truth is that we are together again, and Remy is still all we know how to talk about.

"This is really nice," Callie says. "Hanging out again."

I look away, feeling exposed, like she's somehow read my thoughts.

Callie continues. "Maybe we can do it again tomorrow."

I know I should say something back, but I can't; I feel too vulnerable. I think I might be done with talking. I need to get rid of all of these feelings, Remy, River, Callie. So I lean into the heavy air and start running again.

The next morning I am walking out on the road, watching sunlight filter down through the leaves. I am thinking about Remy again, about River. About all of the times we rode our bikes down this road looking for adventure. No matter how hard I try, I can't figure out when everything stopped being simple. I think I missed the moment when we broke ourselves up into parts and began to hide them from one another. Are there pieces of me that I've hidden? I wonder.

The farmstand is closed today and my mother is at the hospital, so I am all alone when the mail truck pulls up and Mr. Tills places a single white envelope in our mailbox.

When I take it out, I see my name, JULIETTE GREEN, written neatly above the house number in tiny block letters. There is no return address.

My heart flutters like it's full of moths as I hold the letter carefully in my hands. I'm afraid to open it. I'm afraid not to. But there is no choice, really; my fingers are already tearing the top, pulling out a neatly folded piece of paper. I bring it up to my nose and inhale, smelling Remy's vanilla perfume.

The letter is typewritten, the ink of each character slightly different, some dark and sharp, others soft and a little blurred:

Dear Jules,

I'm writing to tell you that I am sorry.

You're right. I'm a fake, a phony, a
prom-queen zombie. All of it is true. My
life is, was, will always be a lie.

Confession: I knew you loved River and I
took him anyway.

Another: It's my fault he died. I broke
his heart. I crushed him. I don't think
I'll ever forgive myself.

I've got this strange problem I've been
thinking about lately: I can't figure
out if I've ever been in love. I have
burned for someone, that's for sure.
But is that love? Was the cool, calm
constant of River love? What does love
feel like? I've seen it on your face
before and it looks so pure.

It's my birthday soon; are you going
to celebrate me? I hate my birthday,
to tell the truth. I bet you didn't
know that. Every year I pretend to want
a party because that's what you're
supposed to do. You're supposed to put
on the dress, apply the makeup, smile.
Be pliant. Be good. It makes me so sad.
And angry. Do you ever get so angry that
you feel like you could kill someone?

I do wonder, what do people think now
that I'm gone? What do you think?
Really, Jules, you are the only one that
matters.

I hope that you're okay. I hope that
you are there, bearing witness to
early summer, noticing the way that
everything is coming back alive. Do
you notice the smell of the violets?
Do you see how leaves cover everything
now? Please notice. Life is brief and
beautiful.

Anyway, I need your help. I'm sure the
cops have searched everywhere by now,
but just in case, I need you to get
rid of something for me. It's under the
green watering can in the garage. Do
whatever you like, tear them up, flush
them down the toilet, set them on fire.
Just make them go away.

Love you. In that life and this one.

Remy

I read the letter three times through, feeling more and
more unsteady, until I have to sit down on the edge of the
pavement. Alive. Remy is alive. Relief floods my limbs. I lie

back into the grass of my front yard, holding the letter to my stomach.

Before I can read it again, I hear the crunching of foot-steps and see Sam walking up the road from the O'Dells'. He is wearing all black, as usual, except for a green base-ball cap on his head that says SPORTS. I sit up, trying to calm myself down.

"What's that?" he says when he gets to me. He tugs the letter out of my hands, then plops down on the grass. I am unable to grab it back. I can't move or think of anything ex-cept: *Remy is alive.*

I watch him unfold the letter and begin to read it, like I am in a trance. My eyes follow his and then stall on the third line: *I knew you loved River.*

The embarrassment of the words starts to creep in, burn-ing like a stain on the skin of my cheeks.

I pick a blade of grass and shred it into tiny pieces, trying to let Remy's other words sink in.

I knew you loved River and I took him anyway.

I crushed him.

Do you ever get so angry that you feel like you could kill someone?

But all of them stay bobbing at the top of my mind, refus-ing to coalesce into anything that makes sense. I only want to keep thinking one thought again and again and again: *Remy is alive.*

When he finishes the letter, Sam sets it down on the grass between us. "Wow," he says. "That was—"

"She's alive," I break in, unable to keep the words inside any longer.

"Okay," Sam says. He scratches at his eyebrow.

"You sound doubtful," I say. I take the letter back.

"It's just that, well. The letter is typewritten." He studies the envelope. "It's postmarked from town."

"It sounds like Remy," I say. "It *feels* like Remy." My voice is angry. Insistent. Still, a million questions about this letter begin swirling in my mind. When did Remy write this? How did she send it? Why?

"Okay," Sam says. "Okay." He looks away, back down the road toward the O'Dells'. "You loved River, huh?"

"No," I lie. "Not like that." I pick another blade of grass and roll it between my fingers. My heart aches, just from reading his name. "I don't know why Remy said it."

I clear my throat. I need for this to sound believable.

"I mean, everything between Remy and me was sort of a competition. She was obsessed with winning. I was too. Maybe she was talking about that."

Sam's gaze feels intense on the side of my face. "You don't need to explain," he says. Still. An awkwardness hangs in the air between us.

Sam sets down the envelope. "We should find out what's under that watering can, though. Don't you think?"

On my way over to Remy's house, my whole body is buzzing with anxious energy. The letter is tucked safely in my desk, but it feels like it's here with me, in the front passenger seat where Remy always used to ride.

I'm alive, Remy says.

You're alive, I say back. I roll down the windows.

Sam is waiting back at the O'Dells. I told him I wanted to go to Remy's alone. This is between my cousin and me.

When I knock on the front door of the house, nobody answers. I wait for a long time on the doorstep. Slowly, worry starts to seep in. Remy's house has no visible neighbors. Nobody would know if something happened to Aunt Stephanie. I can imagine her there, on the ratty sofa, falling asleep and never waking up again. I knock louder and keep waiting. I consider just going in, but Remy says, *Garage first.* I listen.

The garage is a disaster. Walls of boxes, gardening tools, rat droppings, and garbage on the floor at least two feet deep in between old toys, rusty bikes, broken skis. I stand in the opening, looking around, scanning in rows, finding nothing. I'm about to give up when I spot the green spout sticking up from a tall shelf at the very back corner.

Great, thanks, Remy, I think. I start to pick my way through the detritus. I have at least two major scratches by the time I reach the back. One of them is bleeding. I look at the shelf in front of me. It's one of those metal ones and all of the bolts are rusted. It looks as if it might collapse on top of me. *How the fuck did you do this, Rem?* I think. *Why?*

Shhh, Remy says. *Hurry.*

I stretch up onto my tiptoes, but I still can't quite reach. I search around for something to stand on and spot a cinderblock covered in cobwebs. I gingerly slide it over and step on top. I lift the watering can, taking the shoebox from underneath it. I am just stepping down from the block when a deep, velvety voice says, "What are you doing?"

I spin around, clutching the box to my chest, and see Derek Stevenson leaning against the side of the garage doorframe. He's wearing a light blue tank top and black basketball shorts and his shoes are covered in grass clippings. His body is curved gracefully; his eyes are leonine.

Easy, Remy whispers. I loosen my grip on the shoebox. "My aunt wanted me to find a few of Remy's old things," I say.

Derek nods, slowly. "Like what?" he asks.

I look down at the shoebox. "Just some pictures and stuff."

"Remy liked pictures," Derek says. My stomach sours.

Derek takes one big step into the garage. "Let me see," he says. I back up until my shoulders touch the shelf, grateful for the sea of objects between us.

"I'm gonna show Stephanie first," I say. My voice sounds small and unsteady.

"I'm not sure that's a good idea," he says. He runs a hand over the stubble on his chin. "She's pretty upset today."

Something about the way he says this chills me to my core. "What are you doing here, Derek?" I ask.

"Probably the same thing you are," he says. His eyes are glinting. "Helping your aunt."

I start looking around for an object to protect myself. *Always go for the eyes*, Remy used to say while coaching me through a horror movie. *Anyplace soft. Don't be afraid to scratch or twist.* I spot a sharp spade on the shelf near my right knee. My mouth tastes metallic as I slowly start to reach for it.

Derek laughs then, and his whole presence changes. "I'm just fucking with you," he says. Then he turns and walks away. I sink down to the floor and wait there, hugging my knees to my chest.

FOURTEEN

I've almost made it to my car when Stephanie calls to me from the porch. Derek is mowing the backyard now, so I almost don't hear her.

Aunt Stephanie stands in the doorway, a cigarette dangling from her mouth, hands on her hips. She's dressed in wrinkled, pilled pajamas, hair in a messy nest on top of her head. She looks even more strung out than usual, more tired and jumpier at the same time. *Is this what Derek is helping with?* I wonder.

Aunt Stephanie squints at me, taking a long pull of her cigarette. "If you're going to lurk around my house, come inside and make me some lunch."

"There's grilled cheese stuff in the fridge," Stephanie says as she follows me into the kitchen, her voice scratchy. She sits down at the table, a fresh cigarette already lit. Outside, the sound of the mower gets closer.

I pull out the bread, cheese, and margarine. The fridge is mostly empty otherwise, except for a bottle of low-fat creamer, ten Diet Cokes, and a yellow Styrofoam carton of eggs.

"How are you, then?" Stephanie asks, leaning back in her chair. Her eyelids look heavy.

"I'm okay," I say. "How are you?"

Stephanie laughs; it is a deeply cynical sound, hollow, halfway to a racking cough. "I've been better," she says.

The kitchen is a mess. Bowls and mugs are piled in the sink, crumbs litter the counter and floor. A fly buzzes around the overflowing garbage can, and the whole room smells rotten.

"What is Derek Stevenson doing here?" I ask.

Stephanie shrugs, looks defiant. "He's been helping me around the house. More than anyone else has done for me since she left." The way she says *she* is full of bitterness. "Your mother hasn't been here in two weeks."

I don't know what to say to this. Something happened between them the night after the search party and Mom hasn't told me what it is.

"Derek is a good boy," she says, looking out the window. "Only one of Scott's friends that still comes around."

I put together the sandwich and turn on the stove. Aunt Stephanie takes a long drag of her cigarette.

"Do you think she's ever coming back?" Stephanie asks. At first I think she's talking about Mom, but then I realize she means Remy.

Her voice is light, like she's trying to act like she doesn't care. But as she taps her cigarette against the ashtray, I can see the way her fingers shake.

I press the spatula into the sandwich that is now beginning to sizzle in the pan. I think of Remy's letter in my drawer at home. I could tell Aunt Stephanie her daughter is alive. But for some reason I don't want to give her this. I'm not sure she deserves it.

Stephanie bulldozes through my silence. "I guess she's smarter than I gave her credit for," she says. "I never managed to get out of Black Falls." Stephanie begins to laugh again, and this time the laugh sinks all the way down into her lungs and she doubles over coughing. I walk toward her and hover nearby, not sure if I should touch her or not.

"I'm fine, honey," she finally says, wheezing for air. "Don't burn that grilled cheese."

I finish the sandwich and make Aunt Stephanie a plate, adding some chips from a half-empty bag I find on the fridge. "I should get going," I say, setting the plate on the table.

"Of course, of course," Stephanie says. "But come back soon, okay? I'm all alone out here."

As I walk to my car, shoebox in hand, Derek watches me.

I don't open the box until I get to Sam's house. I'm still coming down from the feeling of being in Remy's garage with Derek Stevenson.

Remy liked pictures.

Lili said Fawn was only for students, but it's starting to feel like that was not the case at all.

I smooth the hand that's not on the steering wheel through my hair, tugging at snarls, as though this will calm me. I think the words that I tell myself when I'm walking on the road:

The world is a soft place.

This is not a horror movie.

Remy is not a dead girl.

I have the letter now, so I know.

When I pull into the driveway Sam is sitting on the front porch steps, waiting.

"That took kind of a long time," he says. He looks me up and down, a tight kind of concern on his face. I wonder if I look as shaken as I feel.

"I ran into Derek." My voice wavers a little when I say this. "I think he's been hanging around Remy's house. He was mowing the lawn."

I sit down on the stair next to Sam.

"He really wants that SIM card." I look down at my sneakers next to Sam's. Matching Chucks, his black, mine white. "I overheard Tate talking to Callie's older brother behind the hardware store on Friday." I tell Sam what I overheard, and then I tell him about Zack's user data.

Sam nods, a look of understanding dawning on his face. "If he and Tate were involved with Fawn, then it makes sense why they want the card so badly. It could really fuck up their lives if someone else found it."

Sam and I are quiet for a moment, letting that thought sink in. It feels so big; I don't think either of us knows what to do with it.

Then Sam gestures at the box, which I am clutching tightly with my hands. "Do you think whatever's in the box has something to do with Fawn?"

"I don't know," I say. I take a deep breath and lift the cover.

Inside are a handful of what look like letters, without envelopes, on neatly folded, heavy, expensive-looking paper. The top of one is popping open, and I can see Dear Remy inside. Typewritten. My heart beats faster.

"Should we go inside and look at these?" I ask.

Sam frowns, looking at the door behind him. "I'd rather not," he says. "I hate being in that house."

"Let's go to mine, then," I say. "My mom's at work."

We close the box back up again, not opening it until we are in my kitchen, like we both know how heavy the words inside it might be. Then we set it between us on the table. Sam carefully slides the top off again. I lift the first letter out.

Dear Remy, reads the opening greeting.

Then: Do you know how beautiful you are? I could spend hours looking at the sunlight on the back of your neck. Don't give up. I know this seems unexpected, but trust what you're feeling.

I hold the paper in my hands, eyes tracing the shapes of the typewritten font. I can see Remy's graceful neck, sunlit, in my mind's eye. The little hairs on her skin are glowing.

"I guess this is who she burned for," Sam says, quoting Remy's letter to me.

"I guess," I reply.

"Not River," Sam says.

"Not River," I echo.

My stomach is sinking, fast. I close my eyes, trying to

hold myself here, in my kitchen. I reach into the box for another letter, letting the first one fall to the table.

> My dear Remy. Remy, my dear. My deer.
> Last week I was walking in the woods
> and I saw a young doe, just beginning
> to lose her spots. She reminded me of
> you, the way she floated through the
> trees. So graceful, as if she were made
> of air and light. She looked at me,
> almost playfully. But when I took a
> step closer, she bolted away. All this
> is to say, I know you are afraid. This
> is strange. New. But like the deer, the
> woods, the soft breeze that made the
> leaves dance, it is so, so beautiful.

I read the next letter:

> Remy Valentine. I still can't believe
> that's your middle name, even after all
> these years. A valentine is exactly what
> you feel like to me. A living, breathing
> love letter. A sweet surprise. Poetry on
> fine, delicate paper.
>
> Do you believe that before you I'd
> never been in love before? Of course, I
> thought I had. But now I see that what
> I felt then was only devotion, duty,

friendship. What I feel with you, Rem. I
can't even describe it. It's bigger than
the whole universe.

And the next:

Remy. Can you meet me tonight at our
tree? It's been a hard few days and I
need you. When we're apart for too long,
the darker side of all of this starts to
seep in. Do you feel it too? The guilt
and shame of it? I wish that loving you
didn't feel like a betrayal. Because
Remy, loving you is the only thing that
feels good anymore. Remy. Please come.
I'll be waiting.

And the last:

Remy Green. Eponymous eyes. You say
they're plain blue but I don't believe
you; they're greengoldblue, the color of
summertime. Are you drifting away? Or
is it that I can just never get enough
of you? Look at me. I'm a disaster.
Everything has come apart. You've
brought me to my knees. The only thing
left is the beating of my heart.

Remy. It beats for you.

"Wow," Sam says when all of the letters are done.

I don't have words to give back to him. Only feelings. Remy feelings: stinging jealousy and raw anger. And others: gnawing worry and cold fear. A bottomless well of secrets I will never understand.

"Who could have written these?" Sam asks, stacking the letters neatly on the table.

"I have no idea," I say, looking at the pile of pages.

"Not a seventeen-year-old."

"I don't think so."

"I don't know if it sounds like a cop either." Sam pauses. "Do you think this is the same person who wrote Remy's letter?"

"I guess it could be," I say. I feel sick at the thought.

No, Remy says. *Don't give up.*

I go upstairs and get the letter from my bedroom. We lay them out side by side by side.

"Hm," Sam says. "The font looks exactly the same, but the ink is lighter on the love letters."

I run my fingers over the top of Remy's letter, willing myself not to smell it again.

Sam looks at me like he is sorry for what he's about to say. He taps his finger on the table next to mine. "It would make sense for whoever wrote these letters to want them destroyed. They could have pretended to be Remy to get you to do it."

I feel a deep resistance to Sam's theory, but at the same time I can't say it doesn't make sense. "How would they know where Remy was keeping them?" I ask.

Sam gets up and starts pacing around the kitchen. "I

don't know," he says. "It feels like there's a thread connecting all of this, but I can't see it."

"It's not a thread," I say. "It's a web. Remy was really, really good at making those." I lean my head on the cool wood of the table. "I just miss her so much," I say. "But I feel like I don't even know who she was. Is. Was anything about her real?"

Remy taught me everything I know about love. She narrated every step of her relationship with River, creating a perfect story, better than a movie. But all of it was a lie.

I'm so sorry, Remy says.

Sam stops behind my chair, like he wants to offer comfort but he doesn't know how. I'm not sure if I want that from him, so I sit up straight and take a deep breath. I touch the letters on the table. "These are so . . ."

"I know," Sam says.

"I don't think I can destroy them, though."

"I don't think you should," Sam says. He scratches at his eyebrow. "I think maybe we should give all of this to the police."

I look at Sam. "Zack *is* the police, remember?"

I picture the Remy-red ribbon, hanging from Zack's rearview mirror, and the bruises on Callie's arm. And for the first time, I feel truly afraid.

FIFTEEN

Each year on the first weekend in June, the Black Falls volunteer fire department organizes a 5K run for breast cancer. The event feels like the culmination of spring in Black Falls; everyone comes out either to run or to cheer the runners on. When River died the event was postponed, and then when Remy disappeared it was canceled, but at the last minute the police and fire departments got together to rescue the event, and they decided to donate half of the proceeds to teen mental health awareness.

On Saturday, four days after Sam and I find the letters, Mom and I drive out to Hen Woods for the event. The sky is sunny and clear, a perfect day for a run. We are quiet on the way over, because there is nothing really to talk about anymore.

Hen Woods trail, out near the local ski hill, is where the cross-country team holds their home meets. It's a place that belongs to River and Remy, not to me. It's where their romance began to blossom when we were thirteen years old.

River joined the cross-country team because of his dad and Remy joined because she loved to run. I watched every race, pretending that I wasn't on the outside.

The trail starts and ends in the same open field, ringed with elm and maple trees. The field is full of people, but the crowd is more somber than in years past, without any of the silly costumes or signs that usually mark this event.

I scan the crowd, looking for the person who wrote Remy's letters. I have taken them out every night, reading them again and again. They are so devotional, but something about the words truly scares me. Was Remy really having an affair? With who? A teacher, a stranger? It feels like it could be anyone, like everyone I see could be hiding some terrible secret.

I look toward the starting line, where a large banner with a picture of River's face and the words SUPPORT MENTAL HEALTH AWARENESS is raised over the trail.

The River on the plastic banner—smiling widely against a sunlit backdrop of trees—looks undeniably dead. I feel angry just looking at him, because his face is an empty gesture, the town pretending like they cared about him. The longer I watch everyone lounging and chatting and stretching and moving and *living*, the angrier I get. The more I think about what Sam said in River's room, the more I know it's true. Whatever happened to River, it was the pressure of this place that did it.

"You're starting to come around," Sam says, sidling up beside me, a few yards from the clump of runners who are all getting ready. "I can see it on your face."

I sigh. "I think I am." I turn to him, smiling without meaning to. He sticks out in his usual black jeans and T-shirt, in this field of green grass and people in neon Lycra. "You're not running?"

"I hate exercise," he says.

All week long, Sam and I have been moving around one another in a strange orbit. I think we are becoming friends, and more than that, I think I might be starting to like him. It's strange; the only boy I've ever liked was River. Even Bailey was just an imaginary crush. A mistake.

We stand side by side, watching the brightly colored runners, and I am aware of every inch of space between us. "Why are you here if you're not running?" I ask.

"Rebecca asked me to come. I couldn't say no." He runs a thumb over his eyebrow. "She's the only adult in my life who isn't a complete dick."

I haven't seen Rebecca in a long time, not since my first couple of days at the stand. Sam said she's been gone a lot caring for her mother. I look for her now, finding her in the shade of a willow tree, looking small and pale. She looks so alone.

Then my mother walks up beside her and hands her a muffin. She opens up the camping chairs and offers one to Rebecca, and the two of them sit together, quietly. I've always thought of Mom being a midwife because of the babies, but now I see the way she helps the mothers too. In this moment, when I am otherwise so alone, I feel grateful to have a mother like her.

Kendall comes up to us then and pulls me into a big hug. She smells like something elegant and expensive, and her embrace is tight, strong. "I'm glad you're here," she says in my ear.

"Me too," I say. I feel strange in this hug, not really knowing Kendall, not trusting her. She hasn't been with the other girls when we've worked on finding Remy and I'm not sure why. But when she rests her forehead on my shoulder, I can feel something real, some hurting, inside her.

She tugs me away from Sam, over to where Liliana and Callie and Callie's little sister, Marta, are standing near the mass of runners. Callie and Liliana hug me, just like Kendall did. The three of us have talked a few times this week, to catch up on what I found in the journal and try to figure out what to do next. Each time it feels a little more natural. But sometimes it still feels strange how easily they've let me in after all the time I was on the outside. I still haven't told them about Zack or the letters. My loyalty to Remy is too deep; I can't reveal a secret like this.

Marta drifts off to find her friends and then the four of us stand for a while, just looking around. The energy of the whole group has shifted. At events like this, the girls used to be the center of everything, Remy at the center of them. Now they hover in the background, their energy quiet, thoughtful.

"Seems like everyone came out," Liliana says, leaning over to stretch her hamstring. Lili and Kendall are on the cross-country team too, although they've never seemed to love it like Callie and Remy do. I remember Remy telling me once that they just ran to stay in shape.

What does that mean? I wonder now. What shape are we supposed to be? Long and thin? Straight and angular?

Soft and curved? All of these things impossibly together in one pleasing shape? It makes me think of Fawn again, about the idea of taking control. Don't they know it's an illusion? We will never, ever have it, no matter what we do.

Callie breaks into my thoughts, gesturing over to where Zack is chatting with the other police officers. "Even my brother is here," she says. "I haven't seen him in soft pants in like five years." I study the group of men. They are all wearing matching BFPD T-shirts with American flags on them. I watch Zack as he stretches his muscular arms overhead. Did he write the letters? Is that possible? I still can't remember much about him from when we were younger. He was quiet, alone a lot. Maybe the kind of person who would write a furtive love letter. I'm not sure he's like that anymore, though. He's a cop, and I don't think they write those.

Next to the police officers is the boys football team, Bailey off to the side, stretching his quads. I'm not sure how to think about him now, so my eyes move quickly on to the cross-country team, to Mr. O'Dell standing beside them. He looks tired. Lost, like Rebecca. Like Mom and me. Like he is trying to be here but can't. I wonder if he's still driving around all night, trying to outrun his grief.

Liliana leans over, bending her head close to mine. "Someone here has to know something," she whispers.

I nod. I feel a pang of guilt for keeping Zack and the letters to myself.

"It's so frustrating," she says, scanning the crowd. "I feel like there's something we're missing."

The fire chief, a tall, handsome young man with a rosy-cheeked toddler in his arms, lifts a bullhorn to his mouth and instructs all of the runners to line up at the start. As everyone shuffles into place, I stare at him and wonder, *Is it you?*

Then the race begins with a gunshot, startling me back to the present moment. I begin to run, following the girls down the trail.

Callie, Kendall, and Liliana start out a lot faster than I expect them to. I try to keep up, but we haven't gone far before my side begins to cramp viciously. My lungs are on fire, my legs are heavy. My body is saying no. I slow to a walk, waving the girls on, stepping to the side as runner after runner passes by me. It feels humiliating.

Soon, even the speed-walking PTA moms have gone by and I am all alone, walking this trail. Just me and the sycamore trees. I slow way down, trying to feel my friends in this place that was so much a part of them. *Are you here, Remy?* I ask in my mind. She's been talking to me lately, but never when I ask her to.

She doesn't answer now, but I can almost see the flash of her golden hair moving through the trees.

River moved differently, not like light. Like water. His body was strong and tall and every motion felt inevitable, flowing in a certain direction, in a path made smooth by practice and time. I close my eyes and imagine him, and my heart begins to ache.

When will this stop being so awful? When will the pain of it stop consuming me? It hasn't been very long, but I'm not sure I can take much more.

Suddenly, I hear a sound up ahead. The shrill chirp of nervous laughter. I round the bend and there's Bailey, hand in hand with Marta. From behind, she could almost *be* Remy, with her waist-long blond hair neatly tucked into braids. I've never thought about it before, but the two are so much alike, although Marta is a lot younger than us. She's not even a freshman yet.

I look to where their hands are joined, an uneasy feeling rising in my stomach.

Told you, Remy sneers in my ear. *He is a fucking creep.*

I freeze, momentarily unsure. I know what I *need* to do, but I feel like it requires skills I don't have. I close my eyes, wishing Remy were here.

I'm not, she says. *It's just you.*

I take a deep breath and begin to walk faster, louder, until Bailey, hearing my steps, stops and turns around. His face sours. I don't meet his stare. Instead I look at Marta, who is looking at me with eyes that are nervous, like she is worried she's in trouble, and also grateful, like she is glad I've come upon them. She drops Bailey's hand.

"Marta," I say. "Your sister was looking for you." I give her a meaningful look. "I bet you could catch her if you run." I say that last word with emphasis.

Marta nods once, and then takes off down the trail, like a streak of light, like Remy. Bailey stays where he is, his whole body seeming to block the trail, anger coming off him in waves. My heart starts to thump in my chest.

"What the fuck?" he says to me. I look down at the ground. Bailey takes a step closer.

"Look," he says. "I tried to be nice. But maybe I need to

spell it out for you. What happened between us was not meaningful on any kind of deeper level. I am not, nor will I ever be, interested in you."

His words crawl around like beetles in my stomach, confusing me. I'm not interested in him. But something about his voice almost convinces me that I am. I look up at his neat hair and his square features, his mouth that is drawn into a straight line. It's true; he is handsome. But I can't believe I ever let him touch me.

"You've got to leave me alone," he says, running a hand through his hair. He looks over his shoulder at where Marta has disappeared down the trail. "This is getting kind of creepy."

I'm not sure what he means. I haven't called or texted or even looked at him since the night of the party. Something must have happened. Some kind of misunderstanding. I feel flustered, like I need to say something to right this wrong. There is some explanation I should give. Some kind of comment that will clear this whole thing up. But I can't find words.

Bailey takes another step forward, grabs my upper arm. *Run*, Remy whispers. But I know that I need to give Marta a head start. So I don't move. Bailey leans his head down, his grip tightening.

"I know that Remy is gone," he says. His voice is a whisper, even though there is no one around. "But that doesn't mean you can take her place. I see you talking with her friends, wearing her clothes." He laughs a little. "But you're not her. And honestly, it's a little pathetic."

He drops my arm. "Now I'm going to go get Marta, and

you're not going to go after me. You're not going to say anything. To anyone."

The imprint of his fingers burns on my skin. His hard, painful grip lasts even after he's let go. But as he starts to walk away, something comes over me.

"No," I say.

He stops.

"No. I'm not going to do that."

Bailey turns back to face me.

"I know about your obsession with my cousin," I say. I don't want to say her name in front of him. "You're the pathetic one. Over thirty views, every single day?"

His face begins to redden, a mixture of anger and shame coloring his skin.

"Remy told me everything," I lie. "I know everything." I cross my arms, standing a little taller. "You're the one who should be careful," I say. "Because I'm still not sure what I'm going to do about you yet."

I start walking then, leaving Bailey frozen and speechless in the middle of the path. At the turn in the trail, I break into a run, my legs pumping fast, some kind of unknown force moving my body forward, forward, forward. I don't stop until I cross the finish line.

After the race, the fire chief gives a speech. Everyone is gathered under a giant elm tree near the parking lot, drinking lemonade from paper cups. Bailey is nowhere to be seen. The chief tells us that he is proud of us for coming out today. That we have raised almost three thousand dollars for a mental health nonprofit in Albany. He calls Jake and Rebecca to the front and presents them with a plaque, which will be installed on a bench by the head of the trail.

I stand with the girls, and I know we are all thinking the same thing: *What about Remy?*

Mom and I are quiet as we get back in the car. It takes a while to navigate our way through the parking lot, which is now clogged with groups of people chatting in the sun. I spot the fire chief's wife, carrying the rolled-up banner in her arms. When we are finally free, driving fast down Turnpike, Mom begins to laugh.

"What a pile of horseshit," she says.

Without meaning to, I begin laughing too. Before long we are fully cracking up, until tears stream down our faces and Mom has to pull the car over to the side of the road.

This, Remy says. *This is better.*

That night, Callie invites me to a sleepover at her house. I am not sure whether or not I should go. Bailey's words from this morning left a burn that is still stinging. A question that's worming through my brain. Am I trying to be her? Do I want her life? Is that what I'm doing with these girls?

But when I think about spending another night with Mom hovering around me, I feel incredibly lonely. And I need to find out more about Zack. So at 6 p.m., I show up at her door with a pillow and an overnight bag.

I have always loved Callie White's house. It is neat and

white and square, with short grass and carefully tamed flowers in the front garden. Inside, it opens like a magic box. The foyer has shiny, light wood floors, high ceilings, twin staircases leading to the second floor, and French doors looking out onto a giant backyard with a huge swimming pool. Every decoration, mirror, piece of art, vase of flowers fits perfectly in its place, always clean, always in order.

Callie meets me at the door and brings me up to her bedroom to drop off my things. Everything in Callie's bedroom is different than it used to be. The last time I was here it was a little girl's paradise, with pink ruffles on everything. Now her bedspread is lilac and her curtains are white. She has a white desk, with a neat stack of untouched-looking notebooks and a turquoise Bluetooth speaker on top. A vase of lilies sits next to it.

"You can change in here," she says. "The girls are all down at the pool." She turns to leave but stops at the door. "Whatever you did to help Marta today, thanks. She didn't want to tell me what happened, but I know it had something to do with Bailey. And knowing what we know about him and Remy . . ." She lets out a shuddering breath.

"I'm glad she's okay," I say. I want to tell her about the poisonous things he said to me, but something stops me. Instead I say, "I told him that we know about his stats on the app. And he seemed really shocked." I pause. "Like he didn't think it was possible for anyone to find out."

"Do you think he has the chip?" Callie asks.

"Maybe." I don't tell her that part of the reason I'm here is to find out more about her brother.

"I'm babysitting at his house this week," Callie says. "I'm going to check his room and see what I can find."

"Be careful," I tell her.

You too, Remy whispers, as if she knows my plan.

Callie smiles. "Don't worry. He won't be home."

I am anxious as I put on my black one-piece swimsuit. I feel naked, even when all of the straps are in place. I turn to look at myself in the full-length mirror on the back of the bedroom door.

I think of all the summer afternoons at the river with River and Remy, in this same bathing suit, feeling perfectly free. Happy. But now all I can think of is what I look like through someone else's eyes. How much of my body is bare. My hair is frizzy, my skin is red in places. I try to pose. To be an object. To believe I could be beautiful. It doesn't work.

I pull my shorts on and head back down the stairs. I wonder if Zack is home. In the giant farmhouse kitchen to the left of the foyer, I spot Callie's mother, leaning her elbows on the counter, looking at a magazine. She catches my eye and comes out to say hello.

"Jules," she says, smiling widely. She is a beautiful woman, naturally graceful and neatly dressed. "It's so nice to see you back here again." She squeezes my shoulders with her small hands, and the gesture communicates so much. *I'm sorry that you lost your cousin. I hope that you're not like her. I hope that you can pull my daughter from the path that she is on. It scares me.*

I stand there, trying to smile, until she lets me go.

When I get to the pool, the girls are all floating around in colorful plastic donuts. Kendall tosses me one and I sit down at the side of the pool, donut beside me, dangling my feet in the cold water.

"Cute suit," Kendall says. It feels like she's lying.

Liliana yawns, ignoring her. "This morning was such a joke," she says. She wears an orange two-piece with big, retro yellow flowers on it and her hair is braided into a crown. "It's kind of amazing the lengths that adults will go to ignore what's happening right in front of their eyes." She laughs darkly. "As if any of them give a fuck about our mental health."

Callie glances nervously toward the kitchen, like she's worried her mother will overhear us. Liliana seems to notice and lowers her voice a little. She pulls Callie's tube in close to her, protectively. "I'm just saying that what happened to River is tragic. And donating a few thousand dollars to a teen center in Albany isn't going to fix it."

Callie nods. Her suit is lavender, like her room. "Nobody said one word about Remy today either."

"It's because she's unresolved," Liliana replies. "She doesn't fit into any of the boxes, so it's better to just ignore her."

"I'm glad," Kendall says. "They would have made a banner that was like, 'Keep our girls safe!' When we all know that what they really want is to keep us scared."

"I don't know," Callie says. "It's strange how it seems like nobody cares anymore that she's gone."

"I don't want to talk about this anymore," Kendall says suddenly. She slides out of her tube and sinks down under the water.

I watch her, wondering. I've noticed that Kendall often keeps things at the surface. There has to be more than meets the eye. Maybe she's like Remy, keeping everything light so that darkness doesn't consume her. Or maybe she's hiding something.

"You should get in the pool, Jules," she says when she comes up again. "It's so hot out."

Even though I'm sweating from every pore of my skin, I don't want to take my shorts off in front of these girls. "I'm all right," I say. I feel immediately foolish. Kendall and Liliana have bared every inch of themselves for the entire school and I'm afraid to swim in my bathing suit.

Chicken, Remy whispers in my ear.

Fine. I stand up and awkwardly shimmy out of the denim. Then, quickly, before anyone can notice, I cannonball directly into the deep end.

The water feels unbelievably good on my skin. I sink down to the bottom then float on the surface, looking at the sky. Then I go back under, holding my breath for as long as I can.

SIXTEEN

Over dinner, Callie's mom mentions that Zack is on night duty at the station and won't be home until morning. We stay up late watching movies in the rec room, and I buzz with nervous energy the whole time, knowing what I'm going to do.

I wait for a long time after everyone goes to sleep and then, when I can't wait any longer, I slip out from under the covers of the blowup mattress I'm sharing with Liliana. I sit beside the bed and count to a hundred in my mind, to make sure I haven't awakened her.

It's easy to sneak down the two flights of stairs to the basement apartment, because the carpet on them is so plush. It makes me remember when Callie and I were little and would lie down in the middle of the hallway, making imaginary snow angels on the floor.

When I get to the door of Zack's room, I hesitate. My heart is pounding. I want to turn back, but I have to keep going so I can find Remy. Alive.

I reach for the knob, relieved when it twists smoothly in my hand. Then I push the door open. The room is large and very dark, with only a couple of small windows near the ceiling to let in the moonlight. I switch on my cell phone flashlight and sweep it across the queen-size bed, the bookshelf, the loveseat and flat-screen television, the tiny kitchenette at the end of the space. Everything is neat as a pin.

I walk toward the bed first, because this is where the secrets are usually kept. The bedspread is dark, navy. Perfectly smooth. Two large matching pillows sit side by side on top. Perfectly even. I sweep my hand between the mattress and the box spring. I am very careful not to wrinkle anything.

I move my attention to the nightstand, which is mostly bare like the rest of the room. I see a small metal cross and a silver-framed photograph of Zack with his arm around a girl who looks a lot like Remy but isn't her. I stand looking at it for a moment, feeling the quiet of the house seeping into my bones.

I open the bedside drawer, and it is completely empty. I look under the bed. Nothing. Not sure where to look next, I pick up the photograph again.

"What are you doing in here?" someone says. It's Callie. She looks sleepy; her hair is rumpled.

I look down at the photo in my hands, my heart hammering in my throat. I don't know what to say.

Callie slips inside the room and closes the door behind her. Her face is confused. I try to think of a lie, but nothing seems to fit.

"I'm looking for something," I say.

"For what?" she asks, crossing her arms.

I swallow. "I don't know."

"This is really weird," she says, rubbing her eyes. I can hear something else in her voice now, suspicion.

I clutch the frame to my chest. "I know. It is. But there's something I need to tell you."

"About Zack?" Callie asks, her voice uneasy.

I nod, taking a step toward her. "When I charted out Remy's viewers on Fawn, Bailey wasn't the only one who stood out."

Callie's face falls as she considers all that this could mean. "But he's not a student." She bring her hands up to her face. "Oh my god."

"It's all right," I say to her. I put the photo down on the bed and wrap my arm around her. "Breathe."

Callie leans into me and I hold her tightly. I have been in this exact moment before, my entire world changing shape around me. We all have. But this seems almost worse.

Callie pulls back and picks up the photograph. "That's Amanda," she says. "She was my brother's girlfriend. She died last year in a car accident. Zack was driving. It was awful. He had to come home and almost dropped out of the academy. That's why he's here instead of in the city."

"Was he badly hurt?" I ask.

"No," Callie says, still studying the picture. "I think the guilt was the hardest part."

Callie clutches the photo tightly in her hands as she says this. I wonder if she's thinking the same thing I am.

"They look a lot alike," she says, her voice unsteady. "Remy and Amanda."

I take the frame from her hands and set it back on the nightstand.

"I guess maybe that's why he—" She turns away. I walk over to the bookshelf, giving her some space to let it sink in. Her big brother was Remy's most frequent viewer.

I study the volumes on the shelf: Ayn Rand, Jordan Peterson, a biography of Elon Musk.

"Everyone grieves differently," I tell Callie, repeating my mother's words. I wonder if I should stop searching and bring Callie back up to her room. But this might be my only chance.

I pull a book from the shelf, flipping through the pages to see if anything is hiding inside. A receipt falls out. I pick it up and tuck it in my pocket.

Suddenly, we hear the loud crunching of tires in the gravel driveway.

"Zack," Callie whispers, eyes wide. I shove the book back on the shelf and then we run, as fast as we can, up both flights of stairs, not stopping until we are on the top landing. When I pass the window at the end of the hall, I can see Zack, in uniform, climbing out of his car and walking toward the front door. Just before he gets there, he stops and looks up. We are too far back from the window to be seen, but I swear he knows we are there.

On Sunday evening, Callie and I meet up to run on Turnpike Road again. I tell her about the letters and we go over everything together, trying to make sense of it all.

"Do you really think Remy could be alive?" she asks.

I nod. "I do."

We follow the road past Glen Hollow, cresting the hill by Mill Creek. When I find my breath, I ask, "Are you doing all right?"

Callie squints her eyes at the sun. "Yeah," she says. "Don't worry. I'm fine." It sounds like the kind of thing she says a lot.

By the time we finish the loop and Callie's car comes into view, the light is beginning to turn pink. I slump over, hands on my knees, trying to catch my breath, and when I stand upright again I notice a brick-red pickup truck parked right behind Callie's car, almost touching her back bumper. When we get a little closer I see Derek Stevenson and Zack White waiting inside the cab.

Derek, Zack, and Scott were all friends in high school and would hang around Remy's house together when we were young. In the years after Scott died, though, I thought they'd grown apart. Seeing them together now, two different threads in the tapestry, makes me uneasy.

Callie and I exchange a look.

"Shit," she whispers under her breath.

Zack gets out of the passenger side and starts walking toward Callie. "Dad's looking for you," he says. There's a quiet menace in his voice. Callie's back stiffens. "You were supposed to be home an hour ago."

Callie looks angry, but she doesn't say anything back to him. Instead, she turns to me. "I should go," she says.

I nod, and then watch as she and Zack walk to her car and drive away. They are stiff, not talking at all.

Derek, who has been quiet up until now, turns to me. "Hey, Jules," he says. He looks down at my legs. "Want a ride home?"

"No thanks," I say, crossing my arms over my chest.

He looks at me with subtext in his eyes, "I really think you should come," he says. "I hear it's not safe for girls to be out alone."

"Fuck off," I tell him.

I start walking toward my house, which is about a half mile back down the road, and the truck starts driving beside me, slowly. I'm surprised to see that Derek is on the passenger side, and his brother Tate is driving. I didn't notice Tate before, but maybe he was in the back.

"Come on, Jules," Derek says, leaning out the passenger window. "Get in the truck."

I ignore him.

They pull over on the shoulder ahead of me. Derek gets out and blocks my path.

"Please," he says. "I really think we might be able to help each other."

I cross my arms, considering this. I know Derek is somehow involved with Fawn. Maybe if I agree to talk with him, I can find out how.

"Okay," I say. I follow Derek up into the cab.

Stop, Remy whispers. *What are you doing?*

Derek reaches across me and pulls the door shut. The cab feels small and stuffy; his knee is less than an inch from mine on the bench seat. I slide as close as I can to the passenger door.

Tate puts the truck in gear, then makes a U-turn, driving us in the opposite direction of my house. "I live back that way," I say.

Tate keeps driving like he didn't hear me. My heart starts beating faster.

"Okay, Jules," Tate says, giving me a smile that makes my skin crawl. "It's time. Where's the SIM card?"

I try to keep my breath slow and steady, try to notice my surroundings. *You're safe*, I tell myself.

No you're not, Remy whispers.

"Your guess is as good as mine," I say.

Derek shifts against me, and Tate starts driving faster. Sixty-five, then seventy-five, then eighty. Trees are flying by.

My knee begins to bounce as I realize what an error I've made.

"Where's the SIM card, Jules?" Tate says, his voice frighteningly low and steady. "You really need to tell me, now."

I grit my teeth. "I really don't know."

He slams a hand on the steering wheel, and it startles me.

"Stop," he says. "Just stop. I know you found it in Remy's room. Under the floorboard. Derek saw you."

I watch the needle climb up to ninety as the world around us becomes a green blur. In the middle of the bench seat, Derek looks down at his hands.

"I didn't," I say. "I swear."

"You're lying," Tate says. The speedometer goes to a hundred.

"No." I'm begging now. I don't want to die in this car.

Suddenly, a deer bolts out into the road ahead of us. Everything slows way down, and I can see that the deer is young, a small fawn, light brown, beautiful. She looks at us, as if she is not afraid of anything, not even dying.

Tate wrenches the wheel to swerve around her, and I squeeze my eyes closed.

I feel the car careen to the shoulder and then back across the double yellow lines, and when we finally come to a stop, I open my eyes and see that we are in the gravel on the opposite side of the road. The deer is gone.

"Fuck," Derek says. "Oh my god. Fuck."

Tate grips the steering wheel, hard, as if he is still driving.

I open my door and run, as fast as I can, away from the road, toward the trees. I don't stop, even when Tate starts the truck again and drives off toward town.

SEVENTEEN

Monday is Remy's birthday, and also the summer solstice. I wake up to someone slipping into my bed, and for a half-asleep second I think it's her. But then I smell the warm-baked-goods scent of my mother and I remember walking all the way home in the gathering darkness and falling into her arms.

I cried for a long time but wouldn't tell her why. I still feel uneasy this morning, remembering the flash of the deer running out into the road.

"I couldn't sleep," she whispers now. The room is dusky with the first light of the day. "It doesn't feel right, all this quiet."

She snakes her arm around me and pulls me close; I can feel her heart beating at my back. For a while we lie like that, watching the day come.

Usually, we celebrate Remy's birthday for days. We'll have a big party with all of her friends, a little one with just Mom and me, and then some elaborate adventure with

River. Everywhere we go—the gas station, the grocery store, the post office—everyone will wish her happy birthday.

When we were little, Mom made a birthday scepter that she decorated with glitter and plastic jewels. On the side she wrote QUEEN FOR THE DAY.

Remy was always the best queen. She would think of the most fun things for us to do, from dawn to dusk. Pancake-decorating contest, roller derby in the living room, pillow-fort mansion. Her birthday was the longest day of the whole year, and she would fill every last minute.

I hate my birthday, Remy wrote in her letter. Is that true? Was it Remy who said that, or was it Zack White?

Since the sleepover, I haven't been able to get the smiling image of his girlfriend out of my mind. *I think the guilt was the hardest part*, Callie said. I wonder if that's really true.

Now, lying in bed with my mother in Remy's spot, the longest day of the year stretches before me, hour after hour, empty.

"You could stay home from work," Mom says. She gently runs her fingers through my hair, pulling apart the snarls. "I could make us pancakes."

"I think I should go in," I say. What I mean is that I can't stay here. The thought of so much time together, without Remy, makes me too sad. And lately the sadness has been threatening to pull me under.

"Are you sure?" Mom asks. Her voice sounds disappointed.

"I'm sure," I reply. Then I slip out from under the covers and start looking for my clothes.

When I pull up at the stand, I see Rebecca, struggling with the front grate. I haven't seen her at the stand in more than a week and, for some reason, the sight of her fills me with relief so strong it's almost like a premonition. I watch her for a moment, noticing how even though she looks worn and tired, there is strength in her body.

"Need some help?" I ask.

She nods emphatically, smiling. "Yes, please."

As we work together, I notice that Rebecca looks different today. More animated. More alive. Stronger. The two of us manage to get the door up.

"I've been trying to get Jake to fix this all summer," she says, gesturing to the rusty metal chain. She seems annoyed. She stands for a moment, her hands on her hips, staring off into the middle distance.

"Anyway," she says, voice still terse. "I'm glad you're here early. Jake is sick today and I have to manage the farm crew alone. Do you think that you can close up too?"

"Sure," I say. For some reason, I feel uncomfortable. Maybe because it is so unlike her to ever be frustrated or angry. Or maybe it's that the past few weeks she has been shrinking, but today she takes up space.

Sam arrives at the stand at exactly ten o'clock. I haven't seen him since Saturday, but something about his presence feels instantly calming. He is familiar to me now, with his feline slouch, his soft black T-shirts, the charcoal smudges on the heel of his left hand. He walks over to the back where I'm sitting.

"Morning," he says. His voice is scratchy and sleepy.

"Morning."

He takes a step closer. "Are you okay?" he asks, concern in his voice.

There is so much to tell him. About Zack and Bailey and the Stevensons. But today, Remy's birthday, I am back inside my shell. Fear and sadness cover me like a shroud.

"I'm fine."

The next couple of hours are quiet and achingly slow. Sam draws and I watch the tiny changes in the light as the sun moves slowly across the sky. I wonder if Remy is somewhere, under this sun. I wonder if she is happy or scared or lonely. I wonder if she misses me as much as I miss her.

Remy is not dead, but her absence feels like death. The loss is as sudden and complete. Still, the sadness that I feel for Remy has a different quality from the sadness I feel for River. River's is dull and aching. It spreads over my insides like permafrost. Remy's is a sharp stab. A thorn in my fingertip, drawing blood.

"What's going on with you?" Sam finally asks at lunchtime.

I take a breath. "It's Remy's birthday," I say, not telling him the rest of it.

Sam closes his sketchbook and walks over to my corner of the stand, sitting down on the floor next to me. We are both hidden in the small, rectangular space between the counter and the wall. I can hear the ticking of the old, cheap plastic clock hanging above the cucumber bin, Sam's deep, steady breathing. Even in my sadness, I feel the charge between us.

"I don't know how to feel," I say. "She's gone. But she

isn't dead." There is a hint of stubbornness in my voice when I say that. I cross my arms over my chest, as if expecting challenge.

But all Sam says is, "Sounds complicated. Impossible."

I close my eyes, burrowing down into the heart of my confusion, and I feel Sam's presence, warm beside me. "And River *is* dead," I whisper. "Every morning when I wake up, it's the first thing I think about. My brain has to remake the whole world without him again and again. And then I have to get up and live in it."

Sam leans back, resting his head against the wall. His hair covers his eyes, but he doesn't brush it out of the way. "Sometimes I feel so sad about him that I almost can't stand it."

A deep sorrow spreads like an ache in my chest. "Me too."

We sit like that, on the floor, two bent shapes, inches apart. Outside, on the road, a truck drives by and the scent of gasoline floats in on the breeze.

"I feel guilty," Sam finally says. "I wish I could have known him more."

"Me too," I say again. I wish I knew the parts of River he kept hidden.

Sam reaches over and takes my hand, threading our fingers together. Our sadness seems to swell between us, multiplying, filling the stand and spilling out into the air beyond it. We sit still, for as long as we can take it, letting the feeling wash over us. Then we put it all away again. We let go of our hands and pick ourselves up from the floor.

"Don't be sad for Remy yet," Sam says, dusting off his pants. "She wouldn't want that."

The stand closes at 5:30, and there are still so many hours left before this day is over. That's the thing about the solstice: it always seems to last forever. As Sam and I struggle with the grate, I find myself asking, "Do you want to go for a drive?"

I feel guilty; I know that my mother will be expecting me home, that we should wait this day out together. But I can't face her. Our shared loss is too much.

"Yeah," Sam says. He looks happy. "I do." I stand for a minute, just committing this version of him to memory. This rare smile. A break in the clouds. Deep-set brown eyes and unruly hair. Quiet. Honest. Calm. Present. Sam. Not River. A whole different person. A whole different universe.

"No smoking in the car," I say, turning away from him and heading to the parking lot.

"That's okay," he says, following after me. "I quit."

We slide into my car, which is hot from sitting all day under the sun, and roll the windows all the way down.

"Why?" I ask as we pull out onto the road. I point the car away from my house, then turn right at the crossroads, away from town.

"Rebecca told me that I needed to stop numbing everything out," he says. He begins fiddling with the radio. "I trust her."

"No way out but through," I say. I turn down Route 37

and we follow it toward the sun, which is just making its transition from late afternoon to early evening.

"It's been so weird, living with them," Sam says. "Rebecca is the only adult I've ever known who tells the truth. And she's mostly gone with her mother. Jake is at the farm all day and closed in his office at night." I think again of Mr. O'Dell alone in his car, driving down the dark roads.

Sam looks down at his hands. "The house feels so big and empty. I don't want to be there; I don't want to be anywhere."

He sticks his arm out the window, floating his hand along the breeze. "So I guess I've been escaping more than usual," he says. "Too much, maybe."

I think about that word. *Escape.* In a way it's what River did. Maybe Remy too. It's something I've never known how to do. Or maybe, when the world becomes too much and I begin to drift away in my thoughts, that's my escape. Isolation. That's what I did with River, isn't it? I couldn't handle what was there, so I created a fantasy in my mind. Maybe that was my way of numbing out.

Sam continues. "Two nights ago, Rebecca came home and took me out for a walk. She told me that it was time for both of us to start feeling things again. She spent the whole night in River's room and then, in the morning, there were six black garbage bags lining the hallway. All the windows and doors of the house were open." He pauses as I turn down a narrow road. And suddenly I know where I'm going. "She wants to try to sell the house."

I hear the words as he says them, but I'm suddenly distracted by the route I am taking. Too distracted to let myself think too hard about someone else in River's house. Jake and Rebecca somewhere else. Not here in Black Falls, on the farm.

Sam keeps talking, but I am watching the way the trees begin to close in on the road, the pavement turning to dirt. My heart beats faster, my chest tightens. Each bump of the car jars something inside me, kicking up some kind of sediment from the bottom of my stomach.

When we pass the turnout for the covered bridge, I see a pile of old flowers and dirty teddy bears by the side of the road. I slow down long enough to see a half-melted, blue posterboard with RIVER written across it in gold glitter. Sam stops talking. I keep driving.

The road winds out and back and then finally, I stop at a gravel pullout. We are at the edge of a sea of tall grass, through which a well-worn trail winds down to the riverbank.

We aren't at the covered bridge, not at the place where River went in, but still, we are somewhere I have been with him one hundred other times, with Remy too, and cold cans of seltzer and peanut butter sandwiches and sunscreen-smelling skin and wet hair. A hundred million times we were here, all together, when we were all alive.

I suddenly feel like I've made a huge mistake. I squeeze my eyes closed. I open my mouth, but I can't get a breath in. The world feels like it's starting to spin faster and faster; the grass, the trees, the car begin to blur. Then Sam laces his fingers through mine.

There he is again. An unexpected anchor.

"Open your eyes," he says. "Look. The sun is starting to melt over everything."

I do, and for a moment I see the world through his eyes, artist's eyes. The light gives the tall grass a soft glow. Everything is moving, bugs and birds and leaves and air. It feels full of life here, full of beauty. It's my favorite place. I'd forgotten.

"Are you okay?" Sam asks after a while. "We can leave if you want. I don't have a license, but I know how to drive."

I take a deep, slow, steadying breath. "No," I say. "I want to stay."

Sam lets go of my hand then and gets out of the car, circling around to my side, opening my door. I grab the blanket from my trunk and then we follow the narrow path through the grass and scramble down the embankment until we reach the smooth rocks at the shore. The river is already much less turbulent than it was a few weeks ago, time having balanced out the tumultuous excess of spring. The water flows slowly, steadily; this section of the river is deep and wide. The weather is warm, but not hot, and the air is still. We sit down and watch for a while.

Being here is somehow both better and worse than I thought it would be. It is better in that River's dead corpse is not here haunting me, but worse in that he is everywhere, alive, at a thousand different ages, a million different times in his life. He is perfecting his backflip off the rope swing at fourteen, he is skipping rocks at twelve, he is telling fart jokes and chasing Remy around with a water gun, he is shaking out his wet hair like a golden retriever. Remy is here too. If River is motion, Remy is stillness, floating on her back and looking up at the sky, lying on a towel, blond hair like a halo, dark sunglasses over her eyes. If River is motion and Remy is stillness, then who am I? Where am I? I am a shadow, a void. I watch from the riverbank, never letting myself see the chasm between us.

"What are you thinking about?" Sam says. His long legs are folded up into triangles against his chest, his arms wrapped around them.

"I'm thinking about them," I say. "And also about me." I pick up a small stone and lob it into the water. "We spent a lot of time here. Our entire childhood."

"I can see why," Sam says. "It's beautiful."

I stare off into the thick green trees on the other side of the water. "The most beautiful place in the entire world."

Suddenly, without warning, I begin to cry. Big, hot, uncontrollable tears. All of the sadness from all of the disparate corners of this tragedy gathers together into a giant wave as I realize the sheer enormity of what has been lost. An entire world. An entire lifetime. The two people I loved beyond reason. They are gone and I am here and I don't know if I'll ever know why.

Sam puts his arm around me and pulls me into his chest, and I can tell from the way his body shudders that he is crying too. We stay like that for a long time, and the water keeps rushing by, and the birds keep singing. The river holds us.

When we have finally cried out all of our tears, dusk has fallen. The air is heavy and pink. I get up and start walking down the riverbank and Sam follows me. We pick up flat stones and skip them across the water, we climb big boulders and jump down, we explore like kids in the dusk.

When it's almost too dark to see, Sam turns to me, grabs my wrist, pulls me close so that our chests are a breath apart.

And suddenly, I feel like I am at the center.

"You," he whispers down to me. Just one word.

It's so unexpected. I have tried and tried to see myself—both my body and face and hair and my words and thoughts and expressions—through someone else's eyes. I've tried to imagine someone seeing me and *liking* me. And when I couldn't, I'd begun to worry that I didn't exist in that plane, in that way.

But now Sam is looking at me like I do. Something has changed. Suddenly, I am not just a person to be seen. I am seeing. Both of us are.

Then he leans his forehead down to touch mine and we breathe like that for a while, listening to the night around us. Sadness ebbs and flows, mixing with something else. A feeling that starts as sweet begins to warm, an electricity crackling between us. And then I push up onto my toes and press my lips to his. *You*, I think. *Me.*

He makes a sound when our lips touch. It sounds like *Oh my god*. And then he brings his hands up into my hair. This is nothing like the kiss I had before. There is no wondering, no worrying whether or not I like it. There is no thinking at all. Just mouths and hands and tongues and time stretching out, just feeling.

Finally, Sam pulls back, breathing hard. "Sorry," he says, and I am momentarily crestfallen. It is the exact wrong response to this kiss. But then he says, "You are just so . . ." He looks down, touching my cheek with his fingertips. "You are just so good." Then he frowns, seeming unhappy with that description. "Actually," he says. "There aren't words for what you are. But it's good."

I search his face in the darkness, feeling the gift of his words, wanting to give him something in return. But something holds me back. I still feel so empty inside.

We make our way back to the blanket, going slowly this time because it's hard to see, and Sam holds my hand the whole way, his thumb stroking my wrist.

"Do you want to go home?" he asks. I think about my quiet house, my grieving mother, my bedroom with its drawer of River, with all of Remy's letters on the desk. "Not yet," I say, sitting down on the quilt. Sam sits down beside me and all I can think about is whether he's going to kiss me again. But instead he says, "Should we talk about it?"

I shake my head. I want to stay in the immediacy of this moment, which is still too fragile for words.

He swallows. "Okay then," he says. I lie back on the blanket and tug him down to me. It feels strange and new to have his broad body on top of mine. All of this feels strange and new, but it also feels alive, and good. I push my guilt to the side and let myself feel all of it. The blood pumping in my veins, my lips tingling in anticipation. When he kisses me, it's slower than before. More careful, like I am someone who means something.

It's hard to stay slow for long, and soon we are fevered, our hands everywhere. Sam is kissing my neck and I am tugging at his hair and all I can think is *never stop never stop never stop.* We don't. We keep going, keep going, keep going, blotting everything out except this thing between us.

Eventually we find the edge, the one I raced past with Bailey. And this time, I do stop. I need to feel like I'm in charge of myself again. I think that's going to take a while.

Sam and I lie back, catching our breath, and watch the stars. I let go of his hand and listen to the river and I feel a piece of myself start to click back into place.

EIGHTEEN

When I wake up, I am disoriented and freezing cold. My face is buried in Sam's chest and his arm is around me and I don't know where my shirt has gone to. Sam stirs, burrowing his face into my hair and saying, "Hi, beautiful," in a tired, raspy voice.

I turn my head to look up at the sky and see that it is streaked with a line of light blue; the sun is coming.

"Oh fuck," I say, sitting bolt upright. That seems to wake Sam all the way up. He rises to one elbow, looking around with wide eyes. I leap into action, searching around until I find my shirt, tugging it on, folding up the blanket. My phone is in the car, and when we get there I have ten calls from my mother and several frantic texts. I am in deep shit.

I hurry around to the back of the car to put the blanket back, and as I open the trunk, I notice River's barn jacket. Needing comfort in this moment, I slide it on, hugging it tightly around myself.

I think back to the night of the party, River opening my

car door as soon as we pulled up, tugging me into a too-tight hug. He'd said, *It's gonna be a big night, Jules.* I remember his face when he said it, exuberant, anxious, like all of his emotions were turned up higher than usual. Classic River, with a little twist. Caught up in the memory, I reach into the pocket. And I feel something both hard and soft. I pull out a tiny velvet box. Inside the box is a small, delicate diamond ring.

I stare at the ring, mouth open. Sam comes around to the back of the car.

"Oh my god," he says. He leans down to inspect the ring, which I am holding with trembling fingers.

I feel in the other pocket, pulling out a carefully folded, stapled set of papers.

Numb with shock, I start to unfold them. I look at the papers, but the letters swim around the page, not making any sense.

Suddenly, the night of the party is rushing back again, Remy running up to the car where Bailey and I are sitting. "River is gone," she says. And then, "I fucked up. I fucked up." I can see her in my mind, uncharacteristically disheveled, eyes wild. She is carrying River's jacket in her arms.

"He's going to be fine, Rem," I remember saying. "He just needs a little time to cool off."

"He's not. He's not," Remy said, again and again. Like somehow she already knew.

Sam's voice startles me back to reality, to the pale wash of orange spreading across the sky. He's reading the papers. "It's a job application. For a place called Cloverdale Farm."

As we drive back toward the O'Dells', racing the sun,

Sam and I try to figure out what everything might mean, the job application, the ring. Sam looks up Cloverdale Farm and finds that it's a WWOOFing site a few hours north of here, across the border into Vermont.

"Why there?" I ask. "I don't get it."

"I don't know," Sam says, sounding frustrated. "We must be missing something."

All of it, the engagement ring, the kissing, the cold ache of sleeping on the ground, has made me feel light-headed and nauseous.

By the time we pull into Sam's driveway, the sun is all the way up.

He studies me as he opens his car door. "Are you okay?" he asks. His voice is calm and reassuring. "Do you want to come inside for a minute?"

"I'll be all right." I take a deep breath, trying to snap myself out of it. "I should get home before my mom calls the cops."

Sam leans in for a kiss and it feels so unreal. I reach down and pinch my leg, hard, just to make sure.

As soon as I pull into the driveway, my mother comes rushing out onto the porch. "Oh my god," she says, breathless, crying. "Oh my god, you're okay."

The sight of her panicked, ashen face brings tears to my eyes. "Yes, I'm fine. I'm so sorry. I fell asleep and lost track of time."

My mother pulls me into a tight hug, and I can feel her body shaking. "I thought you were—" She can't finish the sentence. I know then, for sure, that she thinks Remy is dead. I swallow hard, wondering if she's right. I feel so confused, I don't know what to think anymore.

My mother lets me go then, and turns to walk into the house. There is a sudden chill to her demeanor that's unfamiliar and a little scary. I follow her to the kitchen and she puts on the kettle. She is wearing the threadbare purple bathrobe she's had since I was a child. She used to let me wear it sometimes when I wasn't feeling well, and I wish she would invite me in now, cuddle me up against her like she used to.

But instead she says, "I found the letters." She is turned toward the counter, rifling around the tea cupboard, pulling out the strainer and a jar of chamomile. This is the thing that makes my mom special; even when you have betrayed her, she remembers your favorite kind of tea, knows how to calm your nerves.

I watch her, unable to speak. "Why didn't you tell me?" she says. She still won't turn around to look at me. "Did you think you could figure this out on your own?"

I hear something frightening in her voice, a hardness that is never there. I can see that I have pushed her much too far. I should not have left her alone yesterday. I should not have scared her like this.

"I don't know," I say. "They just felt secret. Like they were Remy's secrets." *For me and no one else*, a voice inside me says. *Remy is mine*.

My mom slumps over, leaning her head down onto her hands. "Baby," she finally says, turning around. Her eyes are brimming. "You know that she might be dead, right? That letter might not be from her. It could be from someone who is trying to—" She takes a deep breath, lets it out, lifts her face again.

"That letter is mine," I say, feeling suddenly angry.

"I gave them all to the police," she replies. I see a tired decisiveness in her eyes.

My stomach turns to ice and Zack White's Remy-red ribbon flashes into my mind. "When?"

"Last night," she says. "As soon as I found them."

"Who did you give them to?"

"One of the younger guys," Mom says. "I forget his name."

Regret seeps into my skin, a warm, acidic flush. I should have come home. I should have stayed home. Zack White has the letters. Everything feels like it is closing in.

I stand up from the table, feeling like I have to get away from here. "I need to get ready for work," I say.

"No," Mom says, her lips pressing into a thin line. "You're not going to work today."

I start to protest, but then she says, "I called Rebecca already and told her you weren't coming in. Go upstairs and get some sleep; I'm taking you to the police station at eleven thirty."

Up in my room, I try to calm my breathing, to think all of this through. Zack has the letters. He knows I saw them. If he's the one who wrote them, then I am fucked. And if he did something to Remy, then I am in danger. I take big, deep gulping breaths. *Remy is alive. Remy is alive.* I say it to myself again and again, until exhaustion finally takes over and I fall asleep.

NINETEEN

At 10:30 Mom wakes me up and tells me to take a shower. At 11:15 we get in the car and drive to town.

The Black Falls police station is housed in a small brick building on the corner of Main Street and Avenue B, catty-corner from the Rite Aid. From the outside it looks a little run-down; the inside is much worse. The two of us sit on a wooden bench in the waiting room while the clerk shuffles papers behind the front desk. On the bulletin board by the front door hangs a large poster of Remy's junior year school photo, a giant MISSING across the top. I ate a bowl of cereal before we left, because Mom insisted that I eat *something*, and the milk feels like it's curdling in my gut as I wait, smelling the moldy smell of the building, staring at Remy's vacant smile.

Finally, Officer Kelly pokes his head out the door of his office. "You can come on in, ladies," he says. Tension radiates from my mother in waves as we file into the chief's tiny office and sit on two cracked, fake-leather seats. Bookshelves line the walls of the room, exploding with paper and files. The certainty I saw on Mom's face when we were at home has disappeared.

"I'm guessing you know why you're here," Officer Kelly says, looking at me from behind the desk. He is in his fifties and very muscular; the hair is mostly gone from the top of his head and the skin there is shiny. I don't answer him.

"Your mother gave us the letters," he says, clearing his throat.

I should be relieved, because this means that Zack has not hidden or destroyed them. But why don't I *feel* relieved? There is something oily in Officer Kelly's stare.

"Okay, darlin'." He crosses his arms, flexing his muscles under his short-sleeve uniform shirt. "I get that you wanted to solve this mystery yourself," he says. He gives me a pitying, condescending look. "But you should have let us know." He frowns. "Withholding evidence is a crime." Mom wraps her hand protectively around my arm as he continues. "Obviously we aren't going to arrest you, but you need to be careful and you've got to tell us if anything else like that happens. Whoever took Remy is still out there. And it seems like they might be interested in you."

I say nothing, my eyes roaming over the contents of Officer Kelly's desktop. Crumpled papers and receipts, a stack of old coffee cups, a rape whistle on a red ribbon, like the one he gave all the girls on the last day of school.

I should tell him about Derek, I think. But something stops me.

Then Officer Kelly shifts in his chair, sitting up straighter. "There's one thing I have to ask you, though," he says. He tents his fingers, looking at me over the tops of them. His eyes are small and eager. "Do you know where we can find Remy's SIM card?"

My stomach drops, like I'm on a roller coaster. "No," I say.

He stares at me for a few long seconds. He looks frustrated. "I keep asking all of you girls that," he says. "And everyone says they don't know. But it's clear that you're hiding something. It would be much, much better if you tell me than if I were to find it out myself."

Mom's grip tightens on my arm. "I think that's enough for today," she says. Her tone is firm, protective. "And for the record, I don't appreciate your insinuation that my daughter is a liar." She stands up and ushers me out of the room.

Just as we get to the door, he calls out, "I know you're hanging around with that other O'Dell boy. Be careful, that kid has a record."

Mom doesn't speak to me in the car on the way home. She is clearly not over my betrayal. When we get back, she immediately disappears into her bedroom.

When I walk into my room, I see River's jacket hanging on the back of my desk chair. I reach into the pocket and pull out the blue velvet ring box, holding it in the palm of my hand.

In another version of reality, one where River was still alive and Remy was still here, this ring would break my heart. But now I know so many things I didn't know before.

I never had a chance with River.

River never had a chance with Remy.

Maybe none of us really loved each other at all, not in the way Remy spoke of in her letter. To be in love with someone, you have to know them. And it's clear to me now that the three of us were holding on so tightly that we couldn't know each other, not really.

I turn my attention to the pamphlet attached to the Cloverdale Farm application. The front is a glossy photograph of green grass, blue sky, a big white farmhouse, and three horses with shining manes gathered at the front fence. It's the kind of place Remy loved when we were kids. Young Remy was obsessed with horses. She wanted to live on a farm someday, but not one of the farms in Black Falls. *Everything is too ugly here*, she would say. *Too broken.*

Maybe River did know Remy. Or at least this version of her.

Mom knocks on my door then, and I shove the ring and pamphlet under my pillow.

She comes in and sits on my desk chair, picks up River's jacket, brings it to her face.

"I don't know how to do this," she says. Her eyes look tired, and I wonder if she's slept at all since yesterday.

"Me either," I answer honestly.

She puts the jacket down. "Why are you keeping secrets from me?"

I consider her question. I could just tell her everything, all of it. Fawn and the Stevenson brothers and Zack White and Bailey. She always knows what to do. She could get me out of this.

But these secrets don't feel like they belong to me. They are Remy's. Callie's and Liliana's and Kendall's. If I let

Mom help me unravel this thread, their lives could be ruined. And it feels like they are my friends now.

"Look," Mom says. "I have to go to work. I've had to call out twice this week and now I need to cover an overnight shift." She drops her forehead into her hands, and I can see how overwhelming this must be for her. How helpless she must feel. "I'm really trying to trust you. I want you to understand that things are not safe right now. You need to stay home."

I nod solemnly. "I promise."

She stands up. "The neighbors are watching out to make sure you don't go anywhere," she says. Her face softens. "I'm sorry to be like this. But I honestly don't know any other way to keep you safe."

I lie back on my bed after she leaves, everything swirling and swirling around me. Remy could be out there somewhere. I'm supposed to find her, but I still don't even know where to begin.

Look, she said.

I have looked, am looking. And each new secret I find leads me in a different direction.

I feel completely helpless.

I close my eyes, trying to imagine a different time. Last summer, camping by the river with my two best friends. We'd set up Mr. O'Dell's old, tattered green tent at the Feather Falls picnic area and unrolled our sleeping bags side by side. We played cards and went swimming and watched

Scream on Remy's cell phone. Then we looked at the stars and made up constellations.

"That one is you," River said. "All those little stars clouded together are like the curls in your hair." He pointed to another spot. "And that's you, Rem. See your golden crown?"

"You're that long, squiggly line over there," Remy said. "Because you're so messy."

"Nah," River said. "I'm just the black sky."

I get up, going over to my River drawer. I take everything out and spread it on the floor, considering. There is so much: First-place ribbons, newspaper clippings, folded notes, a lock of hair, drawings, the number 7 cut out of an old jersey. A paper with *Mrs. Juliette O'Dell* written hundreds of times, on every line, front and back. In a way, it feels like I need these things more than ever. River is gone, forever, and this is all I have of him.

But in another way, I feel like I shouldn't have this stuff at all. It's evidence of a long, unhealthy, one-sided crush. A bunch of parts of a River I thought I knew. Thought I loved. A person who I made up, who obscured me from seeing the one who was really there, who needed me.

I consider throwing these things away. Making room for a new River to emerge in my mind. But I can't bring myself to do it. One by one, I put the objects back in the drawer.

TWENTY

I awaken to the sound of something scratching at my window. I have somehow fallen asleep on the floor and hours have gone by. All of the lights in my room are still on. I am hazy and disoriented.

I hear the scratching again, and then the scrape of the sash moving upward, my window opening. For a moment I am back in Tate Stevenson's truck again, watching that beautiful deer run into the road to save me.

I freeze, breathing as quietly as I can, wondering whether I'm about to die.

But then Sam comes tumbling through my window, landing in a heap on my bed.

It takes a moment for me to remember to breathe again, to know that I am okay. He slides down off the bed, crouching beside me.

"Hi," he whispers.

"Holy fuck," I say, rolling onto my back and pressing a

hand to my chest. "I thought you were someone coming to kill me."

He reaches down and tucks a strand of hair behind my ear. "I'm sorry," he says. "I came to see if you were okay. I was worried after this morning and couldn't reach you." He looks suddenly vulnerable "Too much?"

"No," I laugh. I run a hand down my face, remembering this awful day. "My mom took my phone."

"Luckily I am good at scaling tall buildings," he whispers with a boyish smile. Sam has a dimple in his right cheek, and it only shows when he is truly unguarded.

I sit up. "You don't have to whisper," I say. "My mom is working tonight." Sam's smile changes and I feel suddenly nervous. "What time is it?" I ask.

"A little after midnight."

I yawn, rubbing my eyes. "I feel like I haven't slept in days."

"What happened when you got home?" he asks. His voice is softer now.

I look down. "My mom found the letters. She gave them to the police."

Sam sighs. "Is it wrong to say that I'm kind of relieved?"

I run my fingers through the carpet. "I don't know. I'm so confused."

"Me too."

I tell him about Tate and Derek.

"Fuck, Jules," he says. "You should have told the police."

"I don't know," I say. "Zack and Officer Kelly seem to want the SIM card just as badly as they do. I don't think we should trust the police." I take a deep breath. "Let's start at the beginning. Lay all of it out."

Sam looks around the room. "I wish we had a giant bulletin board so we could make one of those charts they make in crime shows."

I laugh. "You and Remy would get along so well."

Sam tears out a page of his sketchbook, ignoring my comment. "Okay. This one is for Tate and Derek." He tears two more. "This is for Zack. And this is for Bailey." He lays out the papers side by side and then adds one more to the top. "This one is for Remy."

I smile. "Because she is the mastermind."

We write down everything we know, eventually adding another paper for River. We start with the money, the SIM card. Tate Stevenson and Scott's overdose. Then we add everything about Fawn. The user data. Zack's girlfriend. The letters. The brochure and ring. My confrontation with Bailey in the woods.

When we are done, we take a step back to look at everything. It all just feels like a big mess.

Some connections have begun to emerge. Zack, Derek, and Tate are connected to Fawn and the SIM card. And Tate gave River the heroin. It seems like there has to be more that they know, but we aren't sure how to find out.

Bailey seems to have moved out of the center of things, but I can't fight the nagging feeling that there's more hiding there as well.

"Is there anything we're overlooking?" Sam asks.

I close my eyes, trying to think, and a line from the letters appears in my mind. *I have burned for someone.* My stomach twists.

This, Remy whispers.

Who? I wonder back.

I drop my head into my hands, frustrated.

"I don't know."

"Maybe we need to step away for a little while," Sam says, putting a warm hand on my back. I nod, and he begins to gather the pages, putting them on top of my desk.

"What do you want to do?" I ask.

Sam scratches his eyebrow, considering. "We need to get out of our heads," he says. "Let's play a game." He smiles. "How about truth or dare?"

I look away. "I hate that game. It's humiliating."

He reaches for my hand. "I promise it won't be." He tugs me toward him, and I fall into his chest. "Come on, it will be fun."

"Fine," I say, my voice muffled in the fabric of his shirt. "I go first." I take a step back and fix him with a serious look. "Truth or dare."

Sam settles back onto my twin bed, crosswise, so his back is leaning against the wall and his feet are dangling over the edge. "Truth."

I look down at my hands. "What did you think when you first saw me?" I ask.

He narrows his eyes. "I thought we weren't doing embarrassing questions."

I frown. "That bad?"

"Not you." He laughs. "Me. The first time I saw you, I

was kind of in awe. You were twelve years old, but there was something so serious about you. Like your eyes held the entire universe. I don't know. It pulled me in. I never forgot."

I am stunned by this impression. I don't know how to respond.

"My turn," Sam says, not giving me any time to dwell. "What did you think the first time you saw me?"

Like River had crawled back from the dead, I think automatically. And then, as if he senses what I'm thinking, he says, "Wait. I forgot to ask. Truth or dare."

"Dare," I say, and I think we are both relieved.

"Okay," he says, tenting his fingers. "Let me see . . ." He stretches the moment out, and I feel more and more nervous as I wait. "I dare you to let me draw you."

"Really?" I ask. "That's your dare?" I look down at my ratty sweatpants and old T-shirt.

"That's my dare," he says. He gets up and grabs my hands, pulling me over to the bed. "Here, let me just . . ." He pushes my shoulders, gently, until I am sitting up at the edge, and he is leaning over me. Having him this close is overwhelming.

Without thinking, I tug the neck of his T-shirt down until his lips touch mine. Even though we've kissed before, for an entire night, I'm still not used to the feeling of it. I wonder if I ever could be. I feel like I am tumbling down and down and down, like there is no bottom, like I will never be able to get enough.

Remy told me once that you aren't supposed to kiss with your eyes open, but I can't help it. I want to watch. I want to know it's real. Sam. Me. This. His hand finds the hem of my shirt and slips underneath to slide up my back, making warm circles on the skin beneath my shoulder blade. I reach for his arms, trying to pull him in closer, and we fall backward, onto the bed, Sam on top of me, blocking out the ceiling, breathing heavy. We kiss frantically, and my shirt comes up over my head and I forget to be shy, even though nobody has ever seen me like this. Not with the lights on. All I can think about is Sam, how warm he feels, how he takes up all of the space until I forget that everything else.

After a while, I feel Sam start to pull back and I reach for him, not ready to stop this yet. It still doesn't feel real; I need to hold on a little bit longer.

"I want to draw you." He laughs, biting at my neck. He climbs off me, off the bed, running a hand through his hair and straightening his clothing.

I reach for my shirt. "Should I put this back on?"

Sam clears his throat, briefly looking up at the ceiling. "It's up to you."

This feels like an important decision. I have spent so much time standing in front of the mirror, doubting that I could ever be an object of attention, affection, but here I am. No turning back now.

I shake my head, and Sam leans down to run a finger across my collarbone. Then he lays me carefully back on the pillow, arranging my hair around my face. His fingers brush the shell of my ear and I shiver.

He takes a deep breath and steps back to my desk chair. He sits down, pulling out his notebook and a pencil, and begins to work.

It's a strange feeling, having someone look at your body so closely. I keep having to fight the urge to cover myself with my hands. After a while it feels like my skin is crawling.

"You seem nervous," Sam says.

"I've never let anyone see me like this." I look down at myself, the exposed skin, trying to like it. "It feels strange."

Sam sets his notebook down. "You can put your shirt on if you want to," he says. I am flooded with relief at these words.

"Yeah, okay," I say. I'm a little disappointed too. But not all the way. Maybe I'm not an object after all. Maybe I'm just a person like Sam is.

I put my shirt back on, and Sam keeps drawing, looking up from the paper every minute or so to meet my eyes.

"I've been thinking about bodies a lot," Sam says. "Ever since I saw River's in the coffin. Isn't it strange how one moment you can be so full of blood and oxygen and whatever else it is that makes you yourself, and then the next you're just . . ."

He stops, taking a moment to smudge a line on the paper.

Even though this exercise is a part of our truth or dare game, it doesn't feel silly anymore. For a while, Sam is quiet, concentrating, and I watch him, as if I were drawing him in my mind, taking in every wrinkle in his clothing, every lock of hair, which is now sticking up in every direction. A warm feeling spreads over me, a tenderness unlike anything I've felt before, even for River. River was golden, but Sam is something different, something precious and rare, something imperfect, made more beautiful by its flaws. River was a dream, but Sam is real.

Finally, he puts the pencil down. "You want to see it?" he asks. I am somewhere halfway between asleep and awake. I look at my bedside clock; it's almost 1:30 a.m.

Sam hands me the sketchbook. When I look down at the paper, I don't recognize myself. The person in this drawing is beautiful, with mysterious dark eyes and full lips, turned down at the edges. I make a confused expression.

"No?" Sam says. He looks nervous in the lamplight.

"No, no, it's beautiful," I say. "This is just not really the way I see myself."

Sam's face looks serious for a moment, almost sad. But then a grin splits it down the middle and he says, "I guess I'd better fix it, then." He takes back the notebook and turns toward my desk. "Do you have an eraser somewhere around here?" he asks, opening the top drawer of my desk.

"No! I love it, stop!" I say, reaching for him.

Sam pretends he doesn't hear me. He rifles around in the drawer for a second, then closes it. I'm so wrapped up in our little game that I don't realize what he is doing, where he is going. By the time I reach out to stop him, it's too late; he's opened the bottom drawer.

I can tell the moment he realizes what he's looking at, because his entire body tenses. "What is this?" he asks.

It's not that bad, I think. But then I look down to see the paper with *Mrs. Juliette O'Dell* written all over it. My blood turns to ice in my veins. I reach around him, trying to close the drawer. "It's nothing," I say. "Just stuff from when we were younger."

But he doesn't even seem to be listening. He's pulling out photos and mementos and drawings, very private drawings, laying it all out on my desk. When I see it through his eyes, it looks a million times creepier and sadder. "I thought you said—" He clears his throat. "I thought you said you didn't love him."

I force my body in between him and the desk, trying to hide the evidence of my most shameful secret. "I didn't," I say. I rub my eyebrow. "Or. I don't. Not anymore."

Sam's eyes narrow. "I see," he says. He straightens then, carefully tearing the drawing he's just made out of his notebook and setting it on the desk, right on top of my pile of River. He starts looking around for his backpack. When I see that he's about to leave, I start to feel desperate. I have to stop him, but I don't know how.

"Is that why you like me?" he asks, not looking at me. "Because I look like him?"

"No," I say, frantically shaking my head. "No."

"Everything in your life is about them," he says. "Were you trying to re-create some kind of weird fantasy world where I'm River and you're Remy?" I can only stare, my mouth open. His words are so hurtful. Wrong. He closes his eyes. "That is so fucked up."

I have to do something. But I can't think of the right words. "It's not what you think," I say. But he just turns away from me and continues to gather his things.

I watch as he puts his sketchbook into his bag and walks back over to the window. I think he's going to leave without saying goodbye, but then he stops. "Tell me then. Honestly. What did you think of me when you first saw me at the wake?"

For a moment my heart stops beating altogether. I feel

frozen, unsure of what to say. If I lie, he'll know. If I tell the truth, he'll leave. "I—" I say, but Sam doesn't stay long enough to hear it. He opens the window and disappears through it before I can decide what to say.

I sit for a long time after Sam leaves, just staring at the open window as I absorb this new kind of loss. It's a fresh sting, starting at the surface, going deep. I feel like a fool for opening myself up, for thinking someone could see me and not notice or care how weird I really am.

Why didn't I just get rid of all those things? What is wrong with me that I couldn't do it? That I still can't?

I get up and close the window. I am alone again. Just like I was before.

I turn off the lights and bury myself under my blankets until I almost can't breathe.

I feel so out of control; everything in my life is flying apart. When the clock shows three o'clock, I get out of bed and pick up Sam's drawing. I turn on the light again and study the face that for some reason still seems unfamiliar. Who is this person? She looks like someone who is fully formed, but I am full of cracks and holes. I am pathetic and creepy and jealous and spiteful. I wish I could disappear like I used to. But Sam is right. I am alive. All I can do is feel this.

TWENTY-ONE

I dream of a place where Remy and I used to play when we were young, deep in the woods behind my house. There was a ring of sugar maple trees that felt so far out no one could ever find it. We pretended we were fairies with long pointed ears and shiny rainbow wings and we made the trees into our cottage. We did magic with bits of spiderwebs mixed with earth and crushed-up poison berries. "This will kill our enemies," Remy would say, and I would nod solemnly. Sometimes, a strong wind would blow through the clearing and Remy would whisper, "The wind is blowing just for me," and I would wonder what it felt like, to be chosen like that.

In my dream, I wake before the sun has risen and I walk out to the sugar maples. I sit there for a long time, watching as the light slowly enters in, waiting for Remy to find me. She doesn't come. And when I finally leave, I find a piece of her instead. A long ribbon, not red but green, under a heavy stone. On it is written *I'm never coming back*.

Mom wakes me up just as light begins to filter in through the curtains. She is still wearing her scrubs. She runs a hand over my forehead, smoothing my skin. "Rebecca called and begged me to let you work today, so you're free for now, but you need to be home by six."

Her measured tone feels like a sting, and she gets up without saying anything else. I roll over and kick off the covers. The thought of seeing Sam today sits heavy in my stomach, and as I get ready I feel sluggish, like a stone is weighing down each of my limbs.

But when I walk into the farmstand an hour later, Sam isn't there.

"Thank god," Rebecca says, pulling me into a quick, tight hug. "Sam is out today and Jake is still sick and my mom has an appointment that we had to wait like seven months to get. I was desperate." She releases me then and grabs her purse. Her car pulls out of the parking lot before I can ask her what she means when she says Sam can't come in today. Is he sick too? Is he so mad at me that he can't even stand to be here?

The morning moves slowly, like sludge, uncertainty clouding my mind and sadness burning in my stomach. Only a few customers come, and no one makes conversation. I begin to imagine that the stand is a boat out on the ocean, and I am drifting, all alone.

I can't stop thinking about Sam. I keep seeing him in my mind's eye, looking at me like I'm beautiful. I have been so tangled up about my body, but somehow in moments with Sam I felt completely clear.

That's fucked up, though, isn't it? Remy says in my ear. She's right; I know this is not how it's supposed to be—a boy saying you're beautiful making it true. That only gives them more power.

Every time a truck drives by the stand, I panic, thinking it might be Tate or Derek. I haven't heard from either of them, but I feel like they're out there somehow, watching me.

At 11:30, Callie's car pulls up and all of the girls tumble out of it. "Where have you been?" Liliana asks. "We've been calling you for two days."

I toss the rag I've been using to clean the counters back into the bucket, my whole body relaxing. I feel so grateful that they are here, that someone has come for me. Callie gives me a hug and I breathe her in, letting go of some of the heaviness inside. "My mom took my phone, sorry."

"What happened?" Kendall asks. She's wearing a gold nameplate necklace and she runs her fingers across the metal, as though she's a little bit nervous.

I consider whether or not I should tell them about Sam. If they're my friends, I should tell them, right? Information builds bridges. Between them and me. Between me and the outside world. But I can't. It hurts too badly today. "I lied about something," I say instead.

"I lie to my mom all the time," Kendall says, sitting down on Sam's stool. She sighs. "But she's too wrapped up in her own world to notice."

For a second I feel bad for her.

I'm about to tell them about Derek and Tate when Kendall says, "Callie found some creepy shit in Bailey's room."

"I was babysitting," Callie explains. "And after I put Delia to bed, I went upstairs and snooped around his room and—"

"He has a Remy book," Kendall says.

"A Remy book?" I ask.

Callie nods. "He printed out all of these pictures of her and pasted them into a notebook." She makes a face.

"He wrote things in it," Liliana says. "Really weird things."

Suddenly, I think about my River drawer. I wonder if I'm like Bailey. Or if Bailey is like me. Then Callie holds up her phone and shows me a few of the pictures she took. There's a photo of Remy from the neck down. I see her heart-shaped birthmark. He's drawn a knife, sticking out from under her rib cage. *Little slut* is scribbled across the top of the page in red ink. I turn away, feeling like I might throw up.

"There's something else," Callie says, putting away her phone. "All night Delia was talking about the trip to Disney they took for her birthday. I asked her parents about it when they came home, and it turns out they were gone the week Remy disappeared."

I look at Callie, trying to understand.

"And Bailey stayed home," Liliana adds, crossing her arms.

The words sink in slowly, the picture of Remy with the knife still just behind my eyes. My chest gets tight, and I feel like I can't breathe. *It's okay*, I tell myself. *Remy is alive.* But I'm not sure I believe it anymore. I sit down on the stool behind the counter, dropping my head into my hands. "We have to show this to the police," I say.

"No," Kendall says. "They'll find out about Fawn and all of us will be fucked."

"But what if he—" I stop, squeezing my eyes shut. "What if Remy—"

I can't say it. I won't say it.

Liliana comes around and puts a hand on my shoulder. "We have to handle this ourselves," she says. Her voice sounds so sure, so final. Suddenly I feel very separate from these girls again. I stand up, letting her hand fall away.

"What do you mean?" I ask. Whatever they are thinking of, it sounds dark.

"We'll get him to confess, we'll humiliate him, we'll make sure he can never do this to anyone, ever again," Callie says.

I nod. But still, it seems logistically impossible.

"We have a plan," Kendall says. She pulls an old, beat-up phone out of her purse, setting it on the table. "We just need a few new pictures of Remy."

I stand there, confused, all three of them looking at me.

"Your birthmark," Callie says, and then it dawns on me.

I open my mouth, then close it again. "No, there's no way. We look nothing alike."

"We only need to capture you below the shoulders. With the right angles and a few filters." Kendall snaps her fingers. "Voilà."

"I don't know . . ." I say.

Kendall puts her hands on my shoulders. "This is about taking control. Bailey made you feel like you were invisible. Worthless. Now you can make him beg for you. You can make him pay. For what he did to you. And for what he did to Remy."

Callie must notice the way all of the blood has left my

face, because she steps forward and says, "Give us a minute."

I sit down on the stool again as Kendall and Liliana walk back to the car, trying to wrap my head around the past ten minutes. The pictures of Remy on Callie's phone. Bailey's book. I take a deep breath, trying to steady myself.

"Did you ever pose for Fawn?" I ask Callie.

"A few times, in the beginning." She sighs. "But I never showed my face. I was too scared about my family finding out."

"I don't get it," I say, shaking my head. "No matter how hard I try, I can't see myself like that."

"Like what?"

I look down at my hands. "I don't know."

Callie sighs and leans back against the counter. "Can I tell you something?" she asks quietly.

"Sure."

"I never liked Fawn. Remy always said it was a way to take control, but it never felt like that to me."

She looks down at her shoes. "For me, sex is really personal. It sounds silly, but I want to save all of that for a person I love."

"That doesn't sound silly," I say. I feel so much regret about what I did with Bailey. I wish I'd waited too. Maybe not for someone I loved, but at least for someone I trusted.

"I don't regret doing it," she says, as if responding to my thoughts. "Everything I've done is a part of who I am. But I understand if you don't want to."

"Thanks," I say.

"Look," Callie says as she puts a hand on mine and looks into my eyes. "You are important to me. I know we haven't been close in the last few years. But you are my friend. Not because of what happened to Remy and River. We grew up together. That means something."

I am quiet for a while, letting all of that sink in. The past three weeks have been a nightmare, and I've been so glad to have Callie here. And the other girls.

"You're important to me too," I say. I clear my throat. "Can I have a minute to think about this?"

"Of course."

When Callie is gone, I slide off the stool, down to my favorite spot on the floor behind the counter. *What should I do, Remy?* I ask.

She doesn't answer.

We take the photos on a blanket in the grass behind the stand at lunchtime. I strip down to my bra and Kendall captures the area from my neck to just below my belly button, making sure to get a clear image of my heart-shaped birthmark. Lying there in the harsh sunlight feels so different from last night, in the warm glow of my bedside lamp. I don't want to be beautiful now like I did then. I want to be brave and strong. I want to find Remy.

Callie edits the photos and sends the photos to the burner phone, and then it's time to begin.

> I'm back.

Who is this?

> Remy, idiot

No it's not

> . . .

The first picture loads, with the date stamp. Bailey doesn't reply.

"What now?" I ask. I'm nervous, sweaty, looking at the photo of myself on the tiny screen.

"Give him a minute," Liliana says.

The four of us stand there in a circle, in the middle of the farmstand, looking down at the phone. We are all very quiet. The afternoon sun paints the old wooden floor golden at our feet, like our circle is something holy.

What do you want?

> I want to see you.

. . .

. . .

. . .

. . .

Who is this?

Remy. There's a party tomorrow night at the Brennan Camp. I'll meet you in the woods at 1am.

TWENTY-TWO

I get home from the stand just as Mom is leaving for work again. She puts both hands on my shoulders and says, "I'm trusting you," as she walks out the door.

Out of habit, I go to the kitchen to make myself something to eat, but I'm not hungry. I pace around downstairs for a while, from room to room, as the light fades, feeling like an animal in a cage.

I go over the text conversation again and again in my mind, analyzing Bailey's reaction. It's clear he thinks that Remy is dead. But is that because everyone thinks that Remy is dead? Or is it because he *killed* her?

No.

As if to prove that Remy is alive, I say the words aloud: "Remy is dead."

I wait for Remy to argue in my ear, like she always does. Nothing comes.

I want to clutch the words back out of the air, but it feels like they are expanding, filling up all of the space in the house. I need to get out of here.

I get my keys and drive the short stretch to River's house. Sam's house. I don't know what I'm going to say to make him forgive me. But I need to see him. I don't think I can do this alone.

When I pull up outside, daylight is beginning to fade. There are too many trees around the house to see the sunset, but the light is dimmer, the bugs are louder, everything feels more peaceful. I sit for a moment, trying to breathe in some of the calm to help slow my pounding heart. Inside that house is a person I think I might be in love with and also the ghost of another person who used to be everything to me.

I feel stuck, frozen in place. I need Sam. I have to get him back. I have to tell him the truth. I never told River how I felt about him, and because of it my feelings spoiled, turning into something freakish and dishonest. I can't let that happen again. But I don't know how to fix this.

I try to force Remy's voice back into my head. What would she say?

Suck it up.

Get out of the car.

I fucking love you. You'll be fine.

I open my car door and the crickets become even louder, the air so humid it feels like I'm walking through water to get to the front door. When I knock, Mr. O'Dell answers. He looks a little scattered but not sick, like Rebecca said.

"Is Sam here?" I ask.

Mr. O'Dell shakes his head. "He's out, I'm not sure where."

"Oh," I say, all of my resolve leaving my body in a single instant. Then I just stand there on the doorstep, not sure what to do.

I can't go home. Not without Sam. Not without Remy.

"Do you want to come in for a minute?" Mr. O'Dell asks. He looks concerned, and I wonder what I must look like through his eyes: scared, exhausted. I wonder if he knows that this is how he looks too.

"Sure," I say, relieved to have some momentary direction. He motions for me to head into the house, and as he closes the door behind me, everything becomes silent and still. Even though Rebecca cleaned it out, this place still feels sad and strange. The kitchen is dark and messy, and the only light in the house comes from one side of the living room.

"Why don't you go sit down in my office?" Mr. O'Dell says. "I'll make you some tea."

I grew up in the O'Dells' house but have never spent much time in the office. It always felt like a grown-up place, like Mr. O'Dell's place, somewhere we weren't welcome. He would spend hours there during the summer, working on his book. The door was almost always closed.

Now it feels strange to walk inside but comforting too. The air is different in here, less stale than it is in the rest of the house. The glow of the desk lamp is warm and inviting. There are signs of work being done, stacks of pages with inked notes in the margin.

I lean forward to read one and can just make out the top line:

Mr. Malone was not a happy man.

This book, like the office, has always been a great mystery to me. Mr. O'Dell has been working on this one novel for years. River always talked about it like it was special, almost sacred. And Mr. O'Dell never talked about it at all.

I move away from the desk, feeling like the pages are private. I step over to the low bookcase by the windows, looking out at the line of trees that are all blending into one inky blob in the falling darkness. I stand there, watching them blur, my heart gradually slowing in my chest, until I hear Mr. O'Dell coming in with the tea.

I turn around to see him setting one mug on the edge of the desk and holding the other one out to me. I take it, and it's hot in my hands.

Peppermint. I take a tiny sip, careful not to burn my mouth.

I sit down on the small, gray couch across from the desk, and Mr. O'Dell sits down on the other end, looking at me with tired eyes.

Mom always says that peppermint soothes an upset stomach, but as I sit there, looking back at Mr. O'Dell, mine feels uneasy. Why am I here? Is this really better than being alone?

"It's been a hard few weeks," Mr. O'Dell says. I nod, not sure how to reply. He clears his throat. In the space that follows, I worry that he wants me to talk about myself, to tell him how I am doing. I don't know what to say. I am not doing well.

I wait for Mr. O'Dell to ask a question, but instead he looks down at his hands, a spot on his thumb that's covered in ink. "Rebecca has been helping her mother a lot. And before that—I don't know if I've ever been this alone." He stops and turns his head to look out the window.

The silence that follows feels full and heavy. I can tell he's thinking of River, and maybe something else too.

"I've been writing a lot, though," he says, looking over at the stacks of pages on the desk. "The past few weeks it's been pouring out of me. Life is so strange."

Mr. O'Dell looks back at me. His hair is rumpled, like he's been running his fingers through it again and again, the way River used to. "River was doing drugs," he says. "Heroin. And I had no idea about any of it."

"I know," I say, surprised that he's telling me this. "I mean, I didn't know at the time. Only after."

"It's all my fault," he says, letting out a slow, hissing breath.

I study Mr. O'Dell's face, trying to think of something, anything, to say. The room is quiet, except for the ticking of a small brass clock next to the desk lamp.

"When I saw you that night, out on the road, I thought you were her," he says. I feel disoriented by this change in topic and by the way he's looking at my face. It feels as if he is searching for the similarity between Remy and me, trying to find it again. "Even though I knew it wasn't possible, I thought she was there, right in front of my eyes." He looks away, back toward the window. "Or maybe I thought you were the ghost of her, after everything that happened."

Everything that happened.

I'm not sure exactly what this means. The conversation seems to be taking a strange turn. We are somewhere different now, in totally new terrain.

"I never thought you looked like her, but I think I see it now," he says. His eyes stray down to my collarbone, the one that matches Remy's, and then back up to my eyes.

"Grief changes us," he says. "It's changed me, and I think it's changed you too."

He stares at me and I can see his sadness like a deep, dark well. I can almost feel it pulling me in. Then he reaches out and puts a warm palm on my cheek.

"It's going to be okay," he says. "We are going to be okay."

I nod slowly, suddenly fighting back tears. He tilts his head a little, and his expression changes.

And then he is leaning toward me. I didn't notice him coming closer, but suddenly he is right there, his arm along the couch behind me. I feel disoriented by the slow, steady way he moves. His nose brushes mine; his breath smells good, like honey, but it also turns my stomach. I don't understand what is happening. I don't understand how to stop it.

"You know," he whispers, a breath away from my lips. His voice is playful. "You're more of a hummingbird, I think."

I pull back. "What?" I ask. I am lost, overwhelmed by his closeness.

"Remy's a deer, but you're a hummingbird." He puts a hand against my breastbone. "Listen to your heart flutter."

Immediately, I am snapped back into myself with a sharp stinging in my stomach.

Remy. My deer.

Suddenly, the color of the whole world changes. Everything clicks into place. Everything falls apart.

I close my eyes. A sound tries to come out of me, but it dies in my throat.

Mr. O'Dell and Remy.

Remy and Mr. O'Dell.

He leans in closer now, shrinking the distance until he is pressing his lips to mine.

My mother once explained to me that humans have four natural responses to danger, rather than the two most animals display: Fight. Flight. Freeze. And fawn.

I always thought that Remy was a fighter, but now I see that maybe it was more complicated than that. Because I let Mr. O'Dell kiss me, even though I know I shouldn't. I don't know how else to keep myself safe. Fight. Flight. Freeze. Fawn. The words cycle through my dazed brain.

I need to push him away.

I need to leave.

I don't know how.

I need to let him kiss me, to keep myself safe.

No.

I don't.

Suddenly all of the threads come together.

I grit my teeth and push Mr. O'Dell away, hard. "What are you doing?" I stand up from the couch and my legs hold me up. My body is animated by a new force, disgust, revulsion, anger. My lungs breathe deep gulps of air.

I watch as Mr. O'Dell's eyes slowly unglaze, as he comes back to himself. "Oh fuck," he says, and then again, "Oh fuck." He gets off the couch and begins pacing back and forth across the floor, threading his fingers through his hair. "What am I doing?" he says to himself. I take one slow, purposeful step toward the door.

Then he seems to regain his composure. He stops. He turns toward me. His hands are up, like I am a scared animal. A deer in the forest. "I am so sorry, Jules," he says. "So, so sorry."

I take another step toward the door. "I'm leaving," I say.

"No," he says. He grabs my wrist. His touch is gentle, but its message is clear. "Please," he says, his eyes soft. "Just let me explain."

Fight. Flight. Freeze. Fawn.

He leads me over to the couch and we sit down together. I look around the room, searching for a weapon.

Mr. O'Dell slumps forward, resting his forehead in his palms. He's quiet at first, but soon his body is shuddering with sobs, like he is completely overcome. I can feel the sorrow and shame seeping out his skin.

I have seen men fall apart before. When Scott died. And River. But this is different. Hard to watch. I think of my mother and Remy as I sit there, and I try to stay strong.

"I am so sorry," he keeps saying, again and again. Then he says, "I never meant for it to happen that way."

These last words make me shiver. I am still looking for something sharp, scanning the bookcase, and that's when I see it, tucked in the bottom corner. A vintage-looking typewriter, the one we used to use when we were kids. My belly fills up with sand, then my mouth, my legs.

I need to leave.

I can't move.

Fight flight freeze fawn.

Next to me, Mr. O'Dell is still crying.

I need to find Remy, I think, trying to slow my breathing. *I need to find Remy.*

I close my eyes, searching inside for my cousin's cool confidence, her quiet anger. But I find something else instead, a rage that is completely my own. I am calmed by it. I am made strong.

Mr. O'Dell hurt Remy. And I need to find her. And in order to do that, I need to stay here and find out what happened.

"I found your letters," I say, looking at the typewriter. "I know about you and Remy."

Suddenly Mr. O'Dell's body stops shaking. A preternatural calm comes over him. He sits up, wipes his tears, smooths his big hands along the tops of his thighs. He almost looks relieved. "I always thought you knew," he said.

I straighten my spine, ignoring the chill creeping down it. I need to think clearly. I need to get this right.

He looks out the window, where the light has almost disappeared, toward the shadowy line of trees. "I told her not to tell you, but I thought she would anyway." He looks at me. "You were her best friend."

He says this like he knows me. Like I should be proud. It makes me sick.

"I loved her," he continues. "She was unlike any person I'd ever met." I look over at Mr. O'Dell and it's as if he is somewhere else, lost in the world of the story he's telling.

In my mind, a memory flashes, the three of us kids in our bathing suits running through the sprinklers in the yard. Mr. O'Dell picking Remy up and tossing her into the air. We were nine, ten, eleven. It's true: Remy was just a fawn, with wobbly, downy legs and a crooked smile, new adult teeth that were too big for her mouth.

Remy Valentine, that's what he always called her. What he did to her makes me want to kill him.

I reach down into myself, past the fear, past the anger, into that calm, sharp place of knowing. "What happened?" I ask.

"River," he whispers. His face is pale in the darkness of the quiet room. "I knew it was wrong, but I never thought he'd find out. And then he did. Everything happened so quickly.

"I didn't know he was going to die," he says. He is crying again. "I didn't know she would . . . If I had known . . ."

He gets up and starts pacing the floor in front of the couch. I take a deep breath, trying to keep my voice steady. "What happened to Remy?"

He stops.

"She lied to me," he says. His voice is darker now. Lower. "I found out about Fawn."

Then he yells, "FUCK," and sweeps a hand over his desk. Papers come fluttering to the floor, a photograph of River, a million tiny handwritten notes.

This is when I should run. Every muscle in my body knows it. But I don't want to run. I fix my eyes on a black geode paperweight that's fallen to the ground.

"She told me she was mine." He turns to me, eyes suddenly angry. "But that wasn't true, was it?"

"What did you do?" I ask. My mouth is dry.

"Did you know he wanted to marry her?" Mr. O'Dell says, veering off course again. He turns back toward the window and I carefully lower myself to the floor. "He created a whole life in his mind. He didn't have a clue," Mr. O'Dell says. "He wanted to take her to live on a fucking farm, can you believe it? What a silly, selfish, childish dream." Then he stops. It's dark outside now, and I can see his face in the reflection on the window. He runs a hand through his hair. "We took that from him," he says. "We took everything from him. I had to find a way to give it back."

"It wasn't your fault," I say, closing my fingers around the paperweight. I feel disgusted by the words, but also like I am being led by something greater than myself now. I have to follow through. "Remy lied to a lot of people."

Mr. O'Dell nods. "Not anymore," he says. His voice is sad, full of regret. "She's gone now."

Suddenly, the whole world stops. Here is my answer. I can hear it in his voice.

Remy is dead.

I've been searching and searching, and now that the truth's in front of me, I don't want it. Every cell of my body fills with something sharp and stinging.

I spring up from the floor, just as Mr. O'Dell starts to turn around, and I swing my hand with the paperweight at the side of his head, the soft spot right in front of his ear. But my anger makes me clumsy and the geode glances off his eyebrow instead.

Mr. O'Dell grabs my wrist, pushing me sideways. We both topple to the floor and my head connects with something hard, a sharp pain across through my forehead. I try to get up, but Mr. O'Dell is on top of me now, holding me down.

"What the fuck are you doing?" he says. He is out of breath, and a small cut on his eyebrow is starting to bleed.

"You killed Remy," I say, struggling against him. I don't recognize my own sobbing voice.

A look of confusion crosses Mr. O'Dell's face and then recognition slowly dawns. "No," he says. "Remy is alive."

I hear him speaking, but the words don't sink in. I fight against his grip. I have to get him off me.

Mr. O'Dell shoves my hands down, pushing me into the floor.

"Jules, she's alive. Listen to me."

I push up as hard as I can, trying to force him away. He fights back, and my head knocks against the floor again. This seems to startle him, and he releases my hands, backing away. He looks surprised, regretful. I sit up and slide back against the wall, feeling dizzy.

"She's alive," he says, looking into my eyes.

I'm afraid to breathe, because I believe him and I'm not sure if I should.

He reaches for the paperweight in my hand, taking it gently from me and placing it behind him. Then he moves back again, sitting on his heels. "She's okay."

Mr. O'Dell moves over toward the couch, giving me space. I feel dizzy and confused. I want to believe him. He sounds so certain. "I don't understand," I say.

"I'm sorry," he says. He runs a hand down his face. "She needed to leave, and I helped her."

I close my eyes. "Where?"

"I can't tell you."

"Where?" My voice is harder the second time, angrier.

Mr. O'Dell reaches forward as if to touch my face and I flinch backward. Then I feel a trickle of blood slide down my forehead.

"Shit, Jules. You're hurt," he says. "I'm sorry. I'm so sorry. Let's just get you cleaned up."

I clench my jaw. "Tell me where you took her."

Mr. O'Dell looks down, regret in his eyes. "It doesn't matter. She's probably long gone by now."

I blink, still not fully understanding everything that's just happened. "I need a minute." I say the words out loud, but I'm talking to myself, to Remy, to all of the information that's racing around my brain.

Mr. O'Dell turns and starts collecting papers from the floor. Still disoriented, I watch him gather them into a neat pile. And then I spot a photograph on the rug near his foot. Remy, freshman year, in her Black Falls Cross-Country uniform.

My whole life, I've tried to be good, without even really knowing what that means. Even though I was born to a mother who is strong and independent, the world taught me that girls are supposed to be quiet, acquiescent, easygoing, helpful, nice to look at.

Girls are not violent. This is very clear. We don't need to be violent, because if we are good, we will be protected.

The boys are the protectors, of course. "Never hit a girl"

is something people say a lot. Men are taught never to physically harm, not to force themselves or lift their hands. This tricks us into thinking that all of the other things they do to us, all of the quiet things, are not violence. But now, sitting on the floor of Mr. O'Dell's office, looking at Remy's picture, I can see that they are all violent in their own way. Bailey. Zack. Tate. Derek. Mr. O'Dell. What they have done to us is violence, clear as day.

Mr. O'Dell knew Remy from the time she was a little girl. He watched her. He touched her. He made nicknames for her and made her feel safe. And then he did violence to her.

Were there other girls before Remy? Will there be someone else next year? I watch him gathering up the pages of his novel and now I see it, the quiet violence that permeates every muscle of his body.

Violence isn't just for boys, says a voice inside my head. But it isn't Remy, it's me.

The anger drains out of me then, and my body fills up with something clearer, lighter, more powerful. I think it might be joy.

I lunge toward him again, sparkling geode in my hand, and this time I don't miss.

TWENTY-THREE

I bring the paperweight down on the back of Mr. O'Dell's head with the force of my entire body. It connects with a sickening crack, and he falls forward. I hover over him, mesmerized by the dark red blood oozing out of the place where the jagged edge of the stone has cut him open. I am shaking with adrenaline, possessed with the rush of my own power.

I watch him for a while, not sure if he is breathing. In my mind, a fantasy plays: I hit him with the rock, again and again, until his skull breaks all the way open. Then I give the stone to Remy and she snaps his neck, smashes each one of his finger bones. We draw a scarlet letter onto his back with blood. We are brutal. Joyful.

Eventually, I become aware that Mr. O'Dell is still alive. His back gently rises and falls; his eyelids flutter and then close again. I can tell I only have a few moments to decide whether or not to let him live.

I close my eyes, reaching deep into my heart for the answer.

Just as I raise the stone to strike him again, I see head-lights cutting through the living room windows, moving through the open office door. I look down at the heavy geode in my hand, blinking as if waking from a dream. And then I start to run.

I tear through the house and out the kitchen door. Rebecca is just getting out of her car as I go streaking by. I can see her mouthing my name as I pull out of the driveway, but I don't stop.

TWENTY-FOUR

When I get home, the house is dark and quiet. I flip on all of the lights and I place the paperweight on the kitchen table, place the kettle on the stove to make tea.

I'm not sure what happens next. Am I going to get in trouble? Should I call my mother?

I take a mug down from the cupboard, spoon some chamomile into a strainer.

Remy is alive.

It hits differently now than it did when I found the letter in my mailbox. Then it was a butterfly dancing around my chest; now it's a stone, sinking to the bottom of my stomach.

Remy is alive. Remy left. Remy burned for Mr. O'Dell.

Remy's web of lies has grown into a labyrinth.

The kettle whistles, and I pour it into my mug, then I bring it to the table and wrap my hands around it for warmth. I am so cold.

I look down to realize I'm still wearing my shorts and T-shirt from the farmstand. I reach for my mother's green sweater, hanging on the back of her chair, and fold myself into it. Then I pick up the geode from the center of the table. I feel its weight in my hands, watch the crystals gleam in the low kitchen light. Liliana said that Fawn gave girls power, but now I'm not sure. I felt a certain strength when Kendall took those pictures today, but I have never felt as powerful as I did when I used this stone to hurt Mr. O'Dell.

What does that say about me? About power?

Maybe when boys send pictures of us to each other, the power is not in the pictures but in the violence behind the act of sending them. Maybe our power is in stopping that violence, in hurting them back.

Or maybe power is something else. Something in us that we haven't even discovered yet. Something bigger than violence. Something bigger than anything.

I take a sip of my tea and feel the warmth of the water and the magic of the herbs start to settle my insides. I pull my mother's sweater tighter around myself and remember all of the times she has made me a cup of tea: to calm my nerves, to soothe my upset stomach, to cure a cough, to heal a heartache. I wonder what she will say when she hears about all of this, how angry she will be. With me. With Remy. With Mr. O'Dell.

I reach up and gingerly touch the cut at my forehead. Everything that's happened in the past hour, day, month, feels like a strange dream. A movie. A murder podcast.

Remy made the perfect dead girl story, didn't she? Beautiful girl disappears. Suspects emerge, all of them men, each terrible in his own way. And in the end, of course, it's the coach, the dad, the one we all knew and trusted. What a fucking cliché.

But that's what Remy loves: a classic, perfectly executed. She created a masterpiece, recruiting everyone to play along. And now we are all here, grieving her, and she is somewhere else, living and breathing and spinning her threads all over again.

I set down my tea and stand up from the table. I need to find her. I need to make it stop.

Upstairs in my room, I spread everything out on the floor, the cash, the notebook, the papers from River's pocket, the pages where Sam and I wrote down everything we knew. I ignore the ache in my chest as I scan his messy handwriting, trying to focus on the meaning of the words.

I don't know how long I sit there, looking for some kind of sign. I feel so lost.

I reach down for the velvet ring box, turning it in my hands. Then I close my eyes and imagine River doing the same thing, in his truck on the way to the party. I can see his hands in my mind: tan, long-fingered, always moving with a hypnotizing, restless energy.

My heart breaks with everything I didn't know about him, all of the ways he was wounded by life. And yet, in this ring box, I can see a part of him I knew so well, a part I loved. Endlessly, eternally hopeful.

I set the ring down, picking up the job application for Cloverdale Farm. Suddenly, I know exactly where I need to go.

I drive through the night, and the time passes slow and thick, like cold honey. I am still in shorts and my mother's sweater, and even though the night is warm, I blast the heat.

It doesn't even cross my mind that I might be wrong, that Mr. O'Dell might be lying, that Remy could still be dead. I just hold the wheel steady and keep breathing.

As the hours pass, I retreat further and further into my own mind. I go past what happened tonight, past what happened to Remy, past what happened to River. All the way back to when things were beautiful and safe and endless. Remy and me, lying under one of my mother's quilts, whispering in the dark.

"Close your eyes," Remy says. She is very small. "I'm going to tell you a story. Imagine a place with green grass, blue skies, forest, thick and dark. A place just like here, but without anything ugly."

She reaches down and grabs my hand. "Do you see it?"

I nod in the dark.

Eventually I exit the highway and begin to traverse the countryside, long, winding, lonely roads. The sky begins to lighten; morning is coming.

The last twenty miles pass quickly, and before I know it, Google Maps has brought me to a long dirt drive with a beat-up wooden sign reading CLOVERDALE FARM. I still haven't thought of what I'm going to say to Remy.

I'm so angry with her. I'm so angry *for* her. I'm so sad and heartbroken and confused.

The driveway leads up to a large, stark white farmhouse

with a weathered red barn behind it. The light is turning pink, and the place looks just like the photograph on the front of the pamphlet, in the middle of a valley that looks just like the one Remy and I imagined on the backs of our eyelids when we were little girls.

Lights shine out of the upstairs windows, the kitchen, and I remember that this is a farm. People work here.

I park in a muddy patch, between an old, rusted-out Ford pickup and a gold Prius, and then I sit there and listen to the sounds of the car winding down. Suddenly all of the doubt I've ignored comes in a great big wave. What if Remy isn't here? What if she's dead after all? I squeeze my eyes shut, lifting the collar of Mom's sweater up to my face to breathe in her scent.

My legs feel unsteady as I open the car door and stand up on my feet. Everything around me is still and quiet. I walk slowly to the house, my heart fluttering like a moth.

I knock on the door and then wait, straining to hear a sound. Long seconds pass. I breathe. Maybe everyone is out doing chores, caring for the animals, checking the crops. Or maybe they are waiting quietly, to see if I'll go away.

I lean over to look in the small glass window next to the door. And I catch sight of a golden blond cloud of hair, messy with the morning, a long white nightgown. Then the door opens and a face appears. It's Remy.

TWENTY-FIVE

S he steps out onto the porch.

Closes the front door behind her.

My knees give way and I fall to the ground at her feet.

The grief comes then, even though she is not dead after all. Every fear, every horror, every loss, every torturous moment of the past few weeks comes spilling out of me. I am sobbing, waves of heat rolling up over my face. Remy kneels down beside me.

"Shhh. Shhh," she whispers in my ear. "It's okay. I'm here."

After the grief comes anger. I get to my feet and so does Remy and then I push her, hard, into the door.

"What are you—" Remy says, but I lunge at her, flinging my arms, scratching, reaching for her hair. She makes a startled noise and then begins to fight back, and then we are eight years old again, rolling on the floor of the porch, going for blood.

Remy calls me a freak and I call her a traitor and we are a flash of arms and legs and scratches. I think Remy is surprised when I don't give up first, but eventually I feel her tire and submit. I hover over her, looking into her eyes.

Who are you? I wonder.

Then I roll off her and we both lie on the porch, side by side, catching our breath.

Remy finally finds her voice. "You should come inside."

I nod.

I follow Remy into the house. As we cross the threshold, I reach up to the cut on my forehead, which has reopened during my scuffle with Remy. Blood, slick and red, oozes onto my fingertips.

Remy leads me down a long hallway, full of framed photographs of the farm and surrounding land, and into a giant kitchen that is bright with the glow of a light hanging over the sink. The fight has gone out of my body, leaving a strange kind of tingling behind, like my limbs are half here, half somewhere else.

"What happened to your face?" Remy asks. Her eyes are narrowed.

I remember Mr. O'Dell pushing me to the floor and am hit with a wave of disgust. I don't say anything. Upstairs, I hear people moving around, the sounds of people starting the day.

Eventually, Remy seems to realize that I'm not going to answer. She leaves me sitting at the table and begins to move around the kitchen with a familiar poise. She checks on muffins in the oven, cracks eggs into a giant bowl, rinses a dish in the sink. She puts herself back together, and as I watch her, I try to put myself back together too.

"Everyone is heading out to do chores now," she says. "But they'll be back for breakfast in about an hour. You can eat with us if you want."

I nod. I am calmer now but still too angry to speak.

Remy pours two cups of coffee and leads me to a sitting room near the front of the house. The windows are thrown wide open and the cool morning air flows inside with the chirping of birds. It is peaceful here. Every bit the happy valley from Remy's childhood fantasy. It makes me even angrier.

"How could you?" I ask, finally finding my voice. "How could you leave me like this? Everyone thinks you're dead."

Remy looks down at her bare feet on the floor. "I wrote you a letter," she says.

I grit my teeth. "You think a letter was enough?"

She sets our mugs down on a side table and sits on an old sofa under the window. Its blue is the color of the lightening sky, with small, bright red patches on the arms. "I didn't know what else to do. I couldn't stay."

"You lied to me," I say. I clench my teeth, thinking about Fawn, Mr. O'Dell, River. "About everything. *Everything.*"

Remy closes her eyes. "I know. I'm sorry."

I study her from the doorway. She looks smaller than she's ever been. "Why?" I ask.

"Because I wanted to protect you."

I laugh bitterly. A month ago, I might have believed her. Because Remy used to be my protector. But now I do that for myself. "You didn't," I say, crossing my arms.

I come closer, and Remy looks up at my forehead. Fire ignites in the center of her eyes. "Who hurt you?" she asks.

"Jake," I say. I don't think I've ever called him by this name in Remy's presence, and I watch as understanding, then shame, slowly dawn on Remy's face. Even though I am angry with her, I hate seeing this. He should be the one who's ashamed.

"Why didn't you tell me?" I whisper.

Remy reaches for her mug and brings it to her lips. She blows across the top of it, then takes a long sip. She closes her eyes. "I don't know."

I sit down next to her, squeezing her hand.

"I can tell you now if you want," she says.

"Yeah," I say, and she starts at the beginning.

The state championships in Nassau County in November. Remy won and on the way home Mr. O'Dell slipped into her seat on the half-empty bus. She was giddy with her win and he seemed light and boyish. They talked the whole way home and just before they pulled into the parking lot, he leaned in and brushed a loose strand of hair from her forehead.

As she talks, I wonder if she knows about the picture of her on Mr. O'Dell's desk from freshman year, if she remembers the way he used to grab her and throw her into the air. If she knows that November is when it started for her, but for Mr. O'Dell it was much longer than that.

Remy goes on. They started running together, in the woods out on Turnpike Road. *Offseason training*, he called it. He would point out the different types of trees, the tracks of animals. He would tell her about his book. He would help her stretch; she would lie on the ground and he would press her leg back, gently, with firm hands.

A seed of something began to grow between them, slowly at first and then wildly, like a weed or a vine, until it began choking out everything else. She couldn't see past it, didn't know how to move. Couldn't stop. Didn't want to. Did want to. She knew she had to tell someone, but she also didn't know how to come clean. She knew it would break River's heart.

Then, in May, River found out that his dad was cheating. He didn't know it was Remy, only that it was someone young, like him. Everything started falling apart. Fast. *River* started falling apart. He was getting nervous. Erratic. Depressed. She knew she had to tell the truth; she couldn't figure out how to do it.

My heart breaks hearing this part, wishing I had paid more attention, had known what to do.

"He proposed to me the night of the bonfire," she says. She closes her eyes at this part, like she is picturing it. "Something was wrong with him. But still. He was so sweet. He described this place, painted a picture of the two of us here, away from everything."

I don't think about it until much later, the way this future did not involve me. *They were leaving either way*, I would think. *They were never really there.* But now, on this morning, in the farmhouse living room, I only see the picture Remy paints with her words.

She stops, looks around, tears in her eyes. "He was right," she says. "It is *so* beautiful here." She takes a deep, shaky breath before beginning again. "He was there, on one knee, looking up into my eyes. Wide open. And I said no." Tears begin to fall down her cheeks, and she swipes at them with the back of her hand. "He just kept drinking. Half a bottle of vodka gone in ten minutes. And then he got into his truck."

Remy's face crumples now. "I told you," she says. "It was my fault."

I ignore this, not knowing how to respond. "Did you know he was on heroin that night?" I ask.

Remy pales. "No," she whispers.

I move closer to her and wrap my arm around her shoulders. I take everything that is strong in me, everything I've learned in the last few weeks, and try to pour it into her. Remy. My cousin. My best friend. "It wasn't your fault," I say.

Remy begins to cry harder then. Big, loud sobs. I let her fall into my arms. I hold her as wave after wave of grief rises up and then recedes again. Just like mine. Even after everything that's happened, it's so good to be here next to her, to finally be able to go through this together.

Eventually, Remy sits back and takes a few deep breaths.

She slides a black rubber band off her wrist and uses it to tie back her hair.

"Anyway," she says. "I had to get away after that. Away from Jake." She makes a disgusted face. "He wanted to keep things going. Said he loved me. I didn't know what to do." She looks out the window. "So I left."

"Does he know you're here?" I ask. "He's the one who told me you were alive."

Remy nods, taking a breath. "He's the one who helped me disappear. I told him I would tell everyone what happened if he said anything about where I was."

I smile at this ruthless part of Remy. "I fucked him up pretty badly with a paperweight."

"What?" Remy asks, looking confused.

"I don't know. At first I thought he'd killed you, but then . . . I just got really angry."

Remy nods slowly. "I know what you mean."

"I'm mad at you too," I tell her. I want to say something more. Something that hurts. Everything she did was so incredibly fucked up. But what was done to her was fucked up too. I don't know how either of us is going to survive this.

I pick up my own coffee and take a sip. It is creamy and sweet. A little bit of cinnamon, just like Mom makes it.

"What about Fawn?" I ask. I know I have to find out now, before Remy raises her guard again.

Remy laughs, and it is an ugly laugh. Full of bitterness.

"Fawn was an experiment," she says. She picks up her coffee again, looking thoughtfully into the mug. "I didn't like how they looked at us. Do you know what I mean?"

"Yeah," I say, remembering how it felt with Bailey in the woods. Like I was a thing that the world had made for his enjoyment and did not exist beyond that purpose.

Remy continues. "I wanted to see if we could control it." She pauses, looking down at her hands. "It was a really bad idea," she whispers. Then she gathers herself again. "And then we started making money. A lot of money.

"I'd always wanted to get out of Black Falls, and this suddenly seemed like a way to do it." She sighs. "But it turns out that creeps will creep, no matter what you do." She stops and takes a long sip, as if to fortify herself. I think about all of it again. Power. Control. Violence. How it felt to send a photo of myself to Bailey. How it felt to smash that geode into the back of Mr. O'Dell's skull.

Remy continues. "I got distracted because of Jake. I lost control for a little while. People found out who shouldn't have. Tate Stevens and some of his friends."

Anger flashes in Remy's eyes. Concentrated, purposeful anger. "It wasn't enough that they took my brother," she says. "They had to try to fuck up my life too."

She sets her coffee back down. "They were trying to blackmail me into letting them have a stake in the business. But instead we reached an agreement where they could add their own users and charge what they wanted."

Understanding slowly begins to dawn. Zack White and his red ribbon. I turn to Remy. "And the new users were . . ."

She nods. "Adults. Mostly men from town. I didn't tell anyone, but I tracked every user."

A sense of unease washes over me again. It seems wrong, Remy letting older men see the girls' photos without their consent. But I don't say anything about that now, because I want to know the truth of what really happened.

"I found your notebook," I say instead.

Remy smiles. "That's only the hard copy. I transferred everything into a spreadsheet on my phone, and a few flash drives."

"That's why everyone wants your SIM card."

"Yep."

I set my coffee down. "Where is it?"

Remy looks down, smiling into her coffee. "I handed it over to the FBI last week when they came up to interview me. A lot of people are going to get in a lot of trouble."

"Derek and Tate?"

"Not Derek," Remy says. "But yes, Tate. Zack White and a bunch of other cops." She takes a small sip. "A lot of people."

"What about the girls?" I ask, wondering how Remy could be so reckless with their lives, their futures.

Remy's eyes fill with regret. "I know. What I did was completely unforgivable." She looks out the window, where the edge of the sun has risen. "Because they're minors, they'll be protected and remain anonymous. Their identities will never be released to the public. People might speculate, but there will be no proof. Everything will go away for them."

I look at her skeptically. I'm not sure if that's true. How can she really know?

My head is beginning to throb and I know that I need to lie down soon.

"Come on," Remy says. "I'll get you a Band-Aid and then you can sleep in my bed while I finish the morning chores."

She starts to lead the way out of the room. I watch her

move gracefully across the floor and I am so, so grateful that she is alive.

Still.

So much has changed between us this summer. Remy used to be my hero, and now she feels like a stranger.

In a way, I'm a stranger too. I'm not the person I was before River died. I don't think I'll ever be her again. "I think it's going to take me a while to forgive you," I say.

Remy stops at the doorway and turns around. "I know."

My mother arrives at Cloverdale at 7:30 p.m.

"I am going to fucking kill you," she says as she gathers Remy into her arms.

"I know," Remy says, voice muffled against Mom's chest.

All three of us stand there, crying on the porch. The sun is just edging toward sunset, giving everything an orange-gold glow.

My mother and Remy go inside, to talk upstairs in Remy's room, because the farmhouse is very alive in the evening, people everywhere, chatting, plucking guitars, playing cards.

I go walking, alone, out on the road, because this is not a dead girl story after all.

Mom has brought ten different kinds of herbal tea in her bag. Because she knows how to fix every kind of broken heart.

"Why didn't we just talk to her?" Remy whispers to me. It is three in the morning and we are sitting together on one side of the long kitchen table, watching my mother at the stove.

"Because we forget that she knows everything," I reply.

My phone buzzes on the table in front of me.

"I should have never brought that back to you," Mom says from across the room.

I pick it up to see a text: Bailey didn't show.

Fuck, I think. I'd completely forgotten.

Remy gives me a questioning look. "We thought Bailey had something to do with you—with what happened," I say. Looking back, there is a fuzzy sense of unreality to all of it. "He had this book of your pictures. It was violent and creepy. We made this plan to get back at him."

Mom comes over with our tea, and I show Remy the photographs Callie forwarded to me.

Mom sighs. "There are better ways to keep yourselves safe," she says. She scoops a big spoonful of honey into each mug.

Then she turns to her suture kit, which is laid out on the table, everything freshly sanitized.

I wince the first time the needle pinches into the skin of my forehead, and I reach for Remy's hand. She squeezes me tightly enough that it hurts, distracting me from the pain of my mother sewing up my wound.

"What can we do about him, though?" I ask, wincing. "We can't risk the details of Fawn coming out."

Mom sighs heavily. "My loves," she says, bringing the needle through my skin again. The pain is white hot. "It's going to come out. This is Black Falls." She ties the suture, snipping the thread with her silver scissors.

"Look," she says. "I need to talk to both of you about Fawn." She keeps working, cleaning the cut, fixing the bandage. I can tell that this is hard for her. "Your bodies belong to you. They are yours. To do whatever you want with.

"When I was your age, I didn't realize that. I kept feeling like I owed something. And sometimes I thought I needed to use my body to pay that debt. Like, if I had invited someone to my house, I would have to follow through on that. Or if I wanted love, I would have to give access to my body in return. You know what I mean?"

I nod, watching my mother's face. She takes a deep breath, looking over at Remy.

"I can imagine how powerful it must feel to turn that paradigm on its head. To be the person that is owed, rather than the one that is always having to pay."

"Sex work is real, honest work. Good work. It's not about holding power over someone, about taking something away or getting revenge." She sighs, and I can see how exhausted she is. "And it's for adults. Because deciding what you want to do with your body is a process. It takes time. You can be hurt if you rush into it. You are *so* young. And right now, sex is a gift, to explore and enjoy. Not a job or a power chip. Do you understand?"

Remy nods, a tear sliding down her face.

"The truth is," Mom continues, "this might come out. You'll need to be strong. But we'll do it together." She looks down at the phone, as if Callie, Kendall, and Liliana are here too. "All of us," she says.

She starts to clean up her suture kit and turns the phone off, bringing everything over to her bag, which is hanging on the back of a chair at the other end of the table. Remy watches her, deep in thought.

She looks down into her tea and says, "I can't go back." Her face is pale, and she looks so young.

"I know you can't come back right now," Mom says. "But maybe someday you will."

TWENTY-SIX

The next twenty-four hours are a blur. We leave Remy at the farm. The drive home feels long; I follow my mother's car, my mind blank and full of static.

In the morning, Mom goes to Aunt Stephanie's house. She's gone for a long time, hours, and when she comes back she looks exhausted. Later in the afternoon, my mom and I go to the police station and I tell them everything that happened with Mr. O'Dell.

He'd been hospitalized for a serious concussion and had been confused about how the injury occurred.

I tell my side of the story, and I notice how different it feels to be in the station now. I feel more powerful, even as Zack White tells me to stand still while he photographs my face.

I have a secret about these men. I know that justice is coming for all of them.

The next day, I mail an anonymous note to Bailey's mother: *Look under your son's mattress.*

Mom is extra gentle with me, even though I have broken every rule, lied to her more times than I can count. She lets me stay in my room for several days, just looking out the window and feeling the edges of the new space inside myself. There is still a yawning, River-shaped hole, but beside it something new is forming.

In the mornings, when Mom is still asleep. I go out to the road and run. I don't go far, just enough to feel the burn in my lungs, and then a little farther, until it spreads out into my limbs. Just enough to remind me that I'm alive. And then I close myself back up in my room where no one can see me.

I think a lot about Sam, going over everything that happened between us in my mind. I know that I need to apologize to him; even if he doesn't want to be with me, he still deserves the truth. But for now I'm like a seed under the earth, resting and tending to my grief. I'll know when it's time to come out again.

Mom checks in on me every so often. She brings me lentil soup and chamomile tea and poppyseed cake. She brushes back my hair to comfort me, and sometimes when her fingers touch the jagged place below my hairline, she looks murderous. Sometimes something else happens, and she smiles at me, like she's proud.

On Tuesday night, the girls come by. They let themselves into my bedroom, sit down on my bed.

"Remy called us," Callie says.

"Jesus fucking Christ," Kendall says.

Liliana lies down and curls up at my side.

"Thanks for coming," I say.

"Always," Liliana says.

"What happened with Bailey?" I ask.

Kendall shrugs. "We waited in the woods for hours, but he never showed up."

"But I heard his parents are sending him to some kind of rehab in Maine for the rest of the summer," Liliana says.

I smile knowingly, but I don't tell anyone what I did.

I still miss Remy, I think all of us do, but it feels like the four of us have filled up the void with parts of ourselves.

"Let's watch a movie," Kendall says.

"Anything but horror," Callie replies.

On Wednesday, my mother wakes me up before sunrise. "Time to get up, chickadee," she says. "Rebecca needs your help today."

I throw an arm over my face. "I can't go back there," I say. The farmstand makes me think of River. Remy. Sam.

"You have to," she says. She hands me a mug of yarrow tea. "It's time."

My day is not as bad as I thought it would be. And in another way it is a million times worse. Sam is off with the field crew today, so I am all alone. All day long, there is a soft, persistent aching beneath my breastbone.

Are you changing? Remy asks in my mind.

Maybe I am, and maybe change just hurts.

At 4:30, Sam comes walking up to the farmstand. I can see that he has changed too. He is still dressed in all black, but his cheeks are red, his arms are brown. He doesn't look angry anymore.

He walks up to the counter, leaning his hip against the wood. "Can you give me a ride to the river?"

The drive is quiet, except for the sound of wind rushing in the open windows. Summer is full-on now, and the air is hot and damp. Every few seconds my eyes dart over from the road to look at Sam's face, at the bead of sweat forming above his left eyebrow, the beauty mark over his lip. He is exquisite. He makes my heart ache.

We park in the gravel at the side of the road, and then we sit there for a few minutes, windows down, listening to the sound of the river in the distance.

Sam clears his throat. "Rebecca told me about what happened with you and Jake." He turns to look at me. "Are you okay?"

"I don't know," I say. I reach up to touch the place where my mother took the stitches out this morning. "I think it's too early to tell."

I open my door and Sam gets the blanket out of my trunk, and then I follow him through the tall grass, all the way down to the riverbank. Then we sit, quietly watching the water.

"I'm sorry," I say. I feel afraid, but my voice feels strong. Sure.

"I know," he says. He looks down at a spot on his shirt. "You don't have to explain."

"I do," I say. "Because you're right, I lied to you." I reach down for a smooth stone, turning it between my fingers. "I did love River. I was kind of obsessed with him. It was way too much. It was weird."

Sam doesn't say anything and I am left alone with my own awkward truth. It feels uneasy in my stomach. But I sit with it. I let it be there.

"I know I should get rid of the stuff in my drawer," I say. "But I can't. Because River is gone, and those things are all I have left of him." I straighten up. "You should know that I felt a lot of other things for River too. He was my best friend. We spent our entire childhoods together."

Sam nods, turning to look me in the eye. I can see his grief, right there on his face. I want to reach out and touch it. "When I first saw you, I thought you were River. I don't want to lie to you about that." I pause. "But that's not why I like you. I like you because you're kind. And you take time to look at things. To notice." I pick up another rock and toss it into the water, watching the rings spread out from the center. "Nobody ever really looks at me," I say. "But you do."

Sam looks down, sifting pebbles through his fingers. "Growing up, I always thought that River was untouchable. I was so jealous. Sometimes I hated him so much that I actually wished he would die." He looks up, tears in his eyes.

"It's so strange being in this place where people look at me and actually think I'm him. I always wanted that, in a way. But now"—he takes a stone and lobs it in the water—"it's so fucking sad.

"It turns out that people thinking you're perfect is the worst thing that can happen."

He swipes at a tear on his cheek. "Anyway," he says. "I know that's not how you see me anymore. And I understand how you feel about River." He turns and looks at me for what feels like a very long time, his eyes moving across my face, down to my lips and my neck and then back up again. "I do see you," he says.

He doesn't say anything after that. And we just sit for a while, looking at each other and feeling the enormity of everything that has happened between us.

Finally, he grins and says, "Let's go swimming."

He stands up, peels off all of his clothes, and runs into the water.

I am sweaty and sticky and my body feels so much like a body, so unwieldy and soft, red marks at my waist from the seams of my shorts, stubble under my armpits. I reach up and touch the small strip of puckered skin on my forehead, where a new scar has begun to form. The uneasy feeling comes back, starts to spread. And I let it be there. And I take off my clothes.

The water is cool. Perfect. I let it close over my head, turning the whole world dark. I hold my breath until my lungs ache, reminding me that I am alive.

And then I resurface and the world is glittering and new

and there's Sam. *Sam.* Treading water, drops like crystals in his eyelashes.

The afternoon passes, and we drift together, two bodies in the water.

When I get home, my mother is waiting on the porch, sitting on one of the two rocking chairs that look out on the road, the valley. She stands as I climb the steps and comes over, setting her hands on my shoulders just as I reach the top. She studies my face, looking for signs.

"How was it?" she asks.

I smile.

"Good," I say. "It was good."

PART 3

July
and
August

Dear Jules,

Can you believe it's July already?
It feels like the summer is slipping
through my fingers. Everything is
getting busier and busier around here.
One thing ripens, and then another, and
there are barely enough of us to harvest
it all. The baby goats are almost full-
sized now. River has been gone for
exactly nine weeks.

I've been thinking lately, about all of
the lies I've told. Lies have a way of
worming into the cracks in a person's
life and then expanding, breaking
everything apart. But maybe it was time
for that anyway.

I am changing. When you were here it
felt like you were too. If we become
different people, promise me you'll
still be mine.

All my love forever,

Remy

The summer wears on. It gets hotter and hotter until the first gold leaf appears in the woods behind Remy's house. Mr. O'Dell loses his job at Black Falls High. We never hear back about my complaint against him. He leaves town and Rebecca puts the house on the market.

In the end, River's cause of death is inconclusive. A poetic word if you think about it. River was a nesting doll just like Remy. We all are, in some way or another. Selves inside selves. Inconclusive.

I go to the river every day of the summer. Sometimes the grief is so big that I can't get out of the car. Other times, I dive down into the water, all the way to the bottom, amazed at how alive I feel.

The FBI raids the Black Falls Police Station in mid-August. Six of the officers are indicted, but Officer Kelly manages to come out unscathed.

Tate Stevenson goes to prison again. One afternoon I see Derek at the IGA. I brace myself, ready for a fight, but he doesn't say anything or even look at me. I feel strangely sad. I remember him, mowing the grass in Aunt Stephanie's yard. I wonder, what would I do if Remy were in the same kind of trouble as Tate?

At the end of August, Sam goes back to the city. School starts. Bailey does not come home. Remy stays on at the farm. In a way, I am alone again. But this time I feel tethered. I have friends. I have my mother. And I have myself. My body.

Every morning, I wake up when the sun is just rising and the grass is still wet with dew. And I run. I run and run and run. And then I go home.

Resources for Readers

Respect Together (formerly National Sexual Violence Resource Center): NSVRC.org

Suicide Prevention Resource Center: SPRC.org (or call or text 988)

To Write Love on Her Arms (mental health and substance abuse support): TWLOHA.com /find-help (or text TWLOHA to 741741)

ACKNOWLEDGMENTS

This book took me on a journey to the scariest, saddest parts of myself. I am different now than I was when I started; I don't think that the person who I used to be was capable of writing this book. Luckily, I wasn't alone on this ride.

Kelsey Murphy, you propelled me forward, forward, forward in this process, always helping me find the deeper truth and get it on the page. Thank you for your kind words and expert guidance. And thank you to the rest of the editorial team, Want Chyi and Meriam Metoui, whose thoughtful feedback helped me to become a better writer.

Melanie Castillo and Taylor Haggerty, dream team agents, thank you for always seeing me. Jasmine Brown and the rest of the Root Literary team, thank you for making the magic happen.

Thank you to the Viking team who have brought this book to life: Tamar Brazis, Gaby Corzo, Krista Ahlberg,

Abigail Powers, Sola Akinlana, Alison Dotson, Vanessa Robles, Kate Renner, Kristie Radwilowicz, Theresa Evangelista, Lisa Schwartz, Lizzie Goodell, Alex Garber, Felicity Vallence, Shannon Spann, James Akinaka, Bri Lockhart, Emily Romero, Christina Colangelo, Amber Reichart, Carmela Iaria, Venessa Carson, Trevor Ingerson, Summer Ogata, Danielle Presley, Judith Huerta, Amanda Close, Sarah Williams, Enid Chaban, Debra Polansky, Becky Green, Emily Bruce, Brenda Conway, Mark Santella, Mary McGrath, Tanesha Nurse, Pete Facente, Robyn Bender, Jocelyn Schmidt, and Jen Loja.

Thank you to my writer friends who read parts of this book and cheered me on: Katharine Davis Reich, Kate Spencer, Julia Collard, Rachel Vine, Stephanie Carrie, Amanda Paley, and the rest of the Write! Write! Write! group.

Thank you to my teachers from these past three years: Nina LaCour, Elana K. Arnold, Abby Tucker, Laura Huff, and the many more who came before that.

Thank you to Shelly Lev Er for creating the container for my transformation and teaching me how to be with all of my selves. I could not have done this without you.

Thank you to all of the caregivers who took care of my son while I wrote this book and to all of the friends who supported and loved me. Thank you to Julie Grant for being the person who will drop everything to be there. Thank you to my chosen family for keeping the record of my life and holding me tightly.

Thank you to my mom, sisters, nieces, and aunts, for bringing so much strength and joy into my world. Thank you to the dads, stepdads, brothers, niblings, and nephews too. Special shout-out to Mia for vetting all cultural references. And thank you to Angelo, my biggest love.

Finally, thank you to every person who reads this book, for giving me the gift of your time and attention. Every day I am grateful for you.

For more from **Kate Sweeney**, check out

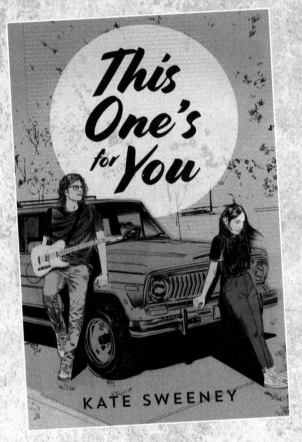

A gorgeous contemporary romance about two
ex–best friends, Cass and Syd, on a life-altering road trip
following the reunion tour of the Darlas—
the band Cass's mom was in when she died

Don't miss **Kate Sweeney's** debut

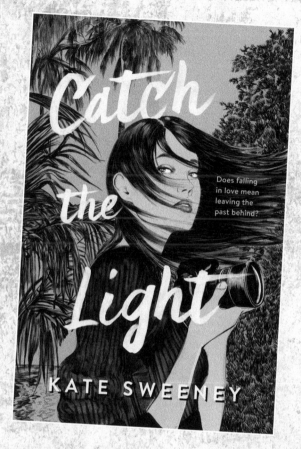

A love story perfect for fans of Nina LaCour and Jandy Nelson
about a girl who moves cross-country and finds herself falling
for someone new who throws her whole life out of order.

"Beautifully captured, like a photograph of a stolen moment.
I ached for Marigold in her journey to move forward while
not forgetting her past. Kate Sweeney's *Catch the Light*
overflows with grief, love, and growing up."
—AMY SPALDING,
bestselling author of *We Used to Be Friends*